THE BEST OF
TM WRIGHT

THE BEST OF
TM WRIGHT

TM WRIGHT

INTRODUCTION BY
STEVEN SAVILE

Published in September 2019 by PS Publishing Ltd. by arrangement with the
estate of TM Wright. All rights reserved by the author's estate. The right of
TM Wright to be identified as Author of this Work has been asserted by his
estate in accordance with the Copyright, Designs and Patents Act 1988.

First Edition
ISBNS
978-1-78636-355-8

Design and layout by Alligator Tree Graphics.
Printed in England by T. J. International.

PS Publishing Ltd
Grosvenor House
1 New Road
Hornsea, HU18 1PG
England

editor@pspublishing.co.uk / www.pspublishing.co.uk

CONTENTS

INTRODUCTION: THE
WINDMILLS OF HIS MIND

There's a reason Stephen King described Terry as a rare and blazing talent, and a reason why, the last time we spoke, Terry said he hated that epitaph. There's no getting away from the fact it's true, for one thing, Terry really was a rare talent. I'm tempted to call him a writer's writer, because when you know just how difficult some of the stuff he attempted to do with his prose was the more you appreciated the sheer skill and down-beat power of those words he conjured with. But that King line was a millstone around his neck, too, because it was a false bill of goods. It got you thinking 'ah, I'm getting another Big Steve' here and became the kind of praise that's impossible to live up to when your main aim, again and again, is to subvert expectation and deliver something new whilst at the same time exploring the familiar themes of death and loss of self.

But for me, Terry had more hits than misses.

I never tired of reading his stories or his emails.

Now, there's something vaguely melancholic about knowing we've reached this point, me writing the last few words that take us to the turn of the last page. After the final story in this book, "Otto's Conundrum," there are no more lost TM Wright stories waiting to be discovered. This is it, right here, in this collection, the rarest thing, the last original and previously unpublished TM Wright story.

Indeed, the fact you're actually able to read it is nothing short of a miracle of a lazy mind, to be honest, and a thank you to my email provider for hanging on to an archive of hundreds of thousands of emails dating back about fifteen years.

A little story for you before we get to the story itself.

Many years ago now, and when I say many, it's more than a decade and then some, I was sitting in a café in Stockholm when one of those bright shining thunderbolts of inspiration struck and I wrote the pitch document for something called *Monster Noir*, which was a shared world concept where all of those monsters we grew up loving were real, and had been hidden away in an enclosure in the Nevada desert, victims of the Monster Alienation Act passed by Nixon, and so on. Terry wrote "Otto's Conundrum" specifically for this book that never was, with us trading a good forty or fifty emails about his ideas for the world, possible storylines and characters he imagined living in it. He wanted to be sure everything he came up with gelled with the world as I saw it, and together try to find out how to best make it fit smoothly in. He had a wonderful habit of sending snippets he was excited about while he was working, just the odd paragraph, a few lines of a description or a turn of phrase that he'd particularly enjoyed during that day's work which made any sort of collaboration with him a lot of fun. Indeed, so many emails were filled with enthusiasm over Nyxon, our fictional town and its inhabitants and what might become of them, so in the slump that followed the failure to publish, we were both very down about everything. We'd invested a lot emotionally in the project and suddenly there was nothing.

It probably sat on our respective harddrives for a year or more before we even discussed it again, but when we did, it was Terry broaching the idea of us working together on a follow-up piece talking about what happened after the last lines of Otto's story, making it something bigger. Maybe a two-part story, or a short novel, or the elusive 'something'.

That was a big deal to me—not least because *A Manhattan Ghost Story* was one of those ten books that made me want to be a writer, and the idea that Terry didn't just like my work enough to write that glorious introduction to *Temple: Incarnations of Immortality* where he half-jokingly called me a mad man who had clearly consorted with devils . . . but that he liked my work enough to want to fuse it with his own.

So, after maybe a year with less contact than there had been for a good three or four years, there was suddenly a mad flurry of emails, ideas building into 'something' and it looked like we were beginning to get there with the story of the Sheriff. Terry actually mailed to say he was starting work on it that day, but when I woke up the next day (thanks to the time zone shift between us) expecting a little sample of Otto's return, instead there was a bullet point outline for something else entirely, a brand new idea that had gripped him as he sat down, a sort of crime noir horror, "Sally Pinup." The story had taken root inside his head, unplanned, he explained, and had gripped him madly. Would it be okay if he saw where it would go before we got back to Otto?

I remember my response, it was the typically sanguine, 'No worries mate, we've got loads of time, we'll come back to it. I've got plenty to be getting on with.'

Only of course we didn't have loads of time, and neither of us realised how little, to be fair. But, the joy for us is that he got to finish that last novella, "Sally Pinup, "while he was still on the top of his game, and it's included here as a rarity along with his better-known short stories.

Terry didn't write much in the way of short fiction, and often what he did was little more than hallucinatory fragments, so the fact we have something complete, and traditional in terms of story, that explores all of his familiar themes, is just this wonderfully unexpected gift from my old friend.

And boy did we get lucky. Terry worked on an old computer—which even in 2008 was ancient, he used to joke that it was a brick even then . . . I seem to remember it was a Pentium, which dates it. During his final months in hospice care that machine, along with all of the digital copies of his old manuscripts and work in progress gave up the ghost and went to silicon heaven. I'll be honest, I thought Otto was gone forever, lost in the crashes, because it hadn't survived the several digital migrations my own files had gone through over the intervening decade. Why would it? *Monster Noir* was never happening. It wasn't my work. It was only when a friend emailed asking if I had a copy of his submission lurking in my email by any chance because he'd lost his that I thought, hmm, you know, I might . . . I'm terrible. I never clear the online storage (there are about 400,000 emails still on the server) and just pay increased fees every year to add gigabytes to the account. I found Terry's original emails, hundreds of them, spanning about six years, a real treasure trove of my dead friend's thoughts and words, which were vital in completing work on what became *Mallam Cross*, and deep in the pile several revised versions of the manuscript for "Otto's Conundrum." Terry was a tweaker. He'd send a finished story, then two days later a version with a couple of changed sentences, then a week later another version with a few words changed, and so on until what you had on paper was exactly how he wanted to read.

I've explained what happened next in the introduction to *Mallam Cross*, and how as a fan of his work Peter Crowther stepped in and volunteered his excellent press to make these two books a reality, he's a champion. But Terry has another champion in David Niall Wilson, who not only came to my aid sourcing digital versions of some of these old stories but with his Crossroads Press has kept Terry's words alive for a new generation of readers. These two gentlemen have, I'm sure, never met, but came together to make this last book possible and for that I will be forever grateful.

Sometimes, just sometimes, it feels like it's not luck at all . . . but then, Terry did spend most of his life writing about how our world and the next interplay, so maybe he had a little hand in this stuff not remaining lost . . .

Steven Savile
26th Feb 2019, SALA

THE BEST OF
TM WRIGHT

RAINY DAY PEOPLE

I love my laptop.
            This thing that glows in the dark.
    I love it.

12:43 p.m.
    It is possible—I believe this—for beings to appear out of the rain who are actually *created from* the rain.
    Remember that always.

12:58 p.m.
    He said:
    I don't believe I've seen such beings, although I admit I've seen something I can't explain. But there's much I can't explain, of course—gravity, for instance, and electricity, and why, according to experts, the universe is expanding instead of falling in on itself.
    I telephoned Fred and told him what I'd seen and he told me I was

tired or hungry or hallucinating. I told him I wasn't; he said okay, and that was that. Fred's never believed me about much of anything, anyway, so to hell with him.

Ronnie was asleep at the time, and when she woke, I told her what I'd told Fred and she said, "Christ, that's creepy! Are you sure?" I said yes, I was sure, then hesitated and added, "Maybe I'm not so sure, really. But I saw *something*."

She nodded in her agreeable way and asked if I'd like some lunch. "Yeah," I said. "Macaroni and cheese?"

"It's bad for you," she said. "Full of fat and cholesterol. You'll die young." I shrugged. "Just like Alexander the Great. That'd be all right."

2:14 p.m.

Odd, that need. Or desire. So fatalistic. If it's going to happen, anyway, shit—why not just let it happen now instead of later.

He said, "I'm your friend. You can talk to me."

3:30 p.m.

It's been raining on and off here for weeks. I like the rain. I like it a lot, in fact, and so does Ronnie. It's comforting, on several levels. But, after a while, too much rain is *too damned much* rain and I've found myself peering at the sky for signs of a break in the overcast. This afternoon, however, there is no break, although, thankfully, no rain either.

Ronnie just came in and asked, "Where'd you tell me you saw those . . ."—she looked suddenly perplexed—" . . . those *things?*"

"Out the back window," I said, and inclined my head to the south. "Near the woods."

"Oh," she said. "That's where I looked." She cocked her head, appeared confused, said, "Creepy," again, then, after a moment, flashed her beautiful and wonderfully appealing *I'm-horny-as-a-goat* smile: "Wanna fuck?"

"Of course I wanna fuck," I said, and smiled back. "Just give me a minute, okay?"

"Okay," she said. "I'll be you-know-where, Josh."

"And I'll be there with bells on," I said.

"I'll help you take them *off*," she said.

5:21 p.m.

Such magic in all that glows in the dark. We don't know everything about magic and that's why it's magic. Maybe everything we don't know everything about is magic.

Maybe if we don't know *all that we can know* about a thing, we don't know *anything* about it.

Maybe *everything* is magic.

Gravity, electricity. Rain.

8:30 p.m.

The rain is constant and unnerving, now. I think I hate it.

Ronnie said, "This rain is incredible. Do you think it's ever going to stop?"

I sighed. "Of course it is. It stopped this afternoon, remember?"

"I mean for good, Josh?"

"For good? Well, that would be unfortunate, don't you think?"

"No."

"If it stopped for good, where would the flowers come from?"

"Oh, crap, Josh, they'd come from my Goddamned ass, I don't know! Can't you at least . . . play along with me!"

I think the almost-constant rain is making her cranky.

10:45 p.m.

Odd what he said. All the odd things he said. All his odd behaviors. And now what? This thing that glows in the dark? The dark. The rain.

11:02 p.m.

Went to the back window, looked out, toward the woods, saw nothing, not even the woods. Ronnie came up beside me. "Shit," she said. "Too dark. Too rainy," I said. "Oh hell, Josh," she said, "you didn't see anything out there and we both know it. I'm going to bed." And that's where she went. To her bed. *Our* bed. And left me to myself and the things I imagine.

5:30 a.m.

Couldn't sleep because of the rain. That's a first. All my life, a good hard rain has lulled me to sleep. Now it conspires to keep me awake.

Ronnie has no trouble sleeping. She sleeps so soundly I sometimes half-believe she's dead (and, earlier, I actually put my hand on her chest to be sure she was breathing).

I wish we had a dog. It would be good company, now that it's just me and the laptop. And the rain. The omnipresent rain. The torturous rain. The unforgiving rain. (What other adjectives can I come up with? Me—the king of adjectives! But I'm stumped. If we had a dog, I'd ask *him.*)

6:12 a.m.

I can not describe what I saw minutes ago. They—these creatures—are as opaque as ice. They smile and grimace all at the same time. They look *at* me and look *away* at the same time. I'm shutting this off. I'm shutting this off.

9:02 a.m.

Josh is asleep. At least he's trying to sleep. He told me what he saw and I have to believe him, I know I have to believe him, but I went to the window too and I didn't see anything at all, only the rain. No "ice," like he said. It's too warm for ice.

He speaks to me and I believe it's real.

He lays his hands on me while I sleep, and I believe it's real.

He comes to me and I believe it's real. Belief is enough, isn't it? Isn't it?

2:33 p.m.

Note to myself: I've mentioned that these beings (*Things, creatures, entities*—Good Lord, who knows?) smile, but that seems unlikely because I don't believe they have *faces*.

4:20 p.m.

Ronnie's upset because I threatened to change the Windows password. She called me a "putz," a word I hadn't heard from her before, then asked what I was hiding. "Nothing," I said, and she said, predictably, "Well then, why would you want to change the fucking password?"

I think this constant, unrelenting rain is wearing us down.

We came here for a reason, she said. To ease the tension, I think. Who knows for sure? But what does it matter? Why "ease the tension" if there's no *reason* for it? And isn't there *always* reason for it? If it exists, isn't there always reason for it? If animosity exists and discord exists, isn't there *always* reason for it?

Let such things exist.

Let discord and animosity create whatever they create: whatever grows from them is natural, after all.

5:30 p.m.

She sleeps as soundly as a still day in winter. Minutes ago, I put my hand on her chest again. Felt for the heartbeat.

7:25 p.m.

I went out into it, into the rain, out to those woods, stood where those things stood, looked back at the house—saw only the house, the windows, Ronnie looking at me from the bedroom. I raised my hand a little, a kind of wave. She did nothing.

So frigid out there, in that cold, cold rain. It will change to snow, I think—the season's right for it. Then we'll be in trouble.

I believe I saw footprints in the wet earth at the front of the woods. They could have been my own footprints, of course, though that's doubtful: these footprints (if that's what they were) lay parallel to the edge of the woods. They could have been made by anything. They could have been made by deer, raccoon, foxes. Then the endless rain made them look provocative. I didn't go *into* the woods. I couldn't.

9:47 p.m.

Ronnie said, "Josh, I saw them. Those things out there."

I said, "When?" and she hemmed and hawed a little and I could tell she was lying.

"Why are you lying to me?" I said.

"I didn't want you to feel like you were alone," she said. "I lied out of love for you."

It's the first time she's mentioned love in months, I think. I don't know how I feel about it. The word slides too easily from her mouth, as if it's merely convenient.

Perhaps because *I* am merely convenient.

I said, "Do you know that I feel for your heartbeat while you sleep, Ronnie?" and she only smiled.

I'm sick of noting the time.

If I do not note it, then perhaps it will cease to exist.

It's early morning. Still raining hard. I'm having coffee—*Jamaican Me Crazy*; good stuff. I just brewed it. And I'm careful, of course, not to spill it on the laptop. I sip the coffee while holding the cup over the floor in front of the laptop because I tend to be clumsy about things like drinking full cups of scalding hot coffee. Sometimes, the coffee even squirrels its way out of my mouth.

We've been here a week.

At least a week.

It could be longer.

3:45 a.m.

Better to note the time, I think. It adds parameters to this . . . thing, this odd experience. Parameters? Reality? Same thing—same function. The laptop's clock says 3:45:23. That's good. Good, tight parameters.

Ronnie's asleep. She sleeps so damned much, now! I want to wake her, want her to sit here with me and wait for first light, want to see if she really sees what *I* see. How could she not?

5:22:42 a.m.

Some light, now. Not enough. It's so weak it might as well be darkness.

Can't see much . . . I can hardly see even the rain because it's so thick and fast. No wind.

Ronnie's still asleep. It's not like her. She always wakes very early. 5:00 am. An hour earlier than I, usually. 5:00 am, always. Even earlier. Makes eggs and toast for herself. Makes them later for me—wakes me up with them, puts the plate under my nose, says, "Good eggs, Josh."

The laptop feels warm against my thighs.

I love it. My laptop. This thing that glows in the dark.

I look out this window, at that wall of rain and near-dark, and I think, It will always rain like this because it has been raining for an eternity.

I love Ronnie. I believe I love her much more than I knew. I need her, too.

I want her to wake.

I wish to heaven she would wake.

I see you there! I see you! No smile, and no frown or grimace.

6:01:21 a.m.

I see you! I see you, dammit!

They speak, I'm sure of it.

I speak and so *they* speak.

6:10:12 a.m.

She's awake, at last! Bustling about the kitchen behind me. She turned the light on. I told her, "Turn it off!"

She turned it off, said, "I can't see to cook."

I said, "Cook later."

"Shit on you!" she said.

"Sure," I said.

"Shit on you twice!" she said.

"I saw them again, Ronnie!" I said.

She said nothing. I turned my head, looked at her; I could hardly see her, as if she were no more than a pale shadow in the dark. I said to her, "You're spooky like that. Turn the light on."

"Shit on you three times," she said, and I know she smiled a little, though I couldn't see it.

She turned the light on.

The rain went away. I could only hear it. I hear it always. I've heard it forever.

She was smiling.

She has a smile as clear as sunlight.

I said, "I love you more than I ever realized, Ronnie."

"It sounds like you're confessing a revelation," she said.

"Of course," I said. "Yes. I am."

"Thanks," she said. "Thanks," she repeated. "I'll make us eggs and toast."

"Yes, thank you," I said. "I'm quite hungry."

8:43

"Do not go to bed with anger or wake with anger," I said.

Ronnie said, "Who wrote that?" because a book lay open on the table in front of me.

"I don't know. Not this guy." I nodded at the book. "Someone else. I don't remember who."

"It's good advice," she said, and yawned. "I like it."

"Why so sleepy?" I said.

She shook her head. "I'm not sleepy. Just yawning." She nodded at my empty plate. "Good eggs, huh? I did something different with them. Did you notice?"

"Yeah," I said. "They were great."

"You didn't notice," she said, collected my plate and silverware from the table, took them to the sink, looked out the window and said, "I feel like Noah's wife."

"You're not Noah's wife," I said. "You're *no one's* wife." I smiled.

She looked at me, smiled back, though it seemed to be as much a frown as a smile. "Do tell," she said, and ran some water on my plate.

12:00

I have seen them clearly. Or, perhaps, as clearly as they'll allow. They're like mannequins made of mist. I can't explain them to Ronnie, and I won't try. I've given up telling her anything about them, or about anything important, for that matter.

I know she won't listen.

She never listens.

She never hears me, no matter how loudly I speak.

She's asleep again.

She sleeps almost constantly now. I check her breathing every five minutes, put my hand on her chest and check her breathing. Put my ear close to her mouth and check her breathing.

The rain is constant.

Breathing is constant.

My laptop glows in the dark.

1:00

It's an approximate time. I have stopped caring about good and tight parameters.

The mannequins made of mist spoke to me not long ago. Who knows what they said. They drew closer to the window, closer to me through the rain, and they spoke to me. What I assume were their mouths moved abundantly, but I heard nothing. Only the hard and constant rain.

1:00

Ronnie woke at last, said, "I had such a good nap, Josh. It's so restful here. Thank you for bringing me," then she added that I might need a nap too. I assured her I didn't. "I may never sleep again," I said.

She said, after giving me a peck on the cheek, "Uh huh, and someday the dead will rise and sing Christmas carols in fulsome voice."

I smiled. I thought it was an unusual remark for her, even interesting. I said to her, "Jesus, that was stupid."

2:00

She's sleeping again.

I don't know what to do about all of this.

I woke Ronnie; I said, "I'm sorry," and she said, without opening her eyes, "For what?"

"For my insensitive remark."

"It's all right," she said, and opened her eyes a little. "It's still raining."

"Yes," I said.

"Christ!" she said. "Christ, the rain!"

"Yes," I said. "The rain."

She closed her eyes.

I can do nothing but write and stare out the window while she sleeps. I can hear her, now, snoring in her soft and appealing way. So odd that I would hear it above the endless drone of the rain.

It wasn't *her*. Good Lord, it was them. The mannequins. Talking.

They were in this room with me, I'm certain of it. They weren't at the window. I'd have seen them; I always see them. And I see them *always* at the window.

If I had turned away from it, the window, when I thought I was hearing only Ronnie, I would have seen them here. In the room with me. Here. In the room.

I've sponged up their leavings. Moisture on the linoleum. They left no standing water.

I am not frightened.

I believe in them, so I can't be frightened. I *know* them, so I am not frightened of them.

The laptop is warm, comforting on my thighs.

Ronnie wakes. I hear her. She wakes.

And then appears.

"Hello," she says. "Hello, Josh," she says. "What a good nap I had. What a wonderful place this is to nap. Thank you for bringing me here."

We made love wildly and urgently.

It's Tuesday, 3:45 pm.

Moments ago, Ronnie said, "That was remarkable. Josh, that was remarkable."

"I agree," I said, and patted her ass. We're in the kitchen. She's making coffee, I believe. A drink of some kind.

She's still naked. She knows I like it—that continuation of her nakedness after lovemaking. Her *reveal*. Her realization of my purposes and need. My revelation, and hers too.

3:46 p.m.

She read over my shoulder what I wrote here, some of it. She tapped
the screen (I don't like that; leaves marks), said, "You're not *very* odd,
Josh, but you're *somewhat* odd." She cocked her head; a coquettish gesture, said, "My 'reveal'?"

I said, "Ronnie, I heard them."

"Heard them?" she said. "Oh yes." She formed quotes with her fingers.
It's a gesture I despise from anyone, even her, even when she's naked,
when all gestures are appealing. It's posturing and false. "*Them!*" she said
and grinned.

"Don't grin," I said. "Please."

She stopped grinning, looked confused, a little anxious, too, I think.
Why not?

I said, "I believe in them. I believe in them."

"No need to repeat yourself," she said. "My hearing's perfect."

"Nothing's perfect," I said.

She grinned. It was a nervous grin. Obviously nervous.

She said, "A little bit, just a little bit, Josh, you're scaring me. Like
maybe you're going to do something strange to me while I'm asleep."

I cocked my head. "Huh? Huh?" I grinned. "I already have," I said, and
laughed a little, which elicited a laugh from her, and when we stopped
laughing, I said, "If I were going to do anything *strange* to you, my love, it
wouldn't be while you were *sleeping.*" I smiled.

She didn't.

"Joke," I said.

"I believe you," she said.

4:25 p.m.

Of *course* the constant hard rain produces creatures such as these—
the creatures I've seen beyond the window. Rain is the offspring of lakes,
rivers and oceans, after all, and those are places of life, places teeming

with life.

So it's no great mental task to believe that the rain can produce, from itself, *within* itself, *of* itself, creatures such as I have seen here, at this house.

4:49

She read aloud, over my shoulder, one of my phrases above: "Rain is the offspring of lakes, rivers, oceans, after all . . ." was as far as she got before I slammed the laptop shut and shouted, "Dammit, Ronnie, dammit, Goddammit!" then wheeled around on my stool and watched her back quickly, quickly away from me.

"Shit, I'm sorry!" she said, and disappeared into the bedroom.

Which is where she is now.

Snoring softly and appealingly . . .

I apologized to her, of course. I needed to. They told me to. And she was very understanding, said it was "all right," said the rain was making us both "contentious and irrational."

"I'm not being irrational, just contentious," I said in an offhand way, so she'd think I was joking, and she said, "I need to sleep again," so I said, "Okay, sleep," and she left the room.

7:23:14

Here I am, on this spot, this tall stool, at my window, and happy about it, even happy about the hard and constant rain because of the gifts it has produced.

Oh, and she appeared not long ago, very sleepy, wiped her eyes, yawned, said, "Oh, Josh, yes, by the way, I've seen them too. Honestly. I believe you now, I really do, and I'm sorry for doubting," then wandered back into the bedroom. I hollered after her, "Thank you, my love!" and got, moments later, what was, of course, an affirmation, a "Yes," obviously.

We go back a long, long way.

High school sweethearts, you know. Proms and hops and so forth. Dated at soda shops. Watched movies that we really didn't *watch* (wink, wink). How many relationships have been spawned by just such scenarios? The world doesn't spin because of such scenarios, of course, but they do spin the world.

I love her as much as I can love anything, anyone, and that's an enormous amount. More than I can hold in both hands.

They told me, "Love her deeply, Josh, love her very, very deeply," and I said, "I do, and have," and they nodded and smiled and said, "Yes, we know."

She's in the bedroom, now.

I have no idea what she's doing.

I'll go and find out.

I'll go and see.

9:02:23 p.m.

Darker than hate in that bedroom. No light. The rain's done it at last—destroyed the light. I should have known, but didn't.

I said in that darkness, "Ronnie?"

"Josh?" she said.

"I'm here, Ronnie. Are you afraid?"

"Yes," she said.

"Why?" I said.

"I think you know why," she said.

"I do, yes," I said.

"Can you leave now, Josh?"

"Yes," I said, "I can leave," and I did.

10:19 p.m.

The laptop's working on batteries only. It's no good on batteries. Never has been. Lasts maybe two hours, tops. What kind of shit is that?

I'll write quickly, type quickly, get lots said.

The rain has not stopped.

And they, whom the rain has produced for me, are pushing against the window *en masse* and grinning, mumbling: odd, they were so articulate not long ago, an hour ago, two hours ago, or three.

Interesting, almost ironic, that the laptop keeps the time beautifully when the lights are gone.

Oh, she said, *Ronnie* said, moments ago, "You shouldn't use it on batteries, Josh. Those batteries are shitty."

"I know," I said.

I like it when she says "shitty." It's a feminine thing—that word.

I said, "Are you still afraid, Ronnie?"

"Yes, I am. I'm going to leave, I need to leave," she said.

"No," I said.

She said nothing. She went back into the bedroom. I heard her packing. Hard to believe she can do that in the pitch dark.

4:15:21 a.m.

And so she's gone. How can I deal with that? How can I deal with her absence? We've been together since high school. We went to parties together, the Senior Prom, you know. We played "Find The Mule" in the backseat of my father's Dodge.

But she's gone.

And that's a very critical thing.

Like the condition of my laptop's batteries.

A very critical thing.

4:22:12 a.m.

I watched her go. The mannequins watched with me. And they kept silence, except for what they said:

Such as:

"Enough of her already."

And:

"That's the end, possibly."

"That's the end of her, possibly."

And:

"Grieve as much as you suppose appropriate, Josh."

And:

"As much as you deem appropriate, grieve, now, Josh."

"Yes," I said, "I will."

6:19:22 p.m.

Odd, yes, how time is wrapped up in static moments that don't represent *time* at all. The moment, for instance, in which a quick inhale is taken. We feel or hear or experience, within us, only that breath, in that static moment of the breath, so it's *apart* from the flow of time. Whether it's the first breath or the last, it is only one breath out of literally millions in the flow of time, the flow of a life.

If I were to construct an analogy, it would be this: time is wrapped up in static moments that don't represent *time* at all, in the *same way* that skin and blood and flesh is wrapped up in microscopic cells that, singularly, have next-to-nothing to do with skin and blood and flesh.

If you think about it, as I do, you will agree.

I love my laptop.

This thing that glows in the dark.

I love it.

Still raining. Very, very hard, now. As if an ocean is draining. I know of it though I can't hear or see it because, at last, I can't hear or see anything. I feel the comforting warmth of my laptop against my thighs, and I feel my fingertips on the keyboard, the little guide bumps on the "F" and "J," which are so important for blind typists and touch typists, or blind touch typists.

Of course.

And *their* touch, as well, is comforting, even warm, surprisingly warm, considering what it's composed of, the small moments of the life-giving rain, the life-creating rain, the rain that is life.

Where do I go now? From here?

Where?

And why?

And why?

I'm the first to admit that I don't have his critical sense, his intelligence, or his lyricism, and his perverse philosophies have always annoyed and eluded me.

And now, *he* doesn't have any of that, either.

I can't be happy about it. I want to be happy about it, but it's not possible.

You'd think I'd have adjusted after so long.

My God, we went to proms together and movies, too, and we played "Find the Mule" in the back of his father's Dodge. So how could I be happy now?

I can't.

I'm not.

I'm as sad and confused as a new puppy blindly searching for its mother's teat.

I have his laptop. It's a strange parting gift for our years of loss and gain and heartache. This thing that glows in the dark.

It *will* rain again. It must rain again. And then he'll *be*, once more, once more, and I'll *see* him, and *hear* him—singing Christmas carols in fulsome voice.

CIRCULARITY

GEORGE

It's not as if I'm haunting anyone, or skulking about, or lingering. But a lot needs to be done. Dogs need feeding, books need writing, leaves need to be carted out of gutters, and people need to be loved. All the *living* (and maybe most of the dead) need to be loved. But lacking time, opportunity, and wherewithal, some of the living do not find it. They get screwed, instead, or lied to, cheated, abandoned, degraded, caught up in bizarre intercourse. And yes, of course I abhor such judgements, and I never made them before . . . *this*! But I find that it matters at this point in my existence to make such judgements in order to protect a past that matters more than any of the living can possibly know, and a future that's barreling ahead without me, and a present that's all too present—at times chokingly, cloyingly present, like the smell of infection.

I have screwed and screwed and screwed, and it's not as if I haunt anyone, now, or linger, or meander around in the moments of eternity.

This late in my existence, I have become poetic—about leaves in gutters, dogs in need of feeding, people in need of love.

But, to clarify—people in need of touch, warmth, *truth*!

ROXANE

He thinks he's found what makes the universe tick. He thinks he's discovered something unique. I don't blame him for that, and I really hated to walk out on him, but it's only temporary, until he flips to his feet again (and the universe being what it is, I know he will. At least I think he will. Perhaps I merely *hope* he will), and discovers what millions or billions already know—that what he and I do, now, we do not because we're unique, or because what we felt, then, for one another (and feel even more strongly, now) is unique, but because it is merely rare, like albino alligators or true poets. And we can share it.

But he's acting like a reformed smoker, for Pete's sake—running about through time exhorting the sinners (in his way) to repent for their own sakes, and for the sake of creation. Poor fool.

GEORGE

When I met her, I did not know her. Okay, that's obvious. We meet others we do not know. We meet them, we learn them, but we do not know them; sometimes we never know them. That's obvious, too.

Who lives to know the guts and heart of another? Who lives to stick his fingers in and poke about, and draw back blood or bile or shit or saliva—the mess of the living, which only the living can endure?

But she was as sweet as maple sugar candy, and as beguilingly untidy in her daunting intellect as cats at a kill. As she moved, I knew the femininity beneath her long dress, and I knew her biology. And as she smiled or talked or frowned or ate, I knew her mouth and all its appetites.

Do you know that sex survives death? Of course it does. It's *about* survival, after all.

Two are approaching. He is filled only with the needs of his penis, and she is filled with the need to be filled up. These two are Humphrey and Paula, and the time is the dead past re-breathing.

He has the remnants of a malted around his lips. She'll taste it when they kiss and she'll dislike it, but will say nothing, because she's used to saying nothing; it's that era.

ROXANE

To hear him talk about it, the first time we made love, it was as if he had discovered a new continent, a new planet, a new *galaxy*. A place, at any rate, which only he, out of billions or trillions of souls who had started down similar paths before him, was privy to.

At the time, I thought of his reaction—"This is heaven, Roxane. No one has ever trod this ground before, I know it! It's holy, it's sacred, it's what God intended when he invented sex!"—as 99% pure bullshit. *And he's bullshitting you,* I told myself, *because he's a man and you're a woman and he believes that it's a man's duty to bullshit a woman.* This was okay, as far as I was concerned, because I thought that his 1% non-bullshit was worth something, that *he* was worth something. And he is, of course. But here, in this place, in this corner of the vast universe, he's so damned *manic.* He's on a mission. And he seems to know nothing about *circularity.*

GEORGE

You see, this is the story. I've lost the beguiling one here, in this ocean of bodies, faces, organs, movement, re-breathing, infection, regret, lust without need, more regret, and more regret, and more regret. That's the whole story. There is no other. I've lost her. No plot. No subplot. No characters, peripheral or otherwise. No dénouement. How can there be any of that in a universe without real change? That's *my* universe, and hers—the universe we've inherited due to a grim tradition set up by a perverse creator who likes to play about with whoopee cushions and exploding cigars. Creates love and takes it away at a whim. Creates death and dishes it out like a cafeteria worker dishing out mashed potatoes. And brings the two together—death and love—as if they are two points on the same circle. And maybe they are.

Here's the circle of Humphrey and Paula, even now. A circle of two. He in well-creased black pants and sporting well-coifed blond hair, and she in a pleated skirt, bobby socks, and pointed bra (Watch out, Humphrey, you'll hurt yourself!). He is as hard as a monkey wrench and she's as soft as a soufflé. It's romance ready to roll around in wet grass, lust snaking into willing orifices, screams already screamed.

Shit, I've got to stop them!

HUMPHREY (OF THE PRESENT)

Listen, I ain't no murderer. You think I wanted to do all that? It ain't like I had a choice or nothin'. Who in hell *does* have any choices in this crazy-ass world, huh? And you think if I had any choices, I'da chose my stupid ass name? No way, José. I would'a called myself Hawk or Ballbuster or Tank. But, hell, my mother—God rest her—gave me that name, so I gotta wear it forever.

So you do what you got to do and things end up okay for everyone. Well, almost everyone. I mean, the guy who gets whacked don't end up okay, I know. The guy who gets whacked . . . gets *whacked*, and that's tough, but so are lots of things, like kittens getting drowned, and forest fires, and floods, and people starving to death, and . . . like that. I cry about these things all the time. You don't believe me? C'mon over!

I mean, all of us got to make a living, right? We all got to put beef on the table and gas in the damned Navigator and baby shoes on the smiling grandkids (here, I got pictures).

So don't look at me funny, okay. Maybe you was born with a freakin' aluminum spoon in your mouth, or whatever, but I wasn't. I was born with my father's Goddamn left foot in one end and his right foot in the other, and nobody ever said, "Hey, here's a break!"

And I had that damned *worm* on my shoulder, too.

GEORGE

I despise not being heard. I despise being *alone* and not being heard. This was never a problem when it was Roxane and I. It wasn't even a matter of being *heard*, it was simply a matter of . . . *being*, of *walking through* and leaving love in our wake.

Look at these two, for God's sake! Look at them! Entangled like the tentacles of an octopus. And to what purpose?

HUMPHREY

I know, I know, you've heard it all before, you got to understand that I didn't whack no one who didn't deserve it. And I didn't do no women, neither. Well, once, I did, but it turns out she had a freakin' sex change operation, so I didn't know. I put my .38 to her forehead and she said, "But I'm a woman!" And I said, "Sure you are," and I shot her, and, later, when I got my money, the client says, "You notice anything strange about him?" which is when I learned that God had made her a woman. Boy, that really frosted my cookies.

But, hell, when you grow up with nothin' but your damn self to keep you company, you got to watch out for number one, first. So when some guy says, "Hey, I got a cash deal for ya, but you gotta kill someone," the first thing you say is, "I ain't gonna do that. I ain't gonna kill no one." But then this someone says, "Sure, I know, but this poor bastard is just about dead, anyway, because he's sick, and it looks like he'll be a long time dying. So he wants somebody to off him, ya know. He'd do it himself, but he's chicken shit. So he asks me to find someone, and I figured you needed the dough . . ."

Well, sure I needed the dough. I had about thirteen cents in one pocket and a hole in the other, and my rent was due three months ago, and a good meal was something you got at someone else's place, and I had this damned worm on my shoulder, so I said, "Yeah, I'll do it."

And I did. But it was tough as pulling your own teeth. Tougher. Because the poor snot wouldn't die quick, and when I put one slug in him, in his arm, I wanted to take it back. I wanted to reach into that scrawny arm and take that bullet back and run away and find a real job— selling fish or something.

But the miserable little bastard looks up at me and gives me this weird-ass smile, and says, "Thanks, but that wasn't good enough by half. Do better with the next one, okay!"

So I aim the gun straight at his forehead and I say, "Gee, I'm really sorry, ya know," and he sighs and shakes his miserable head and says, "Christ, man, I'm hurting here!" and I pull the trigger, and blow his right ear clean off. He goes back a little and grabs the place where his ear used to be and curses real loud, and I pull the trigger again, and get him square in the forehead, but the bullet don't go in, I know, because I hear it ricochet off his freakin' fireplace, for Christ's sake, and he goes down real hard on his miserable skinny back, and he's holding his damned forehead and he's cursing, "Shit, you're fucking incompetent!" and, "Shit, do it right!" so I hold the barrel of that pissant little gun against his freakin' chest, where I think his damn heart is, on the left, you know, and I pull the trigger again, and nothing happens. No blood. No screaming. No dead man.

He sighs again. I think this is amazing because I already shot him so many times. And he says, "What is that thing you're using?"

"I don't know," I tell him. "I got it from my cousin. Cost me twenty-five bucks," which was a lie because I didn't have no money to pay for it and my cousin said, "Pay me later," because he knew what I was gonna do with it.

And the scrawny bastard sits up, with one hand still on his forehead, and the other hand holding the place where his ear used to be, and he says, "Christ Jesus, that's a fucking .22, for the love of God!" and shakes his head a little. "Christ, a hit man who uses a Goddamned .22!" he says, and laughs this gurgling little laugh. "What's the fucking world coming to?"

"Wait a minute," I say. "You got it wrong. I ain't no freakin' hit man!"

"Isn't *that* the truth!" he says.

And I shoot him in the eye. And he dies right away. And I think, *God, listen, I'm real, real sorry for this. Don't hold it against me too much!* and I run from the place.

GEORGE

Do you know that most of the problems in your world are caused by lack of love? I'm not talking about the touchy-feely sort of love you find in progressive churches ("Let's all join hands, now, and experience the power of heaven . . ."), and not because there isn't a place for that sort of love; there certainly is. I'm talking about love between people. Not lust love, or power love, or possessive love, or jealous love. That's all crap. I'm talking about the kind of love that makes you look into her eyes and say, "Will you have our children?" That's sweet, isn't it! But it's more than sweet. It's the *only kind of love* that really works, the only kind of love which makes the evil that dwells in all of us go into an eternity of sleep. And I'm not talking about the actual physical act of having children, or even the possibility of having children. I'm not talking about that at all. Because, of course, not all couples can have children, or even want them. I'm talking about . . . I'm talking about . . . shit, what *am* I talking about?

I'll get back to you.

ROXANE

His ideas are often as half-formed as runny eggs. He depends on intuition as if it were a force as dependable and as immutable as gravity, but he's so damned equivocal at the same time: take, for instance, his last mortal words—"This is going to be quite an adventure." Then he paused and added, "I think."

GEORGE

I wanted to bring the truth of the healing power of honest, pure love to John Wilkes Booth, *before* he did what he did, of course. But I couldn't find him. Roxane was with me, then. She'll tell you; we looked for him in all the places we knew he dwelt, and we even caught glimpses of him now and again, but he always eluded us, though I'm certain he wasn't actively trying to elude us, of course. I'm sure he had no idea we were there.

I think of that as the beginning of Roxane's frustration with me. "How do you know this man *doesn't* have love in his life?" she asked. "Even the kind of love for which you are such an extreme advocate, George."

"Well, it's obvious," I answered. "Look at what he did. He killed Mr. Lincoln at Ford's Theater."

"George, George, George," she said (which was not a phrase she ever used in life), "we're not here to reform assassins, or even to prevent them from *becoming* assassins. Think *circularity*, George."

"Oh?" I had her. "Then why *are* we here?" *Here*, at that moment, was Washington, D.C., in 1864. I would have opted for going back much further, to shortly after Booth's adolescence, when his psyche began flirting with the idea of assassination as a tool for change (though I know, I know—he certainly wasn't thinking, then, "I'm going to assassinate the president one day." But he *was* letting his internal violence begin to lead him, or absorb him, or manipulate him, so it was the best time to give him what Roxane and I have given so many). I would have *opted* for that, but it was not under my control. We don't simply will ourselves into this time period or that time period. We're . . . flung about by what are, in essence, cosmic winds that are random and unpredictable. You see, the "space-time continuum" is like a highway that's always under construction, always imperfect, always subject to change, realignment, restructuring. And I don't believe that it ever really has a destination, *per se*. Just as there are no real destinations on a circle, the maze of the space-time continuum is like a million or a billion circles, ellipses, and dead-ends constantly inter-acting, retreating, reforming, making wholly new combinations. And that interaction, restructuring, and reforming is made possible by formerly non-cosmic beings such as Roxane and myself. There are millions of us, perhaps more, though our purposes may differ (although these purposes are always constructive, positive, and loving, of course) from one formerly non-cosmic being to another. Roxane's and my purpose is simply to put right what the perverse creator didn't get right (or didn't care enough to get right) in the first place—to bring the essence of love (honest, pure, real, and fulfilling love, the kind of love that Roxane and I have shared for such a long time) to those whose futures will be changed by it, like this young man and young woman, Humphrey and Paula. Like everyone, of course. So we're thrown about in time.

It really is that simple.

At least I think it is.

Roxane disagrees, but she likes to disagree.

HUMPHREY

Hey, you got to *be* something. Know what I mean? God didn't put us here to be *nothing*. Why would he? So he made, you know, painters to be painters, and bookkeepers to be bookkeepers, and street cleaners to be street cleaners, and he made me to be a facilitator. At least I thought so. Good word, huh? *Facilitator*. One of my clients used it once. He said, "Humphrey, you ain't no hit man. That's not what you are. You do what you do because you got to do it—for yourself, for your family, for your employer, and even for the people you whack, because they got to find their destiny, right? So you facilitate that, Humphrey. You're a *facilitator*. You help people find their *destiny*."

Like that first poor snot. I helped him find his destiny. I was his *facilitator*.

GEORGE

What can even a creature such as I do when lust rises up and has its way? Look at these two. Tangled like bait in a can. They know only the lusts of their loins, so they're both doomed. I can feel it. And I can give them nothing without Roxane.

ROXANE

Well, you know, I love him dearly. He's always been a good man, and now, as a kind of Angel-on-a-Mission, he's a *very* good man, although he's confused. Heck, who isn't? But when you find somebody who's confused, what do you do? You either help him out of his confusion or you go somewhere else and let him help himself. I had a therapist once, during my existence as a non-cosmic being, who told me, "You know what, Roxane? You can't change anybody." She was right. And I can't change George, even if I love him dearly, and he loves me, as he does, and as we do. But that's really just salad dressing. It's very tasty salad dressing, I agree, but it's not the salad itself. Have you ever noticed that you can dump salad dressing all over a salad, you can mix salad dressings together and come up with an entirely new taste, but you can't take the dressing and the salad, the lettuce and tomato and carrots and broccoli and onions, and grind it all into a kind of yummy pate? If you try, you end up with something disgusting (I did it once, as a non-cosmic being: I even tried feeding it to George, who looked at me, dumbfounded). It's the same with people, living or dead, mortal, crossed-over, time-locked, present or future or past tense. It's the same way with George. He's trying to take these folks, like John Wilkes Booth, before, and this man named Humphrey, now ("now," "before," "then"—such word salad), all of whom are simply the sum totals of all they have been, are, and will be, and he's trying to fold his own brand of everlasting, glorious love into the mix.

"George, honey," I want to tell him, I *have* told him, "it won't work! You'll end up with something disgusting."

HUMPHREY

So, you see, there's this guy, and he's been following me around for years and years and years. Jesus H. Christ, he's like a Goddamned stalker. I even tried telling the cops about him, but they wouldn't listen, because they knew me, and they didn't give two shits if someone was stalking me.

I tell the cops, "Hey, I think he's going to kill me or something." But they didn't care. "Go find someone else to bother, Humphrey," they said.

Every time I turn around there he is, this guy. And he's got this really dumb-ass look on his face, like he wants to sell me something, or give me religion, for Christ's sake!

GEORGE

How amazing the number of permutations, admixtures, time-slips, moments here and gone, past, present and future that comprise the human being. We can, under all the right circumstances, be in many hundreds of places at once, many hundreds of times at once, and we can experience many hundreds of experiences at once. I've explained this to Roxane, but, when I was done, she looked at me, smiled and said, "George, I already knew that. I didn't become a formerly non-cosmic being yesterday." And I could tell that she was telling the truth. But she's never lied, anyway, so . . .

Where was I?

Yes, this poor fool, Humphrey, pulled and pushed around by his libido, driven here and there by the sheer energy that exists between his legs, singing his anthem of *Power to the Penis!* Yes, this poor fool. I've been following him around for so long I can barely keep track. There was even a moment, which still exists, that I came across him during my own time on the earth, which was *his time* on the earth, too, and there we were, face to face on a street in Rochester, NY, and he looked at me and screamed, "Stop bothering me!" I was astonished because I had no idea what he was talking about, because, of course, I was, then, a non-cosmic being—not, as I am now, a formerly non-cosmic being—or, at least, a non-cosmic being unaware of the formerly cosmic-non-cosmic nature of beingness.

Pardon me. Suddenly, I'm a bit dizzy.

ROXANE

It's not that he doesn't mean well. I know that's a namby-pamby thing to say. Most people *do* mean well. As he does. He wants to change the universe, one lost soul at a time. He wants to fill them with the kind of love he and I shared and share and dwell in constantly, on every physical and non-physical plane, plateau, and dimension that exists now, has ever existed, or ever will exist. Jeez, I *sound* like him. Which was why it was so easy to say goodbye to him, because I can't really say goodbye to him— he's always there, everywhere, to varying degrees of what passes (from moment to moment) for reality. But I ask him, "Can you remember how you *became* a formerly non-cosmic being, George?" But, as he often does, he only looked at me dumbfounded. Who can remember the moments of transition, anyway? I can't.

HUMPHREY

So I was in Rochester, which is this town in New York State, near one of the big lakes, Lake Erie or Lake Huron or something, and I'm hunting a guy who needs hunting because it's the way I pay the mortgage, you know, and keep the Navigator fed, and I'm walking down some street and I see this guy who's been stalking me, and he's walking down the street, too, right at me. Jesus, and he acts like he don't even recognize me, like he ain't really been following me around for more years than a dog has fleas, he's just walking and smiling and looking foolish, and when he gets close, I yell at him, "Listen, buddy, you either get out of my life or I'll *get* you out of my life!" Does he say anything? No. He just looks at me like I'm made of bad smells. So I say it again, what I said before, only louder, and he runs away. Fast!

You know what I thought. I thought that if I saw him again, I wasn't gonna like it, and neither was he.

GEORGE

Roxane talks about *circularity*—how we circumvent the proper sequence of events by inserting ourselves into the scheme of things. That's actually the way she puts it. I don't get it, though. I never have. It's like a riddle, a puzzle, a conundrum. But she talks that way, sometimes, because she's just a skooch brighter than I (what can I say?), though she doesn't dwell on it, only lords it over me when she can. No, that's not true. She's a woman who's as good as a warm summer's day. And becoming (as I always was, really) a formerly non-cosmic being did, in fact, make me smarter, though not, I'm afraid, smart enough.

HUMPHREY

You know, sometimes we do what we do because we ain't got no choice, because when we started out in life we were okay, we grinned and smiled and acted like everything was hunky dory, because it was, you know. But then we get these *annoyances* and we can't get rid of them and they change us. They change our lives. These annoyances. Like having a worm on your shoulder and you can't get rid of it. You swipe it away, but it comes back, and you look at it and say to yourself, "Fucking worm!" After a while, it changes you. After a while, you think life is different than you thought it was before. You think, "Shit, what's the use? That worm's always gonna be there." Know what I mean? That worm's always gonna be there, so why not grab whatever there is in any way you can grab it? Why not become a fucking hit man? Why not? People are always gonna look at you funny, anyway, because of that fucking worm on your shoulder.

That worm, this guy, the one who's stalking me, shit, I remember him from *way* back, when all I was trying to do was get laid, and there he was, this guy, this worm, looking at me through the car window like I was killing kittens or something.

ROXANE

I remember, though. *I* remember! Not the moments of my own transition. That's simply not the way things are (don't ask me why. *Foolish rules laid down by a perverse creator,* George would say, George *says*). But I remember the moments of *his* transition, because I was there, for the love of God, and I watched him *become* formerly non-cosmic, and I wept real tears (still can, don't want to), and he said, in those moments, "This is going to be quite an adventure. I think." And I *still wept!*

George, George, my love, give some thought to *circularity*. But then, how would it help? If he never did, he never will, never has, and never can.

HUMPHREY

You do what you gotta do. I said that. I meant it. So it turned out that what I had to do was hang up my .38 and my .45 and my .347, and go to work at the post office. Don't laugh. I really am working at the post office. The one on Elmwood. Great big post office, biggest in the city. The main post office. That's where I work. I sort mail. Junk mail from first class to pre-stamped. Well, I don't do it personally. There's too many damned letters for me to do it personally. The machine does it. I watch the machine and make sure it doesn't fuck up.

Why do I do that?

Because I found out that worms can turn into fucking butterflies. You like that? Worms can turn into fucking butterflies? Yeah, I like it, too. I been taking a course in poetry, because of this thing that happened, this poetic thing that happened (that's what Paula called it—a "poetic thing," and she's pretty smart, so I listen to her. "It's poetic, Humphrey. It's like poetic irony," she said. "Like it's fate or something.").

Meaning that here was this worm, this guy, this schmo, this asshole who's been stalking me since rocks were young, and he's walking down the street toward me again, and I'm waiting at a corner for the god-damned traffic, and he sees me, and I see him, and I go ballistic, I reach for my .38 right there in my shoulder holster, but it sticks in there, in my shoulder holster, who the hell knows why, sweat or something, so I'm getting real mad 'cuz I need to plug this worm, this asshole, this schmo, and I don't know what I'm doing, so I'm walking out into traffic while I'm reaching for my .38, and I see, out the corner of my eye, that there's this truck bearing down on me, and I hear a horn blow, and I look, and the next thing I know, this schmo, this worm, is on the ground next to me, and there's this broad standing over him, and he's saying, "This is going to be quite an adventure. I think." And Paula's standing over me, looking at me, then at the schmo, then at me, and she says, "Jeez, Humphrey, he saved your fuckin' life!"

I look at him. He looks real dead, and his lady looks real sad, and I look at Paula, and she says, "He pushed you out of the way of the fuckin' truck, Humphrey. He pushed you out of the way of the fuckin' truck, and it ran over him. Poor snot! He gave up his fuckin' life for you, Humphrey!"

"Yeah, I guess he did," I say.

So now I don't kill people. I work at the post office on Elmwood.

Because of that guy. Because he was a worm who turned into a butterfly. Because he was so full of love, even for someone he didn't really know, that he gave up his own fuckin' life.

Go figure.

ROXANE

Circularity! Poor, poor George. *Circularity*! But he'll never understand it. I know that. Because he never did understand it. God love him.

GEORGE

Do you know that most of the problems in your world are caused by lack of love? I'm not talking about the touchy-feely sort of love you find in progressive churches ("Let's all join hands, now, and experience the power of heaven . . . "), and I'm not saying there isn't a place for that sort of love; there certainly is . . .

NEW YORK POET

You tell me you need only to see other people—not know them, only see them—and I assume what you mean by this is you need to be near them as they pass—to exist alone with poetry and passion in the city that loves you (as surely it must), to know its strides—purposeful, elegant, stumbling—its brief and lingering glances, its dizzying dances of color and voice, its wide, obtuse and ordinary smiles, its easy talk and urgent business of business and seduction, its lazy afternoons with beer and hip-hop and slow touch, and endless autumns of great achievement—you need, I think, to feel warm exhalations of city air, to know, even, the death of city—this part and that—slow decay of old hands and exhausted minds, and the startling laughter of the new and barely verbal, myriad smells and hurried notations, city chatter and city hum, the soul of its eyes, the taste of its tongue: I believe this, dear woman—you are poetry in a city that steals and cajoles and negotiates poetry from you and gives it back with a strange but human caress.

MR. DEATH

Mr. Death is near. I see him in the hydrangeas peering at me like a chipmunk. Nervous Mr. Death, afraid I'll run over him with a lawnmower.

I also see him in stores, sometimes, and I warn Security; I say there's a shifty person hiding in Women's Lingerie, taking up time in Notions.

He follows me at a safe distance down wide streets: I know his face no better than I know a thousand others, but he bobs as he walks, as if he has heel spurs, and sometimes I lose him by ducking into a theater or catching a bus. When I glance back he looks mystified.

I first met him when I was a teenager playing hearts, and he sat down, pimply and ludicrous in a tie-dyed shirt, and said, "Let's play hearts. I win, you lose!"

And just last week he was hitchhiking, holding a sign which read, "Anywhere," and I passed him up, didn't even glance back. In winter he leaves wide footprints, like a snowshoe hare, and in summer blue jays land on his shoulders and make their raucous noise—he speaks incessantly, makes deals with anyone, reads Chaucer, Baudelaire, Stephen King, Barbara Cartland, loves to play at being knowledgeable, leaves his smell in the corners of any room, where there is no relief from this wall or that, and runs quickly past windows, too, like a streaker. Sometimes, at parties, he slips away with a guest to a place that's quiet and golden—I've noticed if I put the ceiling fan on high, and cup my hands around my ears, I can hear him whistling. And if I take my little dog up and look straight into her big eyes I can see him in her years.

THE MUSIC OF THE NIGHT

I t is not wise to listen to "Unchained Melody" while driving at night through places where deer move from one field to another. It's such a distraction, that bold angst about time and love—who can resist it? One finds oneself listening, not looking, not seeing, really, not knowing, and perhaps one finds oneself singing along in high and bad voice, and carrying on a running inner dialogue about how true such things as song lyrics really are, and how sad, until, in the midst of this blind-glorious immersion, one's luck runs out, and, hell, there you are.

41

THE MAN WALKING

It was the winter Lawrence climbed that damned hill at least twice a day. He had to climb it—even though it was his driveway, because his Jeep wouldn't go up it, or down it; there was too much snow. The winter had turned into one of those extreme winters Lawrence remembered from his childhood, and it always happened that a day or so after he had the driveway plowed—which cost $30.00 a pop, because the driveway was a fifth of a mile long, and had a twelve degree pitch—it was impassable again, so he decided to screw it and simply walk.

He pulled a sled loaded with bags of groceries up that hill. Ten-gallon jugs of water, too, because the water in the area wasn't potable. And sometimes he also had to carry his Boston terrier, because the little thing got cold during the ten-minute walk up the hill. Lawrence imagined he made quite a sight—if there had been anyone around to see him—pulling three bags of groceries up that hill on a sled, and holding his shivering little dog in his arms at the same time.

But having to climb the hill wasn't the main reason he remembered that winter so clearly. He remembered it so clearly because of the man walking on the road.

Every morning, Lawrence drove with his Boston terrier into town for breakfast. It was a routine, and though Lawrence had come to distrust most routines—because, he maintained, they were usually like paths that lead nowhere—he liked this routine because it allowed him to get some exercise, and the cold, early morning air helped him to wake up. He had breakfast at a tiny restaurant called Martha's Kitchen, where he could get scrambled eggs, toast, home fries, and coffee cheap, and he could eat with his Boston terrier, too, as long as the dog stayed inside Lawrence's heavy winter coat. "Wouldn't want the health inspector to close us down," the waitress—a lanky brunette named Iris—told him.

Lawrence encountered the man on the road early into that extreme winter. He saw him first when he was halfway to Martha's Kitchen, on the narrow road he always drove. The road was snow-covered that day. The man was walking on the right shoulder, so his back was to Lawrence, and he was dressed in a loose-fitting black coat and black pants; he wore red mittens that seemed to be attached up the sleeves of the coat by a thick line of blue cloth. His arms moved only a little as he walked, and his gait was stiff. Lawrence guessed, even before seeing the man's face, that he was elderly.

Lawrence slowed the Jeep, made sure no one was driving in his direction in the opposite lane, and swung out, away from the man, so as not to catch him with the cold air turbulence the Jeep created. When he had passed the man, he looked in his rearview mirror and saw the man's face; it was white, puffy, and thin-lipped; the eyes were black slits. Lawrence glanced back and smiled and nodded, hoping the man would see him and raise a hand in thanks for the courtesy of pulling out, away from him as he walked in the cold winter morning air. But he got no response from the man walking. It was all right, Lawrence decided. Some people, he thought, were taciturn; it was possible, too, that the man simply hadn't seen him smile and wave.

He saw the man again on the way back from Martha's Kitchen that same day. This time, the man was walking toward him; because the road was still snow-covered, Lawrence was driving slowly, so it was no problem for him to come nearly to a stop to allow an oncoming car to pass before he swung out, away from the man again, to spare him the air turbulence the Jeep created. Lawrence tried to catch the man's eye as he passed, but the man was looking straight ahead.

It bothered Lawrence a little that the man, for the second time, hadn't acknowledged his good deed, small though it was. Lawrence was certain other drivers weren't so courteous; in fact, he'd seen two other drivers ahead of him give the man no berth whatever, which made the man's loose-fitting coat flutter a little.

Lawrence thought courtesy was a dying art, and that a little bit of it went a long way. Perhaps, on some other morning, the man walking would acknowledge his good deed, and Lawrence hoped to see him again, on the road, simply so he could perform the good deed, once more, and be acknowledged for it.

He saw the man again while on his way to Martha's Kitchen two mornings later. There was blue sky that morning, and bright sunlight created long, early morning shadows. The man was walking on the right side of the road in his black coat, black pants, and red mittens, and, again, Lawrence pulled out, away from him: when he had passed, he glanced quickly back, smiled, and waved a little. He got no response from the man, and he decided it was all right—a good deed, a small courtesy, didn't require acknowledgement; it was its own reward.

He didn't see the man again that day; he saw him the following morning, as he drove back from Martha's Kitchen, Boston terrier in his lap. He swung out, away from the man, glanced at him as he passed, saw the man's eyes, black slits, saw that the man made no acknowledgement of his courtesy, drove home, and began his day.

Lawrence thought every now and then about the man. He wondered where he lived, if he lived *with* someone, if he was a widower, if walking were his hobby. He didn't dwell on the man overly much because the overriding theme of his interest—Lawrence realized—was the fact that the man had yet to acknowledge his—Lawrence's—courtesy. Lawrence decided this was all right. He had decided many, many times it was all right, and he insisted, to himself, that he believed it. The man's lack of acknowledgement for his simple courtesy was perfectly okay. It was even understandable. It was the dolts on the road who *didn't* give the man a wide berth (sparing him a blast of cold air) who should find *bitter* acknowledgement from the man. Lawrence imagined the man should yell, "Give me some damned room, for Christ's sake." So, when Lawrence *did* give him room, the man clearly saw it as simply doing the right thing. No one should receive acknowledgement simply for doing the right thing.

The winter grew steadily colder, windier, and more extreme through December, into January, then into February. Lawrence passed the old man walking many, many times, and he gave the man a wide berth each time. And, each time, he hoped for some slight acknowledgement—a nod of the head, a little wave—from the man. But it didn't happen.

Then, one day late in March, when the temperatures had begun to rise above freezing, at last, Lawrence and his Boston terrier encountered the man when they were on their way back from Martha's Kitchen. When Lawrence—for what he thought was the thousandth time—swung out, away from the man, and when—also for the thousandth time—he glanced at the man for some acknowledgement, he thought he saw the man's eyes shift toward him slightly. It was very surprising, and though Lawrence realized he couldn't be absolutely sure it had happened— because the man's eyes were visible only as black slits, after all—he told himself it had indeed happened, and he smiled. It was a small smile, but it felt good. Lawrence thought he would remember it—the smile, and the slight shift of the man's eyes toward him—for quite a long time. Perhaps for years. It was like a victory. His small courtesy had at last been acknowledged.

For months after that encounter with the man walking, Lawrence watched for him. But the man did not appear again. Lawrence lived in the house at the top of the steep hill for almost thirty years, and he drove to Martha's Kitchen almost every morning. When his Boston terrier passed away, he replaced him with a pug, and when the pug passed away, he replaced him with another Boston terrier. Lawrence tried to live a life that was routine-free and courteous. He thought he succeeded. On his deathbed, his sister—who was five years younger—said to him, "You've lived a good life, Lawrence. You should be happy about that."

And Lawrence smiled a little—in the way dying men smile—and said, "I think so. I think you're right. But I was never sure the man walking actually looked at me. I was never sure of it. I wish I could be sure."

His sister said, "The man walking?"

And Lawrence sighed a little, then passed away.

HIS MOTHER'S EYES

U nder a hot blue afternoon sky, in the squat shadow of a huge complex of wooden towers, bridges, slides, and passage-ways—like an immense honeycomb built by mad bees—Loretta Schoot was frantic. She supposed that the people all around looked bemusedly at her as she moved with quickness and agitation in search of her son.

"Troy?" she called. "Troy? Answer me!" She peered through openings between the vertical slats of the structure as she hurried around it, trying to catch a glimpse of Troy's bright yellow shorts and bright white shirt and big dark eyes, but she saw only other children who were playing at losing themselves.

"Troy!" she yelled. "Troy, answer me!" She glanced quickly at the other parents; they were seated on park benches set up around the play struc-ture. What's your problem, lady? she imagined they were thinking. What can happen to him? Do you really think he's going to get lost in there? She nodded as if in answer to that imagined question.

"Troy?" she hollered. "Troy? Damn it, Troy!" Again she glanced at the other parents; weren't they giving her scornful looks? She centered on one of the faces. "It's my son," she explained. "I can't find him." The face smiled noncommittally and she turned from it and called again, "Troy, answer me!"

She realized she was panicking. She didn't want to panic. It would be unseemly. She had no doubt that Troy was inside the structure somewhere. He couldn't have gotten over the ten-foot-high Empire fence that encircled it, and she hadn't seen him go out the gate.

A flash of yellow appeared between the vertical slats on an elevated passageway in front of her. "Troy!" she screamed. "You stop. Now!" The colors stopped. A small, round, creamy pink face, fleshy lips puckered between the slats, appeared. The eyes were large, dark, beautiful. "Yes, Mommy?"

"You come out of there this instant, do you hear me?"

He hesitated. "Why?" he asked.

Why? Loretta wondered. But it wasn't unlike him to ask why; it wasn't unlike any child. "Because I said so!" she told him.

"Oh." He sighed. Because I said so! was a response he'd heard many times before. "Right now?" he asked.

"Yes, right now. Do you know how to get out of there?"

His face cocked a little, as if in confusion. "Huh?"

She sighed. "Never mind. We've got to get home." It wasn't true. It merely amended her previous remark—Because I said so!—which had been, she thought, so authoritarian, so chillingly like what her own parents had drilled into her when she was a child.

She glanced around, saw a number of blank, adult faces; she grinned. A few faces grinned back knowingly, with approval, she hoped. Didn't she need the approval of the other adults here? Didn't it make her one of them? She said, "He's very headstrong." She looked back, at the spot where Troy had been. He wasn't there. "Damn it!" she whispered.

"He won't get lost, if that's what you're thinking," she heard from behind her.

She looked. A stout woman of seventy, she guessed, nodded at her in a kindly way from one of the benches.

Loretta smiled thinly at the woman. "Well, yes," she said. "It's just that"—she gestured toward the play structure—"it's so big, and I imagine that getting him out of there could be a real—"

"I brought my granddaughter here yesterday," the woman cut in, "and I had a hell of a time getting her out of it, too. I had to go in after her, and let me tell you, that was a chore. It's not made for us, is it?"

Loretta was still smiling; she wanted very much to extricate herself from conversation with the woman. She turned her head a little, toward the structure. "Troy, are you coming out?"

The stout woman went on, "But she didn't get lost in it, of course."

"Of course," Loretta said. "Troy?" she called.

The stout woman said, "That's a nice name. So many nice names today."

Loretta nodded. "Excuse me, please," she said. "But I've got to go find him again."

"Of course," said the woman.

Loretta turned. Troy was standing ten feet away. His beautiful dark eyes sparkled with wonder. "It's great in there, Mom," he said. "Can we come back? Please?"

She hesitated. The question, What if you get lost inside it? came to her. Then, surprising herself, she asked it. "What if you get lost in there?"

Troy smiled. "How could I get lost in it, Mom?"

How indeed? she thought. It, the play structure, was very like a child's mind, wasn't it? It was like the drawings that children made—fantastic, complex scribbles that filled up whole pages. And it was like the things that children built out of blocks—fantastic complex constructions that filled up whole rooms. Hadn't she made just such drawings and built just such constructions herself not so awfully long ago?

That night, Loretta said to her husband, "It's almost grotesque, it's so big. Have you seen it?"

"Yes," he answered. "I see them in lots of places." He traveled quite a bit for his business.

She went on, "I have to ask myself, does it really need to be so big and so complex?"

He said, "It's a place for kids to hide in, Loretta. It's a world of their own."

"Why would they need a world of their own?"

"Because they're kids."

"That's a flip answer. I never needed a world of my own when I was a kid." She paused; it wasn't true. It was simply more adult posturing. She went on, "There was a woman there who said her granddaughter almost got lost in it."

"That seems unlikely."

"It's easy for you to say. You didn't go running around the damn thing, yelling like a maniac. I knew he couldn't actually get lost in it, of course. I'm not an idiot."

Just then, Troy appeared in the doorway. He was smiling with accomplishment. "Come look at what I built," he told them. Loretta and her husband followed him to his bedroom, where he had fashioned a crude but recognizable miniature of the play structure out of building blocks.

"That's great, Troy," his father enthused.

"It's very nice," Loretta said. "Now I think it's time for bed, don't you?"

"But Mom . . ."

"Troy, it's already a quarter of an hour past your bedtime."

"Just a little while longer, Mommy. Please?"

"Don't give me an argument, young man, or I'll—" She felt her temper flare, felt her hand rise. She blinked confusedly.

"Mommy," Troy pleaded, "you promised."

"Promises can be broken," she snapped, "and don't you forget it!" Then she turned, went back to her bedroom, and lay down.

"Why?" she whispered, then repeated it.

"Why what?" asked her husband, as he came into the room.

She looked at him. "I don't know," she said, with confusion. "I don't know."

A week passed before she took Troy to the play structure again, and she took him only because his beautiful dark eyes had registered such mournful disappointment when she'd told him no.

The day was overcast and threatened rain, so she used that as an excuse to give him only five minutes. "Then we've got to go home or we're going to get soaked," she told him.

He pouted. "But that's not very long, Mommy."

"It's long enough," she said, which was also a standard reply, one he had learned not to argue with.

He went into the play structure and soon disappeared. She waited agitatedly for him to reappear. A minute later, he did—at the top of the tallest tower. He waved. "Hi, Mommy!" he called.

She waved back. "You've got just four minutes, Troy," she called.

He stopped waving, pursed his lips, and disappeared again.

There were only a few other adults around the play structure that day. One was the stout woman Loretta had seen the previous week. Loretta nodded at the woman; she had tried to avoid her, but had to look directly at her to see if she was, indeed, the same woman.

The stout woman nodded back. "It's not going to rain," she said.

"Yes," said Loretta. "Well, the weather is always so unpredictable, isn't it?"

"Not always," the woman said. "Let your boy enjoy himself." Her smile altered. "I'm sorry. That was presumptuous."

"No, it's all right," Loretta said. "I'm trying to wean him from this . . . thing, you see." She nodded to indicate the play structure.

"Wean him from it? Why? He loves it."

"It's too complex," Loretta explained. "I'm afraid it will . . . confuse him."

The stout woman grinned. "Children love mazes. And they love to hide."

"Of course," Loretta said. "Troy," she called. "Two minutes." She turned back to the stout woman. "Your granddaughter's here."

The woman shook her head. "No. I simply like to watch the children at play. It reminds me of when I was a child." She paused. "We have so much more real power as children, don't you think, than as adults. We're not bound by the same rules." She gave Loretta an apparently self-conscious grin. "That sounds fatuous, doesn't it? Forgive me. I'm just an old woman who wishes she were much, much younger. But it would be so wonderful if . . . parents could see things through the eyes of the children. Things like this playground."

"Oh?" Loretta suppressed a grin. "Did they have . . . things like this when you were young?"

"Heavens, no. But all of us had such things in here, didn't we?" She tapped her head.

Loretta hesitated, remembering. "Perhaps," she whispered. "But we grow up, don't we?" She smiled stiffly. "One minute, young man," she called. "Just one minute."

"Aw, Mom!" he called back.

"No arguments. One minute!" she paused. "Fifty seconds."

"I assure you, it's not going to rain," said the stout woman.

Loretta ignored her. "Forty seconds, Troy."

"Let him play," urged the stout woman. "It's fantasy. It's just fantasy."

"No," Loretta snapped. "It's wood and nails and cement and steel. That's all it is!"

"My dear—" the stout woman began apologetically. But she fell silent under Loretta's withering gaze.

"Twenty seconds," Loretta called, and moved away from the stout woman. "Ten seconds."

"Just a few more minutes, please, Mom. It isn't raining! See, the sun's coming out!"

Loretta glanced at the overcast sky. "No, it isn't," she called.

"In here it is," Troy called.

Loretta wondered about that a moment, then, "Five seconds and I'm coming in after you!" She waited. "Troy?"

Nothing.

"Troy?"

Still nothing.

"Troy, damn it!" She waited. Troy didn't answer.

Loretta was only a couple of feet from one of the many entrances to the play structure. The entrance was a short cement tunnel that opened onto a kind of tiny courtyard. There were half a dozen kid-sized wooden passageways around this courtyard—the passageways led to the interior of the structure.

She bent over and peered into the cement tunnel. "Can you hear me?" she called. "Troy, can you hear me?"

"Yes," he called back.

She smiled, relieved. "Then it's time to go! We've got to go home, now!"

"No," he called.

She took a quick breath of agitation. "When I say it's time to go, I mean it's time to go. You will not say no to me!"

Silence.

"Damn it, Troy, I am not going to come in there after you!" She realized that this contradicted what she'd told him just minutes earlier. "But if I have to—"

"Here he is," she heard. She turned. The stout woman was behind her; she had her hands on Troy's shoulders. "He apologizes for his . . . inappropriate behavior, don't you, Troy?"

Troy grinned.

Loretta's gaze moved quickly from her son to the stout woman, back to her son, then back to the stout woman. "Thank you," she said coldly, and held her hand out to Troy, who took it reluctantly, his lips set in a huge pout.

"My distinct pleasure," said the stout woman. "I think he has your eyes, my dear. Beautiful eyes." She grinned. "But I think he sees so much more." And with that, she toddled off, through the gate.

When she was gone, Loretta's open hand swept hard across Troy's face. "Damn you!" she hissed. "Damn you!"

He looked open-mouthed at her, his small hand pressed to his chubby red cheek, his huge dark eyes immense and round in surprise and fear and pain. "You . . . promised . . . " he stammered.

Loretta barked, "When I tell you to do something, I do not expect an argument. Nor do I want you being led around by nosy, loud-mouthed strangers! Is that clear?"

He said nothing. He stole a quick, soulful glance at the play structure.

She reached out, took hold of his shirt collar, yanked it. "Look at me!"

He looked. His lips quivered. He clearly was trying hard not to cry.

After a moment, Loretta got down on her haunches and gave him a flat, apologetic smile. "We can't come back here, Troy," she said. "It's a bad place. It's a very bad place. It has bad . . . influences. Do you understand?"

His mouth closed. With effort, he fought back the tears that had crowded to the corners of his eyes. "I want you to go inside it, Mommy."

She shook her head at once. She desperately did not want to go into the play structure. It was a child's universe after all. And she was an adult. "That's not possible, dear. It's just not possible. But I know that you like it here. I only wish . . . "

Troy cut in, his voice a fierce whisper, "It's my hiding place."

"But you don't need a hiding place, dear," Loretta protested. "You have us. You have me!"

He said nothing. He glanced around quickly, again, at the play structure.

Loretta said, "And I just can't see it the way you do, Troy. I'm sorry."

Moments later, she and her son were on their way home.

"I hit him," she told her husband that night in bed.

"I know," he said.

"You do?"

"Yes. He told me."

A moment's silence. "I didn't want to hit him. I didn't mean to hit him. But he . . ."

"Yes?"

"He asked for it."

"Of course he did."

She gave him an accusing look. "Don't use that holier-than-thou tone with me."

"I'm sorry."

"And he's not going back to that play structure, either. We got that straightened out."

"I know. He told me that, too."

"I'm glad you and he get along so well."

"So am I, Loretta. So am I."

It was past two a.m. when Loretta got out of bed, weary of trying unsuccessfully to sleep. She put her robe on and went to Troy's room. The door was closed. Odd, she thought. He always kept it open, especially at night, when light from the rest of the house comforted him into sleep.

She took hold of the knob, turned it, pushed the door open slowly, peeked inside.

His bed was empty.

She flicked the light on, went into the room. "Troy?" she whispered. "Troy?"

The room was empty.

From the gate, under the soft, creamy light of a full moon, Loretta thought the play structure looked monolithic, as if it had been built up from a huge lump of clay.

"Troy!" she called. She got no answer. She thought she didn't really expect one.

"Troy," she called again, and this time kept her voice low because it was night, after all, and there was quiet around her; there was quiet everywhere, the whole world was quiet, she thought, and she did not want to disturb it.

"Troy?" she whispered. "I'm sorry."

Still there was no answer.

"Do you forgive me, Troy?"

Silence.

She tried the gate. The big padlock holding it shut clanked dully against the hasp. She clutched the diamond shapes of the empire fence, pressed her face into it. "Troy?" she whispered. The metal was cool and she liked the feel of it against her skin.

"Troy?"

She hesitated.

"You're not here, are you, Troy?"

The play structure gleamed under the moonlight. It wasn't wood. Or clay. It was glass. It was a castle made of glass and it gleamed in the moonlight.

"Troy," she whispered. "You can play here, now."

It was made of glass. And it was as still as stone. As ancient as stone.

"Troy?"

As ancient as childhood.

"Hello, my dear," said the stout woman.

As ancient and as deathless and as gleaming as childhood.

"Would you like to come in, my dear? Would you like to see this place the way your child sees it?"

"I can't," Loretta whispered.

"But you can," said the stout woman.

"I shouldn't."

"But you should."

The stout woman stepped forward. The gate opened.

"You really should, my dear."

Loretta went in.

The play structure tilted, expanded, contracted. It was made of glass, it was made of diamonds; it gleamed like jewels under the moonlight; it was as ancient and as deathless as childhood, as accepting and as forgiving and as deathless as childhood.

"Enjoy yourself, dear," said the stout woman. She closed the gate.

And stillness and silence recaptured the night.

"It happens," said Loretta's husband some time later, to another woman, in another city. They were seated on a bench in front of another play structure. "She was basically unfulfilled, I guess. I don't know. Wherever she is, I hope she's happy."

The woman took his hand. "It seems to me that you blame yourself. You shouldn't. We aren't as responsible for other people as we might think."

He shook his head. "No. I don't blame myself. I really don't. But he blames himself." He nodded to indicate Troy, who was just then sliding down one of the play structure's several slides, laughter bubbling out of him.

The woman smiled. "He seems well-adjusted."

"Uh-huh. Right now. He has his moments, though."

"Don't we all?" said the woman. "But he's a child. He'll overcome."

There were fifty or more children in the play structure. Several were waving to various mommies and daddies from the structure's tall wooden towers. And from within the structure itself came the incoherent but happy melding of shrill voices.

Loretta's husband saw a pair of beautiful dark eyes staring at him from between the slats of a passageway close by. He stared back. The eyes vanished.

He said to the woman with him. "He has her eyes."

"Sorry?" said the woman.

"Troy. He has her eyes. He has his mother's eyes."

AFTER TIME

At last, you will become a mystery, your skin your eyes and your breasts will become a mystery. And your beautiful large hands.

Your embraces, too, your mouth your vagina your hair your voice nearly the whole temporary you.

But not this, your words which will linger grow vigorous, whisper loud.

CRADLE

We are wandering to the great cradle, pausing over music that's comfortable, pausing over the long days and the brief, pausing over options, taking luxurious delight in things of the mouth—Ferrero Rocher, smooth and rich, chocolate and pecan, and we want to think—I think desperately—that there is no end to it. So I open a drawer I haven't opened in a while and there you are, in a photograph I remember, vividly, taking, and you look expectant in it, glad and hopeful, and it is all I can do to look away, but I do, and it surprises me, but it's all right. You are a thing of the mouth, too, and a thing of the body, whole, and a thing of the tongue, and the insatiable other, and the spaces all filled, but I am wandering, as well as I said, like you, pausing over the view from here to what I can see, what I can understand and have history with—the cold lake, the tall hill beyond.

AT RIKKI'S

At Rikki's Diner in Fairport the only tea drinker is a pretty middle-aged woman who believes in the rituals of silence, and the ritual of tea. She's stacked, smart, has that sexy tea-drinker's grin.

I want to get next to her, talk about the tea, tell her it's civilized in the way poetry is civilized—see that little smile—"Oh, bullshit!" it says—ask her about the tea; "Darjeeling?"

"Earl Gray." Such marvelous words.

I know her. She takes tea alone at Rikki's mid-mornings early in the week. When I visualize her I see what I have shown here, what I have never seen—the teacup in her pale hands, her slow breathing, elbows set and graceful wrists engaged in the tasks of tea. I believe that, in these moments, she is given to the tea, the little cup, the saucer, the heat of the tea—there is no end or beginning, I believe, to the moment of tea; she has the lips for it, parted as much as if for the kiss; she knows what to do with her eyes; her eyes engage, as if her lips and tongue, with the tea, the tasks of tea.

2035-REDUX

T hough the possibility exists, as well, that we will cook our pasta together for an hour, until it melts on our bright tongues, and that we will pour nothing but a pale cheese over it, one that will not offend our geriatric stomachs.

Possible, too, that we will grow similar (at least to passersby) as the years tumble all over themselves to be done, that we will lie naked in some very familiar bed, titillated, grinning, and almost unable.

THE HOUSE UNDER THE STREET

When the Monroe County Department of Public Works tore up part of St. Paul Street so workers could lay new pipe, they found a small green clapboard house twenty feet below street level. Only the front of the house and its rusted tin roof were visible from the street; there was a chimney, though half of it was gone, and small sections of the roof's cap were missing, exposing portions of the framing beneath.

Subsequently, two people from the Monroe County Historical Society were summoned. They peered down at the house and exclaimed it was, indeed, of great and consuming interest, if only a way could be found to get down to it. A way was found; workers widened the big hole, a ladder was carefully lowered in, and the two people from the Historical Society climbed down with hardhats firmly in place and encountered the front door of the house.

One of these people, a man in his late forties, who was wiry and bright and always wore a colorful bow tie, said, "Should we knock?" and chuckled.

The woman with him, also in her late forties—her name was Blanche—said through tight, thin lips, "This is hardly a joking matter, Alex. This house could be of extreme historical importance. And you know, of course, that there may be people in it."

Alex gave her a feigned look of alarm. "People? You mean dead people?"

"Yes," she told him grimly. "Dead people." And she stepped forward in the few feet between the ladder and the oak front door and tried the brass knob. She stepped back.

"What's the matter?" Alex asked.

"It's locked," she said. "The door is locked. It was something I hadn't expected."

From above, a workman called, "You people okay down there?"

Alex said to Blanche, "What do you mean it's locked?"

"I mean it won't open. I need a key."

"Maybe the people who live here stepped out for a few minutes." He smiled. "Maybe we can leave them a note and tell them when we'll be back."

She gave him a hard look. "Alex," she proclaimed, "if there are people here, in this house, then I would say that in all likelihood it is their mausoleum. So my guess is they'd be even less responsive to your so-called humor than I. If that's possible."

Alex continued smiling. "Well put," he said.

Again the workman, twenty feet up, at street level, called, "Are you people okay?"

Blanche called back, "We have a problem. The house is locked."

"Locked," the workman said, parroting her.

"Maybe we can get in through a window," Alex suggested.

There were three windows in the front of the house—two, with lace curtains drawn, to either side of the door, and one very tall and narrow window six or seven feet above it, in what apparently was the attic. Blanche and Alex could not get to either lower window easily because there was water pooled around the house; since the house rested on what appeared to be a natural limestone hump, they had no idea how deep the water could be. ("You got some troughs down there," a workman had told them, "that you could step in and never come out of. It ain't no place for no one to go walking alone.")

Alex got back on the ladder and climbed it so he could peer into the attic window.

Blanche called to him, "Do you see anything?"

He called back, "Yes, I do."

Blanche waited a few moments for him to continue. When he didn't, she called, "What do you see, Alex?"

He answered, "I see . . . toys."

"Toys?"

"Yes. A rocking horse. Some blocks. Wooden blocks with the alphabet on them. A train set. And a doll; no, two dolls. Raggedy Ann, I think . . . Blanche, I think it's a Raggedy Ann and a Raggedy Andy." He smiled. "I had a Raggedy Andy."

And I had a Raggedy Ann, Blanche thought, but she said nothing and, within a few seconds, had chased the thought away.

"That's about it," Alex called. "Toys," he whispered, and when Blanche looked up at him through the gloom below the street, she saw a tiny, quivering smile on his face.

"Come down from there," she told him. Reluctantly, he came down.

She said, "It's remarkably well-preserved," paused, continued, "and it has no business being here, but it is here, of course, so it's something we'll have to deal with." She studied the house a moment. "I think it is possibly pre-Victorian and, well-preserved though it is, it lacks character, of course, so it is clearly the house of a laborer of the day—"

A workman called down, "You two have to come up outta there now."

Blanche called back, "I'm sorry, we can't do that. We've hardly begun our investigation—"

"You don't come up outta there, you're gonna get awful wet."

"I'm sorry?"

"It's gonna rain, sister. It's gonna rain hard."

Blanche noticed, then, that the light had grown even more deeply sullen than when they'd come down the ladder. "We must get into this house. You can understand that, of course."

"You got about a minute and a half, then you're gonna go swimming."

"Dammit!" Blanche whispered.

On the way up the ladder to the street, she looked briefly into the attic. Alex, ahead of her, said, "You coming, Blanche?"

She said, "This is a strange place. This is a very strange place. I'm not at all certain it makes me comfortable." She paused and realized she wasn't sure what she was talking about. "There's light in that room," she said, meaning the attic. She said *room* because that's the way it looked—like a child's room no child had ever used. It was too neat, too much as if in waiting.

"Not possible," Alex said.

"I'm aware of that," she said. "I was speaking metaphorically." She closed her eyes in brief embarrassment, then added, "You understand that, of course."

"Of course I do, Blanche," Alex lied.

She finished, "I would say, in fact, that this house makes me extremely uncomfortable."

"I think it's great," Alex declared.

And she told him, her tone very serious and very instructive, "Alex, I believe you are forty-seven years old going on twelve." It was very similar to what she'd told him many times before: "Alex, I believe you are forty-three years old going on thirteen . . . Alex, I believe you are forty-five years old going on fifteen." She kept him in adolescence because it was very reassuring for her.

It rained that night. It was not a gentle rain, not comforting or restful, not the kind of rain that soothes and heals. It was a torrent, as if an ocean were draining, and the things that got caught in it—hoboes, night workers, trees, cats, flowers—were marked by it and their lives were made shorter because of it.

Blanche was sent stumbling to her window by it and she watched in awe and fear as it wailed at her that there were things beyond her control, after all. It was not something she would have admitted aloud, although she understood it. There were many things she understood. Things about the world she had grown into and become a part of—a world made up of meetings and lunches and decision-making and exhaustion. A world she'd moved about in for centuries. A world that pinched. A world without toys.

She stood for a long time at her window. She watched the storm reach a peak, then watched it groan back to practically nothing; then, as if it were relieved or sated, almost instantly to nothing at all. Then it was morning and there were shiny black streets and a peach-colored sky. And there were people, too. They moved tentatively, like small animals, out of their houses. And they nodded at each other and began to piece their worlds together from the debris left behind by what the earth had hurled at them the night before.

When, late that morning, Blanche arrived at the hole in the street and looked down, she saw that sunlight was bouncing gaily off the sides of the hole all the way to the bottom. She saw, as well, that the house was not there.

She looked at a workman standing beside her and gave him a small, incredulous, quivering smile. "The house isn't there," she said.

"I know it isn't," he said.

Alex came up alongside her. "The storm washed it away, Blanche," he said.

She shook her head slowly. "How could the storm do that?"

The workman said, "Hell, lady, there was a lot of rain last night. It had to go somewhere." He nodded at the hole. "That's where it went."

Alex repeated, "And it washed the house away, Blanche. I'm sorry."

"Sorry?"

"It was probably of great historical importance," he said, and adjusted his colorful bow tie.

She said nothing. She looked stunned, Alex thought. He said, in order to comfort her, "Chances are that it broke up." He had no real idea why such a statement would comfort her. He might have decided, had he examined it, that it would have comforted her because there was much work to do elsewhere. And besides, working below the street was a dirty business, and smelly, too, and was without a doubt extremely dangerous.

"Broke up?" she said.

He nodded. "Yes. Broke up. Into pieces."

"And?"

"And so . . . and so . . . " He smiled. "It got swept away and is beyond us, and we can move on to other pursuits."

She shook her head. "Alex, we have to go and find it."

He shook his head. "We can't do that. We're not equipped to do that."

She looked from his face to the hole in the street, then back to his face. "As you pointed out, Alex, as you pointed out, that house was of great historical importance. And besides . . . " She stopped. She looked confused.

"Besides?" Alex coaxed.

"Besides," she said, "there were toys in it."

The workman said, "Toys?"

"Yes," she said. "In the house."

"Toys?" the workman said again, as if it were a word he just then had encountered.

Alex explained, "There was a rocking horse, yes. And a train set. And some blocks."

"With the alphabet on them," Blanche cut in, smiling a broad, childlike smile that Alex had never seen on her before. "And a Raggedy Ann and Raggedy Andy."

The workman shrugged. "Well they ain't there no more, and that's about as true as yesterday."

It was a week of storms, all of them as angry and as destructive as the first, all of them interrupted, during the day, by sunlight and still, clear air. It was a week that sat on Blanche like a bullfrog, a week she moved about leadenly from place to place, from responsibility to responsibility, as if her world were some grim amusement park where the carousel horses didn't move and the fun house consisted only of darkness and the prize for knocking over milk bottles on the midway was a trip back in time to do it all over again.

To grow up all over again. To be here. And be precisely who she was.

"Did you ever wonder," Alex asked her at the end of that week, "how it got there?"

"It?"

"The house under the street."

"No," she said. "I never wondered. It was there, that was all we needed to know. It was all anybody needed to know."

Alex smiled. They were in a big gray Victorian on Mount Hope Avenue, and they were trying to decide if it qualified for landmark status. "Or why it was there, Blanche? Did you ever wonder why it was there?"

"No," she answered at once, as if the question frightened her.

"You don't need to know very much, do you, Blanche?"

"Sorry?" she said, though she knew what he meant.

He explained, "You don't need to look around the edges of things. You don't need to see around corners. You've got your eyes glued only on the road ahead."

"No," she told him. "No," she repeated thoughtfully, as if to herself. "I do want to see around corners. I want that very much. But I don't know how."

Alex adjusted his bright bow tie. Adjusting it was a nervous habit and he often adjusted it when it didn't need adjusting. He was nervous because he wanted to tell her something had pounced on him just then, but which he didn't have the nerve to tell her. He wanted to tell her that he cared for her.

"It's possible," he said, "that the house under the street wasn't there at all."

He didn't know why he cared for her—now; perhaps it was a fault within himself that had caused it, perhaps some growth had taken over a lobe of his brain and had made him stupid. He'd worked with Blanche for five years and, in that time, she had said only one kind thing to him: "I'm sorry about your hamster, Alex. I had a hamster, once."

"Yes," she said now, in the gray brick Victorian. "I know. It's possible that the house under the street wasn't there at all."

This surprised him. "But it was there," he said. "I was only . . . joking. It was only a joke."

"The room we looked at could have been anything," she said. "It could have been a concoction. It could have been a dream, Alex."

He looked at her and saw that she was smiling oddly, as if at the memory of something that warmed her slowly from the inside, like pudding. "But it was there, Blanche," he insisted.

"And now it's gone," she said. "And that's what matters. It matters that it was there, under the street, and now it's gone, and we can . . . get on to other things." It sounded to Alex like a plea. She looked away, as if embarrassed.

I care for you, he said, but it was to himself, in his head, in preparation for saying it aloud, and he didn't say it aloud because it didn't make any sense to him.

That night, Blanche threw her cool sheets off her cold legs, put on her terry-cloth robe, and her blue slippers, and padded to the window that overlooked her street. *The rain has stopped*, she told herself.

She smiled. Light from a streetlamp below bounced off her face, then off the window, and she saw her reflection. It was, she realized, the first time in a very long time that she'd seen her own smile.

Suddenly she wished she had a cat. Something to talk to. She didn't know for sure what she'd say to it, but she knew that she would make sounds at it and that it would respond, in its way. Maybe she'd tell it what she'd been afraid to tell herself all these years, that there really was a world made up of Raggedy Anns and Raggedy Andys, toy trains and wooden blocks. A world that didn't pinch. A world buried as deep within her as the house and its wonderful attic room were buried beneath the street. "And all I have to do is find it." She turned from the window, hesitated. Her smile broadened. She slipped out of her terry-cloth robe and her slippers. She dressed, left her apartment, and walked out into the night.

The following morning, a little before noon, a workman at the hole in the street, where the house had been, handed Alex a hardhat and told him, "The hole wasn't closed up because we weren't finished working in it." He paused very briefly, then continued, "You know it's going to rain, right?"

"Yes, I know," Alex said.

"And you know," the workman pressed on, "that if you get caught down there, and it's raining hard, then you'll probably drown. There are troughs you could walk into and never come out of—"

"I know that."

The workman shrugged. "You got your lamp?"

Alex held up the battery-powered lantern the foreman of the work crew had given him.

"Good," said the workman. "There ain't no lights down there."

"Yes, I know," Alex said, and, a moment later, he was climbing down into the hole in the street on the same ladder Blanche had used eight hours before.

He could hear the other rescue workers. He could hear bits of conversation, grumbled curses, and he thought, as he listened, that those men could be anywhere in the maze of tunnels under the street, that he could head in their direction and get to where he'd thought they were and find that they were somewhere else entirely.

But he knew this, too, as he listened: he knew that they were not going to find Blanche. He knew that he was going to find her.

He could see their lights, then, and he realized they were moving in his direction. He stayed still. He said nothing. He did not call out to them, as he'd been told to do. For a few moments, he watched their lights—dulled by reflection from half a dozen wet stone walls—then he turned and walked in the other direction, through ankle-deep water. As he walked, the dull orange glow of his lantern showed him only the angles of dark walls intersecting other dark walls.

He walked this way—slowly, through the water—for ten minutes. Then he saw the house.

And, at that same moment, he heard from far behind him, "I found her. God, I found her!"

He smiled. *No,* he thought. *No, you haven't found her.*

"Bring a light," shouted the same voice. "Mine ain't much good no more. Bring a light."

The house was listing in the tunnel, like a ship starting to sink, the left side in one of the troughs he'd been warned about, so his lamp could not show him much of it—only the lower right-hand window, some of the right-hand wall, green clapboards trailing off into the darkness, the softly glistening front edge of the rusted tin roof. And all of the attic window, too, which he could see well because it was illuminated from within.

He heard, then, from far behind him, "It's her. God, it's her!"

And another voice answered, "How are we going to get to her?"

No, Alex called to them in his head, smiling. *No, you're mistaken. That's not her, at all. No. She's here!*

He set his light down on a ledge near where the tunnel wall intersected the floor. He moved forward through the ankle-deep water, toward the little house under the street. He longed to peer into the attic window, but he couldn't; even though the house was listing, the window was still too far above him. He stepped up to the door, saw the reflection of his lamplight on the brass knob, reached out, grasped the knob hard.

He heard from far behind him, "She's rolled over. I can see her face!"

"Can you get to her?" another voice shouted.

"I don't know," answered the first voice. "I don't know. Give me a line."

Alex turned the knob. "Blanche?" he whispered. The door was locked. He heard from behind him, and above—at street level, he guessed— "Come on outta there!"

He shook his head. *No,* he thought. He stepped back from the door and peered up, through the gloom below the street, into the attic.

He saw the attic ceiling; he saw a shadow on it. The shadow moved.

And he watched as a small face, the face of a child, appeared at the attic window.

He heard from behind him, and above, "It's raining. Get outta there!"

He smiled at the face of the child in the window. The face smiled back. "Blanche," he whispered. The child's lips mouthed his name. "Alex."

From behind him, he heard again, "It's raining, dammit! Get outta there!"

"We can't. We ain't got her. We ain't got her, yet!"

"She'll have to wait. Get outta there, now!"

Alex stepped up to the front door of the house under the street. He grasped the knob. Turned it. The door opened.

Above, at street level, it rained. It was not a gentle rain, not comforting or restful, not the kind of rain that soothes and heals. It was a torrent, as if an ocean were draining.

Alex stepped into the house.

THE LIGHTWATER HAWKINS STORY

T he past, the present, and the future, are like paths laid down by chickadees waddling through a windstorm. So malleable.

He wrote:

In that place of night, the old man's shoes are in a closet, but the old man is nowhere to be seen. He was here this morning. He had breakfast—a plateful of scrambled eggs, nothing else. He put ketchup on them because he likes ketchup on his eggs, and he prefers them runny.

Lightwater Hawkins knew with certainty that someone lived surreptitiously in his house, but he had yet to encounter anyone in its several hallways, on one of its three sets of stairs, in one of its living rooms, or its half-dozen bedrooms, its parlor, or its great room, and he had not heard anyone moving about, talking, or using one of the house's splendid bathrooms, nor had he found any food missing, or evidence that dishes had been taken down from the cupboards, used, washed, and put away again. Lightwater was almost certain that he hadn't even *sensed* the presence of anyone else in the house, though he thought he might have sensed another person on the previous Tuesday morning, around eight o'clock, while he brushed his teeth, when he got the distinct though fleeting impression that someone had walked past the open door behind him, peered in for just a moment, and vanished. Lightwater had turned his head a little to look at the open doorway, but decided, within the moment, that he was being foolish: clearly, no one but he and his large and unpredictable marmalade cat Fellatio lived in the house. That fact was clear, as well, he knew, to Fellatio himself, whose feline instincts would certainly have alerted him to the presence of a stranger.

So it astonished Lightwater when he woke early that morning, a Friday, from a discomforting dream about dark roads leading through a small, dark village, and a darker building within the village, and even darker shapes within the building, and realized he was absolutely certain that someone else did indeed share the house with him—and that that someone was as quiet as a bedbug.

He called his brother Jim from the house's only phone, in the cavernous parlor on the first floor:

"Jim," Lightwater said, "someone's living in my house with me."

"Huh?" said Jim. "Who?"

"I don't know," said Lightwater.

"How can *that* be?" Jim asked.

Lightwater sighed and explained, "I don't know *who* it is because I haven't *seen* him." He paused, then added, "Or her."

"Huh?" said Jim.

"But there *is* someone here, Jim. I'm sure of it. And I'd like you to come over right away and help me look for him."

"Is this a joke?" Jim said.

"I'm as serious as a rattlesnake," Lightwater said.

An hour later, Jim showed up in his ancient maroon Chrysler Newport. Jim was five years Lightwater's senior, white-haired, almost mortally thin, and he spoke in a very low *basso profundo* that was at once avuncular, comforting, and exquisitely mournful, as if he were always about to deliver bad news.

"Okay," he said, "where is this alleged person?"

Lightwater, who had just let him into the house, said, "I told you, Jim, I don't know *where* he is. I haven't *seen* him." Brief pause. "Or her."

Jim's abundant brow furrowed. "'S'that so?" He glanced quickly into Lightwater's pale green eyes, then beyond him, at an open door which led to the rest of the house, then at Lightwater again, sighed, shook his head a little, and continued, "Then why in the name of God's green tool shed did you ask me to come here, Lightwater? You know the Chrysler's ailing. You know I hate to drive."

"Yes, I know," Lightwater said, trying to sound apologetic, "but it's very important. I need your eyes and ears. And your other senses."

"Shit, you got eyes and ears," Jim said. "And last time I checked, they were a lot more useful than mine."

"Maybe not," Lightwater said.

Jim harrumphed again.

He looks toward what he hopes are windows, but finds nothing. He stumbles and curses softly because he has stumbled so often.

"What is this place?" he asks himself, though he knows only too well what the place is, what it must be, of all the places in a universe, his universe, that's made up almost entirely of darkness.

He finds that he wants his runny eggs, and so he sits down to eat them.

Two hours later, Jim, with Lightwater at the front door once more—after what they both agreed was an exhaustive search of the huge house—said, "No one's here, my brother, but you and that ill-named cat."

Lightwater said, "Yes, you're doubtless correct, Jim. Thanks for stopping by."

Jim said, "No problem," and drove off moments later.

At a little past seven-thirty the following Wednesday evening, just after he'd enjoyed a dinner of broccoli, salmon and wild rice—he was a marvelous cook, and everyone knew it—Lightwater heard someone whispering to him from out of the darkness in his house. He was preparing for a bath and the water was running, so his first thought was that he'd heard nothing but the softly chaotic harmonics of the water itself, but when he turned the water off and the whispers continued, he said, "Who's there? Who's there?" and heard, at once, "No one," which made him smile a little, because, he decided instantly, some small and playful part of his gray matter was surely having fun with the rest of his gray matter—which, by and large, was not at all playful—so he said again, "Who's there?" although he said it louder, and got once more, "No one!" and it was louder, too, almost insistently louder, and he gulped, glanced around quickly—at the big, shiny, claw-foot tub, the ornate mirror over the sink, the closed door, the row of precisely arranged red bath towels that hung nearby—gulped again, and said, in a small voice, "Jesus, I'm naked! Good Lord, I'm naked!"

"And," he heard, "it ain't at all pretty!"

Small towns on rural highways are as predictable as the sunrise; they're slow and angular and their colors are quiet, faded, unremarkable. Their people are also not much in evidence, and when they are, they seem purposeful, though without quickness or enthusiasm.

Some small towns on rural highways know much about death, though they keep this knowledge much to themselves.

It was three weeks to the day until Lightwater heard that whispering voice again; it woke him from a strange and uncomfortably titillating dream of a bare-footed woman with intimidating breasts and an appealing grin, who lived in a small, ugly village he thought he recognized, but could not name: the voice said, as it had three weeks earlier, and in the same tone, "And it ain't at all pretty!" paused, then said it again: "And it ain't at all pretty!"

Lightwater sat bolt upright in his bed in the pitch dark, in the nearly cold air (he set the temperature at fifty-two in the evening and it was early November) and, without speaking, asked himself, "What was *that?*"

Fellatio meowed loudly at his ear.

He fainted.

He hadn't fainted since childhood, when he fainted often, and for what, he knew, other people considered foolish reasons—when he found that his shirt was buttoned incorrectly, for instance, or when his comely Aunt Betty kissed him full on the mouth, or when the other boys angled to watch him pee into the urinal (because his penis was petite and unimpressive and, therefore, a focus of much amusement).

He hit his head often in those years and, after a while, the multitude of small impacts began, he decided, to have serious effects.

He walks about as if aimlessly, though I know he's looking for something; his gaze moves from place to place, but settles nowhere. I want to call out to him, "What are you looking for?"

Occasionally, his gaze passes over me and I think that, very briefly, there's recognition or curiosity in his eyes. But, in this place, that has to be an illusion.

Lightwater was in his fifty-third year and he didn't like it. He could see Death peering at him from around the far corner, and he had no idea how he was going to deal with it—the complete and utter end of his existence. As un-gratifying and silly as it had become, it was still *his* existence; no one else in all the world could claim it; no one else saw what he saw in the *way* he saw: no one else's thoughts and ideas expressed themselves in quite the same way his did; no one's memories were *his* memories; no one reacted to tuna steak or spumoni the way he reacted. So, Christ, he was *unique*, and, before long—in just the wink of an eye, really—that uniqueness would be a thing of the dead past, a thing for others to remember briefly, and then let go of forever, a thing (awareness, consciousness, *being*) he would never get to experience again, no matter how meaningless it—that *thing*—seemed to be when the room was dark, and the house was quiet.

He became convinced, after the voice fell silent for another month, that he had never heard it in the first place, that it was another of his many manufactured memories (that, for instance, his sister had died of hypersensitivity to olive oil at the age of fourteen; hadn't his mother told him he'd never even *had* a sister, and his mother couldn't be wrong—she was many things, some of them quite unappealing, but she was never wrong: besides, he didn't have any distinct memories of his sister, didn't even know what her name could have been, owned no photographs of her, and no mental pictures either, though he thought she would likely have been short (because he was tall) and dark-haired (because he was light-haired) and able to talk with him engagingly about subjects he usually found uninvolving—gardening, for instance, and the lives of the saints).

He liked to follow Fellatio in his travels through his large house. It was clear that the cat simply tolerated this—glanced back often, with a kind of straight-mouthed cat sneer, and then continued on his way. Lightwater wasn't sure what the attraction was in following the cat: perhaps it was because the cat was a supernatural creature in touch with other supernatural creatures, or that the cat enjoyed leading his owner about, which the cat later sniggered at, in his inscrutable cat way, that the cat had hidden various rodent corpses here and there in the house and needed, daily, to check on their various rates of decomposition; or, perhaps, it was because the cat was a creature of darkness, and so it had answers about the darkness that it would eventually share.

Lightwater *did* have a brother, however. He knew that much, at least. Lightwater's mother had even confirmed it, many times—"Yes, dear, you have a brother. You don't have a *sister*, but you do have a brother." His name was Jim; he was five years his (Lightwater's) senior, and he was, Lightwater had once said to his mother, "helpful but churlish," and then had added, "the way older brothers are supposed to be." Jim had, in fact, helped him only a couple of months earlier with the other person Lightwater had become certain was living in his house.

"How time flies," Lightwater said, remembering Jim's visit (he had yet to visit again). *Almost two months—more than two months, really—since Jim was last here.*

A week and a half later, the voice in his house again woke him from a claustrophobic dream of darkness and suffocatingly thick air and he thought at first that it was simply random harmonics of the hard rain that had started hours earlier, but then he realized that the rain had stopped.

The voice said, "Well, you know, we all die sooner or later—and why not? Is there any reasonable or likely alternative?"

"Huh?" said Lightwater, who'd heard what the voice had told him, but had dismissed it as gibberish.

"I *told you*," said the voice, "that we all die sooner or later. And why not? Is there any reasonable or likely alternative?"

It was dark in the bedroom, of course. Lightwater never used artificial light unless there was a real need for it, and besides, if he switched a light on, it would illuminate whatever was speaking to him, and he certainly didn't want *that*. In fact, he had yet to open his eyes.

He whispered, "Are you . . . can you tell me . . . are you . . . the . . . ghost of someone?"

He heard what sounded like a sigh. He opened his eyes, looked very quickly right, left, then closed his eyes again. He had seen nothing, only darkness.

The voice said, very close to his ear, "Well I'm not the friggin' *cat!*"

Lightwater lurched, wanted to faint, as he had done so often in moments of stress, actually *tried* to faint—gulped great mouthfuls of the cool air very quickly, in/out, in/out, in/out, in/out!

"Oh for God's sake, *stop it!*" the voice cried.

Lightwater stopped hyperventilating, felt suddenly dizzy, reached out, as if there might be something to hold onto, felt what could only be thick cloth—a coat, a sports jacket, who knew? And fainted.

When he woke it was morning, the room was bathed in deep yellow sunlight, and a stout, heavily bearded man dressed in gray herringbone sat at the foot of the bed, in an equally stout bright green chair which, if he'd had his wits about him, Lightwater would have realized he'd never seen before.

The man said, nodding at Lightwater's crotch, "You peed yourself! Christ, you peed yourself!"

"Uh!" Lightwater managed.

The man pointed stiffly; his arm was massive, and quite hairy, too. The man said, "You peed your fucking long-johns, Quicksilver! You don't clean yourself off, you'll get a rash, and how will *that* look?"

"Uh!" Lightwater said again, and quickly added, "Uh!"

"Jesus," the man said on a long exhale, "this is getting us nowhere far too quickly!"

He vanished.

"Uh!" Lightwater repeated, and fainted.

"The end of life," he wrote once, *"opens our eyes in several ways. But the pupils dilate and so we are effectively blind, except where there is no light at all, but what is there to see then?"*

When he was barely out of his teens, Lightwater remembered, he reluctantly visited a chiropractor named Dr. Lewis O'Sullivan, who told him, "You have a very, very unique disorder, Mr. Hawkins." The man's nurse, Lorraine, came into the examining room, then, gave the doctor a chart which, Lightwater could see, had his name on it, and left the room. The doctor added, "I've heard all about it from your mother." He smiled quickly. "Your disorder, I mean." He smelled of witch hazel and it made Lightwater's eyes sting. "She's a very fine woman, your mother," O'Sullivan continued, and, as he talked about her, Lightwater thought there was entirely too much sparkle in his eyes. Images of his mother bending naked over a pool table, an ironing board, and the back of a car seat, while Dr. Louis O'Sullivan, Licensed Chiropractor, inserted himself into her came and went fleetingly from Lightwater's imagination, and he realized, as the images developed a sort of despicable rhythm—on/off, on/off, on/off—that he was watching the images in rapt fascination, for he had never supposed that his mother would actually have intercourse with a *chiropractor*. He had never supposed, of course, that she would have intercourse with *anyone*, not even Lightwater's father—identity unknown—who had doubtless arranged that his sperm be taken surgically from him and inserted directly through his—Lightwater's—mother's uterine wall and into the awaiting egg, *sans* sexual contact.

"So," said Dr. O'Sullivan, when he was, at long last, done with talking about Lightwater's mother, "would you like to discuss this very interesting dysfunction of yours?"

"Why?" said Lightwater.

"Simply as a favor to your mother," O'Sullivan said, and smiled broadly. "She's an exceptionally fine woman, as I told you." His eyes sparkled again. "And she's asked me to discuss your dysfunction with you because, apparently, *you* won't discuss it with *her*."

"But you're just a chiropractor," Lightwater said.

"Ah yes, true," said O'Sullivan, and pointed his index finger into the air, "but I've also studied the behavioral sciences, as it were, and I have a keen, if not professional knowledge of mental dysfunction, so to speak."

Lightwater looked nervously about the room.

O'Sullivan said, "Well, then, how about it? Are you up for a little discussion, *mano-a-mano*, as it were?"

"No," said Lightwater, "I'm not." And he left the building.

Lightwater told himself, now, that those events had happened decades ago. They were an indelible and immutable part of his past, and so they existed and, at the same time, did not exist. There was comfort to be taken from that, he thought. And *comfort*, not simply pain and regret and fear, was what should come naturally with age.

He waited months for the man in gray herringbone to reappear, and when he didn't, Lightwater searched exhaustively in the house for him.

He even spoke to him, now and then: "Could you show yourself again, please," and, "I mean you no harm," which he thought was awfully foolish, and, "I need to know your purpose for being in this house," which he also thought was foolish because the man hadn't seemed the type to explain himself and his "purpose" to anyone.

Lightwater finally concluded, after a week's searching, that the house was just too damned big, that he could search in the parlor, for instance, find nothing there, go to the dining room, and find nothing there, either, because the man in gray herringbone could easily have slipped out of the dining room and into the parlor through one of its three entrances and exits, or into one of the other rooms, through as many entrances and exits, or he could have been in none of these rooms, could have been, for instance, in the cavernous attic, where there was decaying bric-a-brac in abundance, or in one of the half-dozen bedrooms, which contained huge walk-in closets that could, under some circumstances, have served as rooms of their own, and the man in gray herringbone could have been in any of these places, chuckling as he kept Lightwater at several arms' length, and he, Lightwater, could have played this game of cat and mouse for a very long time, never knowing who was the cat and who was the mouse.

Of course, there was the fact that, two months earlier, the man had simply vanished from his green chair in front of Lightwater's bed. Lightwater had thought about this at length and had decided it had been simply an illusion. People, of course, seemed to "vanish" all the time. They vanished around street corners or into stores, they got on buses when you weren't looking, or secreted themselves behind clothes racks, refrigerators, armoires. Clearly the man in gray herringbone had pulled just such a sleight-of-hand. He hadn't *actually* vanished from in front of his—Lightwater's—bed; he'd merely been there one moment and *not there* the next. It was the sort of thing that probably happened a million times a day.

It was, Lightwater thought, nearly a year before the man appeared again, just five weeks after Lightwater's fifty-fourth birthday. It was a mid-afternoon in late September, rainy and unseasonably cold; Lightwater was sure, in fact, as he peered out one of the living room's big, oval windows, that he actually saw snowflakes falling with the rain. He liked that. It was comforting, somehow.

He heard from behind him, "Your mother's *very* dead, you know!"

It was the man in gray herringbone—Lightwater knew it immediately. He recognized the man's voice (*basso profundo*), the flow of his words—insistent but vaguely comic and ironic, very like the voice of one of Lightwater's English teachers, a voice he'd enjoyed but one which intimidated him, too (as did the breasts of the anonymous, barefooted woman who lived in the small town that Lightwater could not name).

He started to turn from the window, the rain and the snow, felt a strong hand on his shoulder, turned his head just a little to see it—the hand—and heard, "Please, Mr. Hawkins, don't, for God's sake, faint again."

Lightwater looked at the hand, then at the round, craggy face of the man in gray herringbone, at his eyes, saw that they were as gray as the herringbone, saw humor in them, and compassion, too. And fainted.

"We have so many memories," he heard. "As one, all of us have so many billions and billions and billions of memories. The number is truly uncountable, I believe. And who would try?"

"To count them?" said Lightwater.

"To count them, yes."

"Who would try?" said Lightwater.

"And for what purpose?"

"There would be no purpose," said Lightwater.

"It is un-quantifiable."

"Memories?"

"Yes. Un-quantifiable."

"Are you a mathematician?"

"Mr. Hawkins, we are all mathematicians."

"We?"

"All of us. Everywhere. Mathematicians. One, two, three, four heart-beats. Five, six, seven blinks of the eye. Eight, nine, ten dreams, lovers, days, weeks, months, years. Comings and goings. It's all so complex and unwieldy. It makes the past, as far as we are concerned—and that's a collective *we*—very much like a path laid down by chickadees waddling through a windstorm. So malleable."

Lightwater knew this wasn't real, knew he was dreaming. He dreamt often, and almost always in a riot of color (except recently), and heard voices that were loud, confident, and human.

"What would be the purpose, then," he said, "in counting memories?"

He got no answer.

He woke himself up.

And realized at once that he'd been awake all along. Realized that his gray matter had been playing games with him again. *This* is real, Light-water! No, *this* is real, Lightwater! He thought often that he would love to tear his brain from his skull and replace it with something more reli-able, less predictable, more boring. After all, most of living *needed* to be predictable, didn't it? Even boring. Otherwise the human heart would simply pop, and where was the comfort in that.

The room was empty. It was the living room and, beyond the big oval windows, the rain and snow still fell, and the sky was salmon-colored, though Lightwater couldn't see it because his back was to the wall beneath one of the windows.

But he said, because he simply *knew* it was true, "Christ, it's the same day." He hoped for a reply. He got silence.

He liked oatmeal very much, liked its flaky consistency, the way it played with his tongue. He put only brown sugar on it, no milk, because milk made his stomach queasy ("You have a lactose intolerance, Light-water," a doctor once told him; he couldn't remember the doctor's name—he'd make one up, he knew).

He was eating oatmeal this morning. He'd dumped a lot of brown sugar on it because he needed a sugar fix—his energy level was dangerously low because his night had been tumultuous, in and out of rooms he did not recognize, among people he knew well, but not, it turned out, well enough. And they talked *at* him, not *with* him, or even *to* him: they peppered him with advice, told him he was humorless, that he was possessed only of a past, and no future, and that, indeed, his past was littered with inaccuracies.

At one point, a tall, buxom, red-headed woman he needed very much to recognize, used her body as a sort of bulldozer and pushed him against a wall, where she glared down at him (she was taller than he by several inches) and reminded him more than a few times, and in great voice, that he could "do better": "You can *do better*, Mr. Hawkins!" she said, again and again. And he knew, of course, that she was right.

His oatmeal didn't come close to satisfying him this morning. What a disappointment. Oatmeal with brown sugar was such a *real* and *tactile* thing. Like mouthwash that stung the tongue. And tight shoes. Acne, too.

He pushed the bowl aside and the cat, Fellatio, who'd been sitting expectantly at his feet, leaped onto the table at once and began noisily devouring the oatmeal—*slurp, slurp/slurp, slurp.* Lightwater looked on with wonder; it was strange that Fellatio liked oatmeal, strange that a killer—and cats were the most efficient killers on the planet—liked oatmeal, especially sweetened oatmeal, because, unlike dogs, cats had no sweet tooth to speak of; or maybe he was simply imagining all that.

Who knew?

Perhaps, in the universe that really mattered—wherever that might be—he had no cat at all.

Perhaps it was some other creature (rat, vole, ferret) noisily licking the bowl and he had, simply, using his fertile imagination, wrapped a big, marmalade cat around it—one he called "Fellatio," ("ill-named cat," said his brother, Jim) because it was easier to deal with a cat than a rat, vole, ferret.

He stroked the cat as it slurped the bowl. The cat purred, though it sounded like a low growl, and Lightwater imagined that the cat was half-contented, half-uneasy (guarding his food). He—the cat—was a creature of the darkness, Lightwater thought—a killer in the darkness, the world's *finest* killer in the darkness. And he was licking out a bowl of oatmeal. Something was not quite right about that.

Lightwater pushed himself away from the table, noted the harsh scraping noise the chair made on the bare oak floor, and decided that he liked the sound because it was so real, and *real* things were, by nature, quite appealing (thus, he concluded in that moment, the unappealing oatmeal was actually and essentially *appealing* because it was *real*. He smiled at that: such logic could allow him to find even very bad news or great pain appealing and comforting, and that was a huge plus).

He watched as the cat, finished with its oatmeal, at last, lifted its big, bright orange head from the dull green bowl, licked its chops a few times, leaped without fanfare from the table, landed on the floor with barely any noise at all, then trotted off into the parlor.

Lightwater said, "Thank you, cat," because it had given him a valuable life lesson this morning, which was quite dandy. He didn't encounter valuable life lessons every day, and to have one provided by a cat was a valuable life lesson all by itself—it proved that even lesser creatures could give him the means to manage the ups and downs of an unpredictable and often chaotic existence.

Oh, this was turning out to be a rollicking good morning, indeed! He heard a knock at his door.

"Christ," he whispered, "it's Mother again."

But it wasn't Mother; it was Jim, his brother, and Jim's wife, Charlene, who was dimpled and charming and who always brought a pie to Lightwater's door (mincemeat, which Lightwater hated, but that was all right; the gesture was admirable, and what was life without admirable gestures?).

"Hello!" Lightwater said brightly.

"Hello!" said Jim in his *basso profundo*.

"Hello!" said Charlene, and pushed a pie at Lightwater, who took it, sniffed it. "Cherry?" he said, and she said, "For a change, yes. Change is good!"

"Lightwater," Jim said, "are you going to ask us in?"

Lightwater nodded earnestly, said, "Of course," opened the door wide and gestured expansively toward the darkened interior of the house. "Come in, please. We'll have this cherry pie. And some coffee, too. Would you like that?"

"Sure," Jim said, "coffee would be wonderful," and added, as Lightwater was letting go of the doorknob, "Mother died this morning."

Lightwater dreamt once of a building that was dark at all hours of the day and night, and, in this building, there were structures that were even darker, and these structures were comforting, though, in the dream, Lightwater couldn't say why they were comforting, only that when he touched them, or saw them—amorphous shapes darker than the dark-ness in the building—or simply became aware of them, he *felt* comforted, and at rest, as if he were an infant, again, and had just finished a meal at Mother's breast.

And this dark building, and its darker shapes, were in a small town he could not name or visualize; and he knew, while he dreamt of this town and the building in it, that he needed to be there (again?), for his own sake.

When he woke from the dream to a bright morning, full of noisy birds and insistent sunlight, he grew sad and wished he could find his way back to the place from which he'd awakened.

Charlene's cherry pie was as tasty as cherry pie should be, and Light-water complimented Charlene repeatedly on it, until Jim said to him, "Can it, already!"

Lightwater looked confusedly at his brother and mumbled through a mouthful of pie, "I was only giving credit where credit is due," but Jim apparently heard only the words "credit" and "due," so Lightwater swallowed his pie and said, "I don't understand about Mother."

"What's to understand?" Jim said.

They were in the parlor, which was decorated in a mixture of Mission Oak, Queen Anne and Mediterranean Swiss: Jim sat stiffly in a large, dark blue chair, Charlene sat in a smaller chair nearby, and Lightwater sat smiling vaguely between them. Two empty plates, bearing forks and the detritus of the pie, lay on a Mission Oak coffee table in front of them. Lightwater still held his empty green plate on his lap; he was trying to gauge the proper time to set it on the coffee table, given that the subject had just turned again to Mother's untimely death.

"I don't think I knew about it," he said.

"Well, Christ, how could you, Lightwater?" Jim said. "It happened just this morning."

Lightwater nodded quickly. "Yes, Jim, I understand that only too well. She died this morning, just this morning—"

"Can it!" Jim said.

Lightwater closed his eyes quickly, opened them, gave Jim a flat smile, and Charlene, too, then leaned forward and put his empty pie plate and fork on the Mission Oak coffee table.

Jim said, "She died at 5:12 a.m. That's pretty early."

"Pretty early to die, you mean?" said Lightwater.

"Huh?" said Jim.

"You said that 5:12 a.m. was pretty early . . ."

"I know what in the name of Gretchen's pink elbow I said, Lightwater."

"Of course you do, Jim. I simply didn't understand . . ."

"She's being buried on Saturday," Jim said.

Charlene said, "More pie, Lightwater?"

"That's six days from now," Lightwater said..

"Don't you want to know *how* she died?" Jim said.

"I'll get you some more pie," Charlene said, leaned way forward in her small chair, retrieved Lightwater's plate and fork, stood, and wiggled quickly into the kitchen, while Lightwater watched.

Jim said, "Put your eyes back in your head, Lightwater!"

Lightwater looked at him, surprised.

"I know you have a *thing* for my wife," Jim said. "But you don't need to broadcast it to all and sundry."

"All and sundry?"

"Everyone. You know. You don't need to let everyone know about your lust for my Charlene."

"I thought we were talking about the death of Mother."

"Well, that's past, isn't it. Her death, I mean. And there's nothing at all we can do about it. You must begin to live with more *linearity*, Lightwater. Mother is *dead*, yes: that's a fact none of us can do anything about. And her funeral's on Saturday. We'll all attend, pay our respects, have some good food, engage in sad talk, blah, blah, blah. But for now, I would very much appreciate it if you wouldn't drool all over yourself when you look at my wife. Am I clear?"

"Yes, you are," said Lightwater. He wanted to add, "But I don't lust after your wife," because, as far as he knew, he *didn't* lust after her, but Mother was dead, and that was the item *du jour*.

He said, "You know, Jim, I really thought that Mother died years ago."

Jim took a deep breath, held it a moment, then let it out wearily. "Lightwater, Lightwater, Lightwater," he said. "Your fantasies are crippling, though clearly first-rate." He stood abruptly, looked toward the kitchen. "Why is Charlene taking so long?" he said.

"She's getting more pie, I think," said Lightwater.

"Well, it doesn't take a stinking half-hour to get *pie*," said Jim, and moved quickly through the parlor, into the kitchen.

When he hadn't returned after several minutes, Lightwater called out, "Is everything okay in there?" and, getting no answer, repeated the question, still got no answer, and went into the kitchen. It was empty. No dirty pie plates. No pie. No comely Charlene or churlish Jim. Empty.

Lightwater sat on a tall stool, elbow on his knee, chin resting in his palm. *Life is a mystery*, he told himself. *Though it is truly only one of many, many mysteries.* He liked that. It was a good thought, he decided, and good thoughts were comforting.

When, some time later, he looked it up in one of the many family albums that littered his cavernous attic, Lightwater discovered—and possibly not for the first time, he supposed—just how Mother had died, and when. It had been September 17th, eight years earlier—the news story told him—and Mother had been walking on Clarence Avenue in her hometown of Albion, New York, had been on her way to see her sister, Rebecca, who'd been waiting impatiently for her visit, the first in nearly a decade, when an Albion yellow taxi driven by a man named Michael jumped the curb and slaughtered her in a nanosecond. Lightwater was very surprised, sickened, really, to see that the reporter who'd written the story had actually used that phrase—"slaughtered her in a nanosecond": *How inappropriate for a story about death*, he told himself. But when he considered it for a minute, he realized how true it must have been, because, according to the news article, the taxi had been traveling at a very high rate of speed and had all but torn several of Mother's limbs from her body, and her head, too, which lay connected to her neck by only a slim cord of muscle.

"Oh," said Lightwater, and threw the album down, "this is awful, so awful!" He thought he'd remembered the circumstances of his mother's death—long illness, many painkillers, tearful last goodbyes—but this news story told him he'd been horribly wrong.

After a minute or two, he picked up the album, reread the article, rechecked the date of its publication, the name of the reporter (Anthony Ji-John), the name of the newspaper (*The Albion Ledger and Rule*), fingered the article beneath the clear plastic sheet that had protected it these past eight years, grimaced, sighed once, twice, exhaled slowly, and whispered, "Who in the name of Gideon's red shoes could die this way and remain at peace?"

"No one," he heard later that night as he lay waiting for sleep . . . "No one," he heard again. "I'm surprised you'd even ask such a question, Lightwater. Happy, too."

He didn't faint, but he did not open his eyes, either, or speak.

"Look at you," he heard. "You're like a new puppy in a cocoon."

He thought he remembered the voice. He'd heard it recently, within the past year or two. He tried to speak, said, "Umph!" softly, fell silent.

"I can't understand you, Lightwater," he heard. "You're thinking, perhaps, that I must be omniscient, or omnipresent, or omnipotent, but I'm not any of those things, of course. I know little or next to nothing about anything, but I know, at least, my real name and my place in the universe and, shit, what universe I'm *in*, exactly. That's all any of us can know, or should *want* to know. Don't you agree?"

"Umph!" said Lightwater.

"You scare me, Lightwater. I don't understand you; you're . . . what? Vaporish? Sure. You're made of vapors, or smoke, or some sort of greasy ectoplasm. I've heard so much about ectoplasm. Spooky damned stuff. *You're* spooky. I think you'll possess me if I let you, if I let my guard down, and then you'll lead me off into some small, cramped, dark and smelly place where I won't be able to think or breathe, except rapidly, in a panic, and who wants *that*! Shit, Lightwater, it's Halloween all year long with you." Brief silence, then, "Hell, I'm outta here!"

And then, Lightwater knew, the room was empty.

"Jim, I've got to see you."

"You sound awful, Lightwater. What's wrong."

"Everything, Jim. Just damned everything."

"Did you hear," said Jim, "that Mother died?"

Lightwater hung up.

His mother had once told him, "You know what, Andrew? It's clear to me, now, that you live on dreams and moonlight." He liked the phrase; he even thought he understood it. He said, "I do?" and she nodded once, smilingly: "Yes, you do. More people should, but they don't."

She was kind, beautiful, tender, caring, exceptional. He realized all this when he was in his mid-forties; she'd been dead for several years, and he had been hoping for her magical return—perhaps on moonlight.

His lover—Where was she, now?—once asked, "Would you miss me that much if I went away?"

"Oh yes," he told her, "of course I would."

"I don't think so," she said, and gave him a forgiving smile. "It would be great if you did, but it's not going to happen. I'm not going away, first of all, and if I did, how could I come back? It just doesn't happen." She gave him a flat smile, as if, oddly, in reassurance. "No one comes back, Lightwater."

They were the saddest words he'd ever heard.

Almost without his knowledge, his name was changed a short time later by forces beyond his control.

His earliest recollections were of pain. He'd once (years earlier?) polled all his friends and acquaintances and "pain" was not high on their collective list of first recollections (it was, in fact, not on their collective list at all), so he decided he lived, and had lived, a very strange life, in a very strange place.

He remembered driving, long ago, through a very small town that had disturbed him quite a lot, although he couldn't recall, now, *why* it disturbed him. He remembered he'd been in his early twenties and had driven very slowly through the town, as if transfixed by it: later, he'd written about it:

This isn't the Arctic or the Antarctic, but it's always night here, and there's nothing anyone can do about it. It's in the slant of the buildings, the lay of the streets, the tilt of the people. Even the animals—a few ragged cats, apparently disinterested dogs, and half a dozen barely conscious chickens—carry night around with them; it's in their eyes and their lack of speed. They seem to do everything surreptitiously, even the chickens.

But, on second thought, the people in this place appear to do nothing surreptitiously; they move about as if each step requires sad reflection. They look straight ahead, except when a car goes by, and then they turn and watch. They continue watching even after the car has long since passed.

No one comes here to stay, except the people who have always been here—Raymond, Lucille, Charles, Constance , Jack and Thomas.

Others have always lived here, too, and they have names, as well. Most of the dogs and cats also have names, but not the chickens.

He'd saved that piece of writing in the bottom drawer of a tall armoire on the house's third floor: he thought the piece of writing was the only "creative writing" he had ever done, though he had done much, much writing in his life (check writing, contract writing, the writing of lists and the writing of addresses on envelopes). He wasn't at all sure, on the day his brother Jim told him of his mother's death, that the piece of creative writing reflected reality—whether it was, indeed, based on a real town (one that could be located on a map, or actually visited), one where real-though-desultory people resided whose names were common and uninteresting. But it didn't matter. His memory was reliable, after a fashion, and was therefore undeniable, and verifiable, too.

He woke up on a Wednesday, some time after his brother's visit, and remembered dreaming of the town about which he had written. He remembered that there was a building—dark and ugly and made of metal—in the town, about halfway down its main street (of only three or four streets), and that he had gone into this building and seen things he did not want to see, things that disturbed him as much as anything had ever disturbed him.

When he woke, and remembered having dreamt about the town, he didn't remember what he had actually seen in the ugly building. This was very frustrating because he thought the things he had seen in it were quite important to him, like unexpected but welcome embraces, or breasts offered abundantly in the night, or eyes that possessed great understanding (which was always the better equal of love) in faces that were otherwise unbearable.

He was thinking about the building, and trying hard to remember the things he did not remember in it, when Fellatio came in, meowed once, from the floor near the bed, jumped on the bed, and attacked his hand. Fellatio was large, so his fangs were large, as well, and his claws, too, so, when Lightwater at last disengaged the cat from his hand, he saw that the hand was as bloody as a horror show, and that the blood was dripping all over his Mother-made quilt and the exquisite Oriental rug. He glanced about, decided Fellatio had run off—after his lightning-swift attack— and decided his hand needed bandaging, at least.

He got out of bed, while holding his hand high in the air to stop the bleeding, and went into the bathroom.

He looked at his face in the mirror and told himself that he did not recognize it. But he did recognize it, he knew, and that was the problem. Better, he thought, to look in a mirror and see a startling face, a face that needed introduction, than a face he knew too well, one which was depressingly unremarkable.

He held his injured hand under the cold water faucet. Minutes later, he realized that Fellatio hadn't done as much damage as he'd thought, and got some flex bandages from the medicine cabinet, applied them to his very minor wounds, and called his brother.

"Jim?" he said.

"Yes, Lightwater?"

"Jim, I've been attacked by the cat."

"Uh-huh," Jim said, "well it was bound to happen, don't you think?"

Lightwater sighed. "You're not demonstrating a lot of sympathy, Jim."

Short pause, then, "If you're able to call to let me know the cat attacked you, Lightwater, then I'd say you don't really *need* my sympathy. Unless you're calling from the hospital. *Are* you calling from the hospital?"

"No, Jim, I'm calling from home."

"Okay, then," Jim said. "Demonstrates my point, right?"

After a moment, Lightwater said, "Yes, it demonstrates your point. I'm sorry for disturbing you," and began to hang up, but, when the receiver was halfway to the hook, he heard Jim call out, "Wait a minute, Lightwater!" and put the receiver to his ear again. "Yes?" he said.

Jim said, "Lightwater, Mother is very ill. Gravely ill, in fact."

Lightwater felt faint.

Jim went on, "The doctors give her only a few weeks or months, possibly less."

Lightwater hung up the phone. It rang moments later. He ignored it.

Later that day, he wrote this:

The old man's shoes are in my closet, but the old man isn't in the house. He was here this morning. He had breakfast. Scrambled eggs. Nothing else. No coffee or orange juice. Just scrambled eggs. He put ketchup on them—he likes ketchup on his eggs, and he likes his eggs runny. He said once: "Look here, runny eggs. How beautiful!"

He was in his favorite chair in the living room this afternoon, too. Reading. Mickey Spillane—one of his favorite writers. He reads a Mickey Spillane mystery from cover to cover in one sitting. He devours them.

I say he's an "old man" because, compared to almost everyone else on the planet, he's very old. I don't know his age exactly, and I won't guess because his age in years doesn't matter, only the fact that he's old.

When I look at him quite closely, I can see that there's much clutter around him—newspapers, old shoes, open books and magazines and love letters, ashtrays full-to-overflowing (odd, because he hasn't been a smoker for years), tall green drinking glasses, and lamp parts, too; the wiring and the fixtures of lamps, as well as the interiors of watches, which do not tick.

He has needs which can't be met any longer, though most of these needs were never met, anyway.

He stares at me when I see him and I know he doesn't see me. There's a reason for this, though I can't think what it might be.

He dialed his mother's number later in the evening. He was certain it was she who picked up the receiver, but she said nothing, so he hung up. Seconds later, he heard from somewhere else in the room, "If there were ghosts, Mr. Hawkins, we would hardly know it."

"No one comes back," Lightwater said dryly.

And the voice—which was the voice of the man Lightwater had encountered in the house several times in the past year—said, "Well, of course, there's a very obvious reason for that. It's because they, these people we hope will come back, never . . . "

"I know," Lightwater said, with exasperation, "I know."

"Good then," said the voice, "then you aren't completely ignorant."

"No more than anyone else," Lightwater said.

He remembered, at last, the name of the very small town he had driven through many, many years earlier; it was "Friend," and it was located in upstate New York, between two small cities whose names escaped him.

He remembered going back to Friend at least once, and breaking into the metal building he had lately dreamt of: he'd gone back to Friend because he was attracted to its desultory people, its animals who acted surreptitiously, as if—he decided now, many, many years later—they were putting something over on their people. And the ugly metal building whose purpose was almost a mystery was a strangely comforting place, perhaps *because* it was a mystery.

He thought, too, of dead Mother and her invisible, unbearable face.

He thought, as well, of chickadees waddling through a snowstorm.

When he called Jim, with whom he supposed he needed to talk, because the house was dark, now, as it often was, he got Charlene, and he said to her, "Do you know, Charlene, that throughout life, throughout this life, we have only one great need, only one, and that is the need, always, always—Jesus God, *always*—to suckle?"

"You think so?" Charlene said, and hung up.

He walks about as if aimlessly, though nothing is aimless, not even the movements of asteroids or amoebae.

He's looking for something; his gaze drifts from place to place, but settles nowhere. I want to call out to him, "What are you looking for?" but I've tried talking with him many times without success, so, at last, I must think about giving up the effort.

Occasionally, his gaze passes over me and I think that, for a nano-second, only a nanosecond, there's recognition or curiosity in his eyes. But this has to be an illusion because, in this dark place, among these darker shapes in this dark place, how can he see me? And how can I see him?

THE SIGN AT VERA'S RESTAURANT

At last, the road is quiet. Too much traffic for a town so small—It's like a myth in the making; why all the traffic? Where's it going? People passing through, I think, heading somewhere else; who can blame them? I don't believe anyone stays here—what would be the reason? To buy overpriced bread at the village grocery, chat with the postmaster (he'll ask what you got in the mail), nod at folks staring from porches, compress time into long, hot afternoons, dissolve in the steamy dusk?

But it doesn't matter *where* the day is—I've learned that much, at least, after so many. What matters are cool nights passed in dreaming (any dream will do, as long as it travels), and learning to live despite the steamy afternoons and the yellow haze of morning, the squat houses, the flat streets, the big mongrel dogs barking in a dutiful way, mostly disinterested rural folk driving slowly to breakfast at Vera's ("Still a buck and a quarter for eggs and toast!"). Chris says, "There are so many obese people in rural America." I don't think it matters, neither does she; we're just talking, it's better than dwelling on the heat, the cranky neighbor (he's grown old here, plays golf in his backyard, sells used bicycles at the end of his driveway), the beginning of the end of another summer, another year down the tubes. Who, I wonder, will come to this place in fall, when the trees are dressed and ready for visitors? Slim people, people with money, people whose trees are not so well-coifed, perhaps, or so numerous, or maybe they'll come to see the running deer, the Amish moving their poor mares along, the church with its truncated steeple. Or perhaps they'll simply pass, on their way to country garage sales, or roadside stands ("These really are the best peaches I've ever tasted!"), farmers plowing their fields under, people moving without hurry near squat, gray houses, lifting heavy boxes into trucks, pausing to watch autumn traffic. "We need rain," Chris says, and I agree. It's easy to agree about such things. "Let's walk to Vera's," she says, and we start walking and find the picked-over remains of an opossum by the roadside.

"He was whole," I say, "just the other day. Pretty tri-colored ears. Fat."

The traffic drones past. It almost never stops in this wayside village, this place caught between somewhere and somewhere else—a phrase I share with Chris, who winces and says it's cliché, and when we're at Vera's, sipping coffee ("Strong coffee!" a sign proclaims, but it isn't), I look out at the bright sunlight, past the other people eating here, and talking ("We're patriotic, at least; I'll say that much."), into the dense blue rural sky, and I imagine nothing, I feel the warm coffee cup against my palms, smell bacon frying, hear words scrambled around me, and Chris says, "Look at that sign." I look at her. She's nodding; and I look where she's nodding, at a sign which reads:

OUR CUSTOMERS MAKE IT POSSIBLE FOR US TO BE HERE.

"So many philosophical possibilities," Chris says, "in that," and I say,
"No, I don't think so. Not in this burg."

Our breakfasts arrive. I eat hungrily. "Damned air conditioning's too
high," I mutter as I eat. "What are these people—Eskimos?"

ONE OF THOSE POEMS
AGING WRITERS WRITE

I still have the hands of that boy who did marvelous things—ran for hours, built bicycles out of spare parts, wrote stories, hiked a dozen miles in a blizzard for love. His hands are my hands. I could show you, you wouldn't believe me, you'd think I'd done it with moisturizing cream—I think it's a miracle, the way a tall hill is a miracle, and dreaming, the very weight of the air, breasts leaking milk, a life that changes. I don't look often at my own eyes. I think I'm afraid of them. Perhaps I should be drinking, by now, or smoking again, driving very fast, making loud noises in restaurants—all the myriad cacophonies of the dying. Bring a stout chair, I want to sit down.

SUNSETS IN 1962

I was made of lead and romance, then: I ate all the mashed potatoes and peas and meatloaf my mother cooked on her Tappan stove, in her tiny kitchen, in the small farmhouse my father did not build. Carol visited twice and, at fifteen, she really was no beauty, but she believed in winter, and so did I—we walked in it until our toes grew numb, then we went back, with reluctance, to the small farmhouse, listened to Chubby Checker, and ate corn on the cob. We kissed a half-dozen times, tremblingly, in the part of the kitchen where my mother slept, after my father had gone out too often. Carol let me fire her shotgun, once. I aimed it into the dark woods, aimed it at the darkness, and pulled the trigger, and the recoil knocked me down. I saw her smile; she was no prettier, then, when she smiled. But what did it matter? She believed in winter, and so did I. She's gone, now, in this new century, forty years after that shotgun blast, the small farmhouse leveled by rot, my mother aged, my father dead. Pain is almost behind me and that's a blessing. I don't remember the sunsets—they must have been magnificent.

A VISITOR ENCOUNTERS
THE SMALL SCREEN

Bach is here, watching CNN's endless coverage of war; he wants me to tell him what a Bradley Fighting Vehicle is; he looks confused, skeptical, says the desert is the wrong color, says the sky is the wrong color, says the only music he hears is the massive, insistent grumble of gears, earnest voices talking in goosey hiccups about missile attacks, over-flights, collateral damage. And I say I'm not sure what a Bradley Fighting Vehicle is; I say it carries troops into battle, and that it's very expensive. He asks for wine. I tell him I have none, only Pepsi. He looks at me a long, long moment, then looks at the TV, again, at the orange sand and the aqua-marine sky and the olive drab machines moving inexorably into the moment, and then into the moment. He says he wants to know about Pepsi.

ONLY TWO LEGS AND NO SILK

One wonders how the spider lays a single strand of silk out ten or twelve feet on a diagonal—from tree to porch railing, or flagpole to chair, sunflower to park bench.

I've read that he flings himself into the breeze, and I wonder if he does it with a cheer—a crisp "Whoopee," and a broad grin?

But, in the midst of this compulsive behavior (which he shares with many spiders), I wonder if he worries that a starling will come along and snap him up, or if the breeze will stiffen or die before he reaches his destination, leaving him stranded.

He's got guts, I'll give him that. Or maybe he doesn't care. Maybe, for him, the flight's the thing, the whole thing, or most of the thing anyway. Or perhaps he has no destination at all—maybe any destination will do.

GRATITUDE

For lifting me into a place I did not know existed before, ever, and for staying there with me hour upon hour, again and again, and then again, for longer than you wanted,

thank you

for sharing the largest part of yourself in those same hours and for letting me take you with me when we went to our separate cars and drove to our separate houses,

thank you

for existing, which was not your doing, I know, but without which I would have been poorer, and sadder, and would have gone through my days with fewer grins. Thank you

and thank you too (though this is not the end of the poem), for all of those things for which lovers do not thank each other, and which I will not name, but will remember day upon day upon day, thank you

for all of those days, and for the hours, and the moments which consumed them, and still do, and for consuming me.

MORE MIDDLE-AGED CRAZINESS

After a shower, naked in my comfy bedroom chair, (bending over to search for socks and underwear in the bottom drawer of my four-drawer chest), I realize I exist inside the softly lumpy body of a middle-aged man with hair in some of the wrong places, two or three liver spots, and a novel that's finally dipped below seventy thousand on the Barnes and Noble website.

And I'm not unhappy with any of it—not the lumpy body, or the cliché of middle age or the distressing fact of failing vision (new bifocals last year, and new again, next) or grandchildren nearing puberty, time nipping at my ass, women looking the other way after cursory glances (which once weren't so cursory), extracting a moment's peace in petting the cat, finding a poem, acquiring silence.

Not at all unhappy with any of it, or happy, either. Simply aware that there are more important things to think about, and that, now (in the simpering exhaustion that is middle age), I can wonder, at last, what those things might be.

THE GODLY GREETINGS OF DOGS

Each time I visit her little brown house and begin to make my way down her walk, I see, first, her two yellow labs and her edgy Jack Russell tied on long leads near her door: I stop; "Hello, hello," I call. "Hello, Myr, hello, Fionn," I call. "Hello, Mac." And they look, and wag, and bark, stare and smile (in the earnest and honest way that dogs smile) as if I really am okay.

And, for an instant, I look inside, here, into my own alien heart, where I have never before enjoyed looking, and nod, and go forward, into their good embrace.

PROCESS

W hen Jack Morgan set off for the woods that chilly November morning, he had little idea he was being followed.

Jack was angry. He shook with anger. It made him very uneasy because he thought he was capable of *anything* when he became this angry— capable of hurting himself, of hurting someone else, of killing someone (anyone), capable, even, of slashing someone's tires or ruining their day.

He'd seen two ceramic gnomes in lederhosen lurking in his neighbor's prim garden when he'd moved down his driveway toward the woods nearby, and he'd thought how wonderful and liberating it would be to kick those Goddamned garden gnomes into pieces, then to throw the pieces through his neighbor's Goddamned picture window. Wake his neighbor up. Spit curses at him. Make his neighbor's bright morning into something ghastly. It was a fantasy that gave him great pleasure within his inarticulate anger and made him grin. But that was one of his many abilities—finding pleasure *within* his anger. It was an ability that always frightened his statuesque wife, Loretta, and his two young children—timid Sue and brash Joe. Even his just-grown Shih Tzu, Sobig, had seemed frightened of it, though Sobig, too, was no stranger to anger.

Jack often made his way to the woods in the morning. He found solace from his anger—or, he told himself, solace, at least, from the many causes of it—there. It didn't matter the month, or the weather. It could be ten below in January or ninety-five above in July and it would be all right. It was the trees themselves that brought Jack solace. Not their leaves, but their trunks and branches. Yes, in autumn, it felt nearly orgasmic to push through the leaves, whose vivid, dead colors were so stimulating, but the trees themselves—their trunks and branches, their patterns and purpose, their sharp odor and voice and uncompromising need—were what gave him the kind of solace others like him the world over had, he felt certain, never known.

Sometimes he thought if he got close enough to the trees he would become one of them and one *with* them. (Then he would be blameless for anything he might do and he could go on living his days and nights as he had always lived them.) He could block the sunlight, or be a home to the creatures of the woods, or let sap run through him, and he would be honored by it, because of it, *within* it.

He liked to stand with his long, muscular back straight and tight against the trees in the woods. He didn't stand this way against any particular tree for long—usually a few minutes at most, and almost never more than an hour or two, sometimes three, depending upon the day and its horrible needs. He could sense the life of a tree and its green warmth through his back, his ass, his heels, his hair. Often, he could even sense the root system beneath him, and, from it, sense the very health of the tree. Sometimes, if he found a tree whose root system told him the tree was unhealthy, he avoided that tree on future walks in the woods. And sometimes he returned, on the same day, and took an axe to the tree. Sometimes he merely hacked at its lower branches and cursed it. If a tree returned his curses, he gave it his quiet apologies and went on his way.

On this morning, Jack didn't look back at his lemon-colored split-level house as he made his way to the woods—and this wasn't unusual—he rarely looked back because it always leavened his anger with memory and heartache, which made him feel suffocatingly mortal, which made him weak and fearful.

And, as he made his way to the woods, he thought about the gnomes in his neighbor's prim garden. They were new, Jack realized, because he hadn't seen them the day before, and they had a new look about them, too. They possessed a dull shine, even beneath the morning's dreary overcast. He thought briefly about going back to his neighbor's garden and destroying the gnomes, or pissing on them at least. It was foolish to put ceramic gnomes in your garden. Your personhood was suspect if you put ceramic gnomes in your garden. It meant you lacked taste and brilliance. It meant you invited destruction upon yourself.

But he didn't turn around. The gnomes were no more important than a single tear, today.

Jack liked to watch the approach of the trees as he walked, liked to watch their perspective change, *his* perspective on them change, liked to see their definition sharpen, their height increase, their width, too, and the alteration of their colors, which—at a distance—was usually shades darker than when he was within a stone's throw, or, soon thereafter, at arm's length. And, as the trees approached, he loved to listen to his footfalls on the earth—in the leaves, the grass, the mud, the snow, whatever the season or the day dictated. Sometimes he counted his footfalls as the trees approached. *One-two-three-four-five . . . (And there were days, yes, or moments, when he counted his footfalls this way—"One, one, one, one, one" . . . and so on.)* All of this was *process.* He enjoyed *process.* This process—watching the trees approach, counting his footfalls. Other processes—anger rising, then abating: love rising, then abating: voices rising (in anger or in love), then abating: the rise and fall of women weeping and men in horrific pain. Neither happiness nor sadness was eternal, and that was a truth he depended on. Only mortality, of course, was eternal—odd though that idea doubtless was to all the fools at large.

If he'd turned his head and looked, he'd have seen the thing following him, and he would have recognized it, too, at once, but he would also have looked away at once, as if the thing weren't there, and had never been there, as if he were merely looking at the tract houses, the gardens, the driveways, the windows, the neighbors (chatting, working, staring, depending upon the time and the weather and the *processes* in which they were involved).

He didn't like gunfire. He heard it often from within his house and he knew it came from the woods, that there were hunters loose there, and that they were slaughtering the wildlife. What a sad thing—slaughtering the wildlife. Slaughter the wildlife and you slaughter the soul of the earth. It wasn't like other slaughter. The slaughter of prim gardens, for instance, or the slaughter of expectations and memory.

Often, in summer, spring and autumn, he heard the buzzing of flies as he approached the woods. And he smelled the flies and their food, too—it was a confluence of unmistakable odors that made his lips rattle. But it was late November, too cold for flies. And he knew the source of the buzzing, anyway, so he didn't look about in the fallen leaves for flies, or in the cold, damp air.

He thought, as he walked, that the blast of gunfire and the buzzing of flies were similar, that they involved similar processes, or, at least, parts of processes that involved the same thing. So he decided, then and there, that he didn't like the buzzing of flies, either. This process of decision-making pleased him; it was a way of codifying the universe, the world, his neighborhood, the people who made him angry, or didn't listen, or put gnomes in their gardens, or stared, laughed, wept, or pleaded.

He still shook when he reached the woods. He'd counted the usual three hundred and fifty-four steps (though, on some days, it was, indeed, only *one* step) from his driveway to the first trees—a pair of maples; they were both taller than most maples, but one, because he had read its root system, was unhealthy, so he avoided it.

He stood with his strong and muscular back against the other maple. He wasn't facing his house when he did this; he was facing the woods, which quickly deepened until, after only a few dozen yards, the light itself was changed by the density of the population of trees, even though it was autumn, and the trees were bare. He much enjoyed this change in the light, the increasing density of the trees, the solid wall of trees further in. He thought that if he walked slowly enough, or quickly enough (*What was the process?*), he could become one with that solid wall, that mass, that density, that appealing and dark light.

He heard his wife's voice. It said, "Believe me, this is fucking serious!" and he smiled, hearing it, because it was so very like a phrase she had used often. It was part of her lovable predictability, her *process*. He wanted to say, "Oh yes, I know how fucking serious it is," but he said nothing because he was always quiet in the woods, he barely even breathed, barely even moved his legs and arms.

Arms!

Their arms were the arms of dancers caught in a moment. Beautiful arms, and precious. Arms were things of such grace and motion and necessity, even as *theirs* were, now—splayed out and incapable, the arms of dancers in an interminable moment of *process*.

He stepped quickly away from the tree.

God, he was still shaking.

God, I'm still shaking.

It was a fearful thing. Like standing up against a wave as tall as the trees themselves.

He stepped with quickness and agitation away from the tree and moved forward, toward the darkening of the light, toward that density and release. He counted his footfalls—*one, one, one, one, one, one* . . .

The thing following him counted, also.

It couldn't help itself.

That was *its* process.

His process.

The thing quickened its pace.

One, one, one, one, one, one . . .

Jack heard it breathing, counted its breaths—*One, one, one, one, one* . . .

Felt its cool exhales on his neck.

Turned.

Saw it.

Rattled his lips at it.

Said nothing.

Turned (again), and quickly, toward the trees, the dark light, the release.

And the thing fell on him.

And consumed him.

Digested him.

And let him go.

To dream. And remember. And begin. The *process*.

THE MARYBELL WOMEN

Grissom read the names—Abigail, Caroline, Rebecca, and Mary Anne Marybell—and wondered again (because all the names were on the same tall tombstone) if the women were buried in the same grave. He asked his wife about it and, again, she answered, "That would be impossible, don't you think?" She gave him a smile he generally thought of as patronizing—and which often made him angry—and realized she was right: how, indeed, could four women share the same grave? "Maybe there are four coffins," he said.

His wife shrugged. "Sure," she said. "Four coffins." Then she looked about, sighed, and gave him a glance filled with agitation. "Are we done here?"

"Uh-huh," he answered, but he was studying the Marybell tombstone, again, and hadn't really heard his wife. He was looking for more information somewhere on the tombstone—dates of birth and death, a notation which would indicate that no one, in fact, was actually buried there: "In

131

Memoriam," for instance. The story demanded more information. But the tall, dark gray stone bore only the women's names (in heavily stylized script), which Grissom, once more, found hugely unsatisfying.

His wife said, "You know there are wood rats out here."

He looked at her. She was scowling. "No there aren't," he said. "The town keeps things clean."

She shrugged. "Wood rats don't care about clean."

Grissom said, "I've never seen a wood rat here. Shit, I've never seen a *wood rat*. I don't think you have, either." He wondered briefly if he'd told her this before, and how many times?

She was only a few feet away; she came forward, leaned over—because he was on his haunches in front of the tombstone—and said into his face, "I've *seen* wood rats. I've seen lots of them. They're bigger than other rats—city rats. They're furry; they have long brown fur. And they're not afraid of anything."

He stood, which made her move away suddenly and stumble backward. He reached quickly for her, caught her hand, kept her from falling. She looked momentarily confused. He still had a hold on her hand; she looked at it, then at him, and said, "Thank you. I'm sorry."

He was thunderstruck. She never said she was sorry. He didn't know how to respond.

She said, "Can we go, now?"

He let go of her hand, which she let hover in the air a moment, and said, "Yes. We can go."

He went back to the tombstone of the Marybell women later that week. It was an early morning as bright as midsummer allowed, and not unpleasantly hot, but the sole of his right foot ached—a chronic ailment; he had many—and walking was difficult. He didn't ask his wife to come with him. He thought he must have had some kind of tell-tale look on his face when he came into the kitchen, where she was having toast with jam, and coffee, too, because she looked up from the table and said, through a mouthful of toast, "You're going to that cemetery, aren't you?" She gave him a small half-smile.

"Yes, I am." He nodded at her. "There's jam on your lips."

She harrumphed. "I'm not going with you. I can't."

"You wouldn't want to, anyway," he said.

"I don't know if that's true," she said, and wiped her lips on her napkin. "You need looking after."

"No I don't."

"Yes, you do. You always have. You just don't know it."

He sighed. "Whatever you say." Another sigh. "I won't be long. I'm just trying to get some ideas for the story."

"Of course you are." Another half-smile. "The story," she whispered, as if it were a phrase whose meaning eluded her. She bit into a piece of toast. "Good jam," she said. "Raspberry." She pointed at the opposite side of the table. "You should eat, first."

He shook his head, said, "Not too hungry, I guess," bent over and kissed her (a routine he could not break: in the time they'd been together, he had always kissed her upon leaving the house, no matter what his mood, or hers), added, "I'll see you later," and was at the grave of the Marybell women half an hour later.

He found three names. Not four. Caroline, Rebecca, and Mary Anne. He couldn't remember what the fourth name had been and he felt certain he'd only imagined it because names do not simply dissolve from tombstones in a couple of days. And the remaining names were etched deep into the stone; certainly it would be centuries before the elements erased them completely. It was a puzzle he found intriguing and he thought about it for a while, though he came to no conclusions, found no solutions; he did notice a small jagged, horizontal crack in the gravestone, just below the names, and he decided it was possible it had made him imagine the fourth name, whatever it had been.

Three dead women, then. Not four. And dead how? Accident?

Misadventure? He liked that word. *Misadventure*. It seemed oddly comforting and familiar, like an old glove. He decided he'd use it in the story.

When he arrived home, his wife was sewing a button on his long-sleeved gray shirt. She liked to sew, said she found it relaxing, but he couldn't remember if she'd ever sewn any of *his* clothes.

She looked up at him from the couch and said, "You've got to be more careful, Grissom. Buttons are hard to come by." She gave him a smile that was clearly designed as rebuke and forgiveness at the same time, and he noticed, after she'd spoken, an odd odor in the room, as though it had come from her mouth.

"Are they?" he said.

She was looking at his shirt, which she'd lain across her lap, and her long, white fingers were busily and expertly sewing a button on it, though the button was black, and the other buttons were white. "They?" she said, gave him a quick glance, then busied herself with the button again.

"Yes, buttons? Are they really hard to come by?"

"As hard as hen's teeth," she said, held the shirt up, looked admiringly at it, stood, went over to Grissom, and said, "Okay, fixed. Watch what you're doing next time, okay?"

He took the shirt from her and said, "Have you been eating peanut butter?"

"No," she said, "nothing."

"That's an odd answer," he said.

"Yes," she said, "I'm odd," which, he thought, was also an odd answer, and he nodded and went to his office/bedroom. He'd wanted to add, "Or garlic," but thought it would be rude, and he was rarely rude.

She came to him some time later, after he'd fallen asleep in his office chair; he was awakened by her hands on his shoulders, her long hair on his cheek, her warm breath on the top of his head. She smelled good, now. Her usual scent—a perfume or essential oil which blended nicely with her natural, earthy odor.

He said, "That feels good, Abby."

She said, "Oh yes, I'm sure it does. We all need these little pleasures. These small comforts."

He turned his head a little to look at her, though, in the early evening light, he thought he'd see little. She gently turned his head back, said, "No, it's all right, Grissom—no need to look."

He said nothing. She rubbed his shoulders for a long while, until the light in the room was all but gone, then she led him to the bed, stripped, stripped him, and they made love. When they were done, and lying beside each other, hands clasped, he said, "We're together simply for this, aren't we?"

She didn't answer at once, so he repeated the question. She said, on an outflow of breath, at a whisper, "Who's to find anything wrong with it? Grissom, you're a foolish man."

He couldn't tell if she were joking, and he didn't want to pursue the matter. He knew it would simply make him angry. She'd become much more pleasant than usual in the past few days and he thought that if he questioned her about it, she'd become the Abby he'd known for what seemed like a very long while, now.

The next morning, he asked her to go with him to look at the tombstone of the Marybell women and she said yes, which surprised him.

"You're sure?" he asked.

"Have you ever known me to say yes when I meant no?" she said.

He hadn't, and he told her so.

They were standing in front of the Marybell tombstone a half-hour later. She stood just beside him, her hand touching his lightly, as if she wanted to hold hands, but when he tried to take her hand, she moved it away quickly and he gave her a glance: "You know I don't like to hold hands, Grissom," she said.

He didn't know it, he told her.

She nodded at the tombstone. "I think they're all buried here," she said.

"All three of them in one large coffin. One on top of another. One decomposing onto the other."

"Who's to know?" Grissom said.

"Who, indeed?" she said, and gave him a flat smile which he did not understand.

The morning was oppressively hot. Grissom had begun to sweat. There were times when he actually liked to sweat, but this was not one of those times.

"You're sweating," his wife said.

"It's hot," he said.

"I don't like it when you sweat," she said. "It's disgusting. You become befouled with it."

He glanced at her. "Befouled?"

She looked at him. Her gray eyes were wide, her lips set. "Don't sweat," she told him sharply. "It attracts mosquitoes. And wood rats."

He smiled at her. She didn't return his smile. She said tightly, "Grissom, I *know* about wood rats." Her breath smelled of meat. "I have been beset upon by them as I lay in my bed."

He furrowed his brow, cocked his head. "'Beset upon by them'?"

She stood on her tiptoes so her face was very close to his: "And they've taken vital parts of me off into their hidey holes in the hellish woods!"

He wanted to tell her about her breath, but didn't know how to broach the subject without upsetting her, which would upset him. And he wanted to tell her she was acting very oddly. He considered a moment and said, "Jesus, you sound strange."

She settled back on her heels, looked silently at him for a few moments, glanced quickly about. "Oh," she said, while looking away from him, "it is all your business, is it not? All the stuff that you have made!"

"Sorry?" he said.

She looked at him, again. Her large gray eyes were distant, as if she were looking through him. "Take my hand, then, and we'll leave this place, for who would want to fall here and not be rescued?"

Over a dinner of lamb, greens, and mashed potatoes, she asked him, "What's your story about?"

He looked questioningly at her across the small table and said, "I'm surprised you'd ask."

"I'm asking," she said, and popped a forkful of mashed potatoes into her mouth. "I'm interested," she added as she chewed. And she smiled a little, too, though her potatoes were not yet completely chewed.

The overhead fixture and its five 100-watt bulbs washed the room in light and Grissom hated it; more than once, he'd removed three of the five bulbs from the fixture, only to find, later, that his wife had replaced them. He glanced quickly at the fixture, now, sighed, glanced at his wife's face—ghastly pale in the bright light—and the remnants of potatoes at one corner of her mouth (she was still smiling, as if expectantly), and said, "It's about the Marybell women."

Her smile became crooked. She cocked her head. Stopped smiling. Chewed her potatoes. Swallowed. "Whatever the hell for?" she asked; he thought he heard a note of anger in her voice and he wondered, in so many words, *Why is she angry?* He shrugged and began to speak, but she interrupted, "Why in the name of all that's holy would those women interest you, Grissom? They're . . . " She paused. "Jesus Christ, they're . . . " She glanced quickly about, as if searching for the right word, then looked at Grissom again. "They're Goddamned boring!" she said. "They're as boring as . . . as . . . " She glanced about again, then leaned over her plate and gave Grissom a hard look. "They're as boring as *death!*"

He shrugged once more. He wanted her to simply finish her meal and leave him alone. He thought he would become angry if she didn't. "Abby," he said, and he could hear his voice tremble a little as he tried to keep his temper, "*I* don't think they're boring. I don't even know them. The real Marybell women. Neither do you."

She continued to look hard at him for a moment, then at her plate, then at her fork, which she clutched in her hand, then at Grissom once more, at the plate, again: she said, as she stared at the plate—she'd eaten half the greens and lamb and potatoes—"Well, Grissom," (she spoke nearly at a whisper; if her words had not been sharply enunciated, he thought he wouldn't have understood them) "okay. Yes. I acquiesce."

He smelled her from across the table. The odor of meat. He wanted to say something about it. After a moment, he said only, "You *acquiesce?*"

She looked at him. Her gaze was soft. The fork fell from her hand and clattered to her plate, which made Grissom lurch a little. She said, "This opportunity to rise"—a quivering smile spread across her mouth—"and to love and to lust . . ."—her smile broadened—" . . . Grissom . . ." She looked softly at him for a long time, while he looked back, and then she looked at her plate, again: "And to *eat,*" she said.

Grissom said nothing.

"And to *eat,*" she repeated.

Grissom saw the wood rats at the cemetery that afternoon. They were as large as dinner plates and they regarded him as if he were of no consequence—a shadow moving among the stones.

He thought there were dozens of them, but he was wrong. Three or four or five wood rats in a place such as that can appear to be dozens, and he knew it, but he saw dozens, anyway—they moved with an ambling, jittery gracelessness that was jarring in the stillness, and threatening enough that he stepped quickly to one side as they moved past, though he knew, down deep, that it was unnecessary.

But as he stood at the grave of the Marybell women—and the sun through the trees dappled the gray stone with a cheerful yellow light—the wood rats ambled away and were gone, and he read the names on the tombstone to himself, at a whisper—"Caroline, Mary Anne, Rebecca"—and reached out and fingered the names as he said them, one after the other.

"The Marybell women died unhappily," he said, still touching the stone, and quoting the little story he was trying to write, which was many, many words shy of being done, because he was no writer. "Victims one and all of horrible circumstance."

He dropped his hand.

And heard his wife move toward him through the short grasses: she moved, always, in near-total silence. He felt her hands on his arms. Such strength in her hands. She said, her voice no less musical and urgent than the voice of wind, "You have so little to say, Grissom. And you will never say it."

He put his hand on her hand. It was no warmer than the summer air, no softer than bone.

"You must tell me what *is*," he said, without turning to look at her: he had looked at her more than once. "It is only fair and just."

"We are no more fair and just," she said, "than anything that breathes, my love. How can it be otherwise?"

He had no answer.

She asked again, "How *can* it be otherwise?"

When he arrived home, he did not find Abby in her usual places—at the kitchen table, a good meal in front of her, or in the bedroom, splayed out on the bed, or in the cavernous attic, where she often rummaged through the musty old things Grissom always assumed had been left by the house's previous owners. He found her, at last, around the back of the house. She was smiling very broadly, as if her face had acquired strange new muscles, and her large gray eyes were open as wide as eggs, and she was sitting in a stiff wooden chair, long gingham dress dreadfully askew, and so inappropriate in the suffocating summer heat.

He spoke to her—to her improbable smile and her eyes as big as eggs, to her graying skin, her blood:

"Would that I were sorry," he said, "then this would be only a moment that passes."

"It was his anger," he read aloud, and squinted to read the rest of the sentence because his handwriting was awful: "and their quixotic natures—always unpredictable, which delivered him daily into madness. What else could he do? Only that which was just and right, for his own sake.

"But he was a good man—too good to be held accountable, even to himself, for such acts.

"Though how not accountable? How not accountable?"

He paused. Read on:

"The Marybell women died unhappily, one after the other. Victims one and all of horrible circumstance."

Grissom read the names and wondered again (because all the names were on the same tall tombstone) if the women were buried in the same grave, perhaps the same coffin. He asked his wife about it and, again, she answered, "Yes, all one on top of the other, all decomposing into each other, all but the woman on the bottom, who suffers from the weight of so much decay."

Grissom looked at his wife and smiled. "You have a dreadful sense of humor, Becky," he said.

She smiled back. "I do, yes," she said. Her breath smelled of newly fallen leaves. It was a good smell and fit the season.

Grissom reached out and touched the tombstone of the Marybell women. "Odd," he said, "but I could swear there were four names, yesterday. I was sure of it."

His wife reached out and put her hand on his, as it touched the stone: "The dead cannot be accounted for by name, my love," she said. And their hands were no colder than the late autumn air, no softer than bone.

THE PEOPLE ON THE ISLAND

This winter morning, when we crossed over the dune, we saw a man lying face-down in a shallow tide pool half a dozen yards from us. A gull waddled about agitatedly near him and squawked now and then.

"Oh God," Elizabeth said, and stopped walking, as I had. She put her hand to her mouth, said again, "Oh God," and added, after a moment, "Another."

I love such winter walks on the beach. Even before we came to the island, I found them bracing. I claimed to the skeptical that they made me "feel alive."

The man in the half-frozen tide pool wore a black suit, and his shoulder-length hair also was black, as were his shoes. He wore several playfully grotesque rings on his right hand. One was purple, another green.

Elizabeth asked, "Do you think he drowned?" She looked questioningly at me, then at the man, again.

I answered, "Who's to say?"

She looked at me again and frowned a bit. "*He* would. If he could."

Over lunch, we discussed the morning. Our discovery of the black-suited man was, of course, at the forefront of our conversation.

"I'm sick of these people," Elizabeth said, and sipped her tea. She was having a chocolate scone with the tea, but had not yet touched it. "Where do they come from?"

"I think we should go and look at him, again," I said.

Elizabeth broke off a small piece of her scone and popped it delicately into her mouth. She is a very courteous woman. Very aware of etiquette. "Go and look at him again," she echoed as she chewed.

"Yes," I said. "But more closely this time."

She glanced sadly toward the window, which overlooks the water.

I said, "Perhaps we should even . . . turn him onto his back."

She looked at me, brow furrowed, as if she were troubled. She looks at me like that quite a lot lately.

"Perhaps we really should do that," I said. "Turn him onto his back. Look at his face. It's possible we know him, Elizabeth."

"I don't think so," she said. "We know none of these people."

"But you're so wrong," I said. "We know them only too well. They're simply what they are. They are organs, flesh, hair. And blood as thick as pudding. How can they be any more or less than that?"

"I don't understand you," Elizabeth said. "I don't think I ever have."

I nodded. "Maybe that's for the good."

She shook her head. "You only think it is, George."

"And what of the woman in the parlor?"

Elizabeth sighed. "She'll keep. Every one of these people will keep."

"Yes," I said. "It's amazing, isn't it?" I smiled a little. "They keep so damned well."

Elizabeth awoke screaming early the following morning. I took her hard into my arms, gave her kisses and whispered assurances that "everything is all right," until at last she became calm, and she said, "How long is this going to continue, George? How long do we have to endure it?"

I shook my head and held her more tightly. "My love," I told her, "our needs and our dreams can be demons. I've learned that much, here, at least. But our demons will bring us so much, if we let them, if only we can hear and understand their song."

This house is small, comfortable and easy to clean, a plus when the wind is fierce, as it usually is, and the fine sand insinuates itself through every crack and crevice. Winters are the best time for that, and this winter has been no exception. Often, it seems as if the wind blows in four directions at once, and the house shivers, shrieks, and complains. But although the house is small, it's quite sturdy, and I have never worried about being tossed into the elements late one evening, or of coming back from one of our winter walks to find the house not where I'd left it.

Elizabeth says she's waiting impatiently for the first snowfall. She says it brightens the landscape, reflects sunlight (should we ever have it), masks the grotesque. I tell her there's no reason to mask the grotesque; I tell her it can be beautiful. She merely shakes her head and scowls.

The black-haired man in the black suit was missing from the tide pool. I assumed several possibilities—he had been carried off by the tide itself, carrion eaters had quickly dispatched his remains, others on the island had spirited him away. That last possibility is remote, however. As far as I've been able to ascertain, there are no others living on this island. I've circumnavigated it several times (quite time consuming), and, except for a few scrubby trees, and the poor excuse for a lawn I try to maintain around the house, there's an almost complete lack of flora; animal life is restricted to a few gulls and herons (they seem confused, somehow, even a bit logy; I can't imagine why), and an animal I've only heard, but have never seen. I believe it's a stray dog.

The woman in the parlor in the other house is perched on an exercise bike. She has both hands tightly on the handlebars and both feet on the pedals. She's wearing bright red nail polish, and she's leaning forward slightly, in the position a bike rider would use. Her head is up a bit, her gaze forward, her eyes open halfway. They're robin's-egg blue. Her hair is blonde, straight, long, and stunning. She's wearing a gray, loose-fitting exercise suit with the words "Find Out For Yourself" emblazoned across the chest in green, art deco-style letters.

I believe her name is Jane. Elizabeth is skeptical about this: "It could be anything," she said. "It could be Barbara, or Helen, or Jacqueline."

"No," I said. "I believe it's Jane."

Elizabeth gave me a puzzled look. "She doesn't look like a Jane to me. Where do you get these ideas, anyway? Why assign names to these people at all?"

"Because it amuses me," I said. "They amuse me."

She scowled.

We went to visit Jane this afternoon. It has been three days since our last visit, and she was precisely as we had left her. The parlor was cold, as was the entire house, I assume, since it's not heated, and there was even a little frost on the backs of Jane's hands, on her forehead, and on her eyes. I gestured to indicate the frost, because I found it almost decorative.

"Look there," I said. "Look at the frost." I smiled.

"It's sad," Elizabeth said.

"I don't think so," I said. "I think it becomes her."

"Good Lord," Elizabeth whispered.

She doesn't like to visit Jane. She likes visiting none of those who exist here. But she most dislikes visiting Jane because, she says, Jane looks angry. "It's in her eyes," Elizabeth said. "And in the line of her mouth."

I agreed, and added, "But I can't imagine that she would have any reason to be angry. She is, after all, beyond anger."

"And everything else, as well," Elizabeth said.

"My point exactly. Don't you see? Isn't it obvious?"

"Nothing's obvious," Elizabeth snapped. "Nothing's obvious!" she repeated. "And *that's* the whole point, isn't it?"

She's right. That is the whole point. Nothing's obvious. Is the wind actually fierce and cold? Is the landscape actually barren? Is there a stray dog loose somewhere on the island? And what is Jane doing on the exercise bike in the parlor of the other house? Who put her there? And why? And what of the others? Henry, Joanna, and the rest. They're fascinating. Complexity to simplicity to eternity in one effortless outflow of breath. Past and soul, needs and lusts and longing gone forever in a moment without oxygen. And perhaps their purpose is simply to be fascinating, grotesque, and predictable. Like chess pieces. Pets. Stories told around a campfire.

But there are some givens. My fingers actually do have ink on them from the leaky fountain pen I'm using. Elizabeth's hair has indeed begun to turn gray since we've come here. And I'm positive this is winter, positive about the wind and the barrenness of the landscape. Positive that the grandfather clock in Jane's parlor predictably strikes the hour and the quarter hour. Positive there's a purpose to my presence on this island. Positive it is an island. That it sits in an ocean. That the ocean churns and throws whitecaps at sandy beaches which—I'm positive—are eroding rapidly. Positive no one walks these beaches except Elizabeth and I, a few logy herons and gulls, and a creature that barks hoarsely at a distance. Positive this landscape has as much to do with heaven as it has to do with hell.

The others in that other house may have once believed in their immortality, and so they have it now, in a way. Caught forever in the positions of life—eating, taking a bath, arranging shoes, feeding an absent cat, making love, becoming old, drowning. I am not surprised that there are no ghosts on this island. The others in that other house, and on the island in various places, are stationary ghosts we may touch, if we wish. But Elizabeth says that the touch of death is miserable, that it stinks. I disagree, of course. I tell her that death is as necessary to us as a beating heart.

Elizabeth and I have stopped having sex. She no longer parades around naked in front of me, nor I in front of her. It's something we used to revel in, something we found exciting and necessary—after a shower, or just before bed, or simply as an enticement. But we don't do it, anymore, though I believe desperately that I want it for us both. We don't know why we've abandoned our nakedness—at least I don't know why.

We don't prepare meals for one another, either. Various pasta dishes were our favorite, and I had become something of a pastry chef. But we don't prepare meals for one another, anymore. We hardly eat, anymore, and hardly ever together. We eat when we're hungry, and I think that neither of us finds any pleasure in it, though we have all the food we need, and the little kitchen is delightful and well-equipped.

It strikes me that Elizabeth and I are necessarily together here, on this island and in this house, and necessarily drifting apart. She is drifting off to a world that's more confusing, complex and gaudy—in a Technicolor way—than I like. And though I hate to do it, I think I have no choice but to let her go there.

"How do they arrive?" Elizabeth asked.

"By boat, I imagine," I answered.

She turned her head toward me, and, in the half-light, I could see her frown. Prior to coming here, her frowns were elegantly expressive of much more than I had come to expect from any frown; but here, they're merely expressive of sadness and confusion. "You mean they pilot a boat to this island—they get in a boat and, start the engine, and . . ."

"Of course that's not what I mean," I answered, regretting my abruptness.

We were lying in bed, comforter and blanket pulled up to our necks. The air in the room was cold, good for sleeping. "I meant that they're brought here."

"By who?"

I shrugged. "By elves," I said, and grinned.

She said nothing.

"Did you hear me?" I said.

"Large elves," she said. I tried, unsuccessfully, to hear a tone of amusement in her voice.

"Elves with grunt and grit and muscle," I said. What a fascinating and grotesque idea, I thought. Elves piloting boats filled with the dead. Elves unloading the dead on my island and arranging them in various positions of life. It was an idea I could embrace, and which made me warm.

"We would hear such elves," Elizabeth said. "We would hear their boats."

"Above that wind?" I asked.

She said nothing.

The others who've been put here do not argue or cajole or laugh or make meaningless conversation, though one might expect from looking at them that argument or cajoling, laughter or meaningless talk could well be their intention, had they any intentions left. But they are at the mercy of the wind's intentions, now, the intentions of the winter, the intentions of those—unseen—who move them about, from place to place, and from attitude to attitude. I have never seen this being done, but I'm sure that it is done.

Jane is no longer perched on her exercise bike. I don't know where she is; Elizabeth says she's reluctant to look elsewhere in that big house in fear we'll find still others in the attitudes of life. We believe, however, that Jane is indeed in the house because we can see what appear to be drag marks in the thin layer of sand throughout the house's first floor. The drag marks stop halfway up the flight of stairs that's off the parlor, where the layer of sand ends. So we assume that Jane is on the second or third floor of the house. We have no idea why she's been moved.

Tonight, the creature that barks hoarsely, and which I assume, perhaps incorrectly, to be a dog, seemed closer than it has on previous nights.

I have never seen the sunrise, here. From time to time, on our walks,

I see a diffuse patch of light through the overcast and I assume it's the sun—it can be nothing else. I've seen a sunset or two, but these are dull events which possess nothing of the brilliance of sunsets in other places. The sky does not turn to fire, the pale and fragile blue at the horizon does not become a delicate, short-lived rosé. No pale and fragile blue exists here, only a horizon the color of lead, which, in its own way, is quite remarkable.

I went to the other house without Elizabeth and found Jane lying on her back in a four-poster bed on the house's third floor. She was wearing her gray exercise outfit, and her hands were clasped over her stomach, legs straight. Her sneakers were on the floor beside the bed. Her socks had been put neatly into the sneakers.

One of the room's tall, thin windows was open wide, so the room was very cold.

Jane's faded blue eyes were open wide, too, as if someone had forced them open. Her look of anger seemed to have passed. This confused me, and made *me* angry. It passed quickly.

"Whose world is this?" Elizabeth asked.

"It's not a world," I answered. "It's an island."

"That's the same thing as a world." She sounded petulant. It's a tone I used to find amusing—as if she had momentarily become a small girl; it reminded me of our first few years together, when we were young children, before we started noticing, in earnest, that we were different sexes.

Her petulance, now, is merely annoying. Like her frown.

I think I would find even her laughter annoying, if she laughed anymore.

I wish she were someone else.

"What are we going to *do* with them?" Elizabeth asked.

I shrugged. "What *can* we do with them?" I shook my head a little. "I'm not even sure we're *supposed* to do anything with them." I grinned. "We can arrange them," I said.

"Arrange them?" She seemed astonished by the idea.

"Sure. We can make them be . . . what we want them to be. We can make them smile. We can make them look attentive and interested."

"That's pathetic, George. They're not dolls. They're not marionettes."

"What are they, then?"

We were on one of our walks, which have grown less and less frequent because there are so few areas on this island, now, that are unsullied by the others propped up in their various positions of life. I find it very disconcerting to come across one of them—even those with whom I'm familiar, perhaps because they are, as well, so grotesquely *un*familiar as their positions change from day to day and week to week. I maintained to Elizabeth that the others should, at least, remain predictable. If they are in an attitude of repose, then that is as they should remain. If they are in some other attitude—an attitude of life, as I call it—then that is as they should remain, as well. They have no choice.

Elizabeth had no idea what I was talking about. I think, at times, that she does not appreciate the situation we have here as much as I. I believe that she sees it as a burden.

Sometimes I wish that she were somewhere else.

We've spotted the black-haired man in the black suit, though at a short distance. He was seated in a high-backed wooden chair on a dune overlooking the ocean. He was facing away from us, though we knew it was the same man we'd discovered two weeks earlier. When we saw him, we both stopped walking and Elizabeth whispered an obscenity. We were perhaps fifty yards from the man and the brisk wind was blowing his black hair about.

"He's watching," Elizabeth said, then added, "or waiting."

"How could he be watching anything? Or, for that matter, waiting for anything?" I asked.

"Why not?" she said. "Why couldn't he, or any of them, be watching? And waiting?"

"They've nothing to watch, and nothing to wait for," I said.

"They have everything to wait for," she said. "How do we know they don't? How do we know anything about them? We don't even know their names."

"You're being argumentative," I said.

"No, I'm being realistic," she said.

"And you're being confrontational, too," I said.

She shook her head. "No," she whispered, then nodded at the black-haired man. "He is." She paused. "They all are."

I managed a brief and unsatisfying glimpse of the creature we supposed was a dog. It awakened Elizabeth and me early in the morning, when the sky had begun to lighten. It sounded as if it were very close to the house, perhaps on the little patch of scrubby lawn that I have tried hard to maintain. I could hear a slight warble in its hoarse bark, as if it were attempting song.

"Listen to that," Elizabeth said. "Listen to that," she repeated. "It's awful."

I looked at her, saw the pale oval of her face in the semi-darkness. "I don't think it's awful," I said.

"It's grisly," she said. "It's awful," she repeated. "This entire island is awful. These people all around us are awful. They're sickening and awful, George! Look at them!"

"I have."

"Not in any meaningful way. You've looked at them as if they're merely . . . lawn ornaments."

"I haven't!"

"But you have. I know you have. You always have."

"Always? We haven't been here that long."

"Haven't we?"

"It only feels that way, Elizabeth."

"We've been here since we were children. I know it."

The creature near the house barked again. Its warble was longer this time, more pronounced, as if it really were attempting song.

Then what passes here for morning came, and when I went to the window, I saw the creature moving off, toward the center of the island. It was larger than a large dog, though it was vaguely the shape of a dog. I saw only its dark silhouette against the gray light, as it moved away from me. When I study it again, with the eye of memory, I don't believe that it was a dog, however. I believe that it was human, or something trying to be human, or something which may have once been human. I said as much to Elizabeth, while I stood at the window and she lay in bed.

She laughed. It was a joyless noise. "You live for drama," she said. She grimaced. "More precisely, you live for the drama of death. I think you always have."

I didn't like her laugh. I liked her grimace even less. It made me quite angry. I could feel it in my hands and arms; I could feel it in my ears and my mouth. "Damn you!" I whispered.

She turned over, as if to go back to sleep. I was certain she hadn't heard me.

One of the others is a woman I call Joanne. She's young, pretty, and she wears a black bikini, which fits her well. She sits upright in a two-seat wooden rowboat that has the words "The Arrangement" painted poorly in black on the port bow. Joanne has red hair and green eyes and, unlike so many of the others, she looks happy. I could be wrong, but I'm almost sure there's the ghost of a smile on her broad, red mouth. She has her hands on the rowboat's oars, which are at right angles to the rowboat, in the sand—which is where the rowboats sits, at the bottom of a dune about a half-mile from the house Elizabeth and I share.

Sometimes I speak to Joanne, as I do to many of the others, though I've never shared this fact with Elizabeth. "Hello, Joanne," I say. "Beautiful name—Joanne. I've never known anyone with that name, except you."

She never responds, of course. I think that I would jump out of my shoes if she did.

Her skin has a pale blue cast. All of the others on the island have that same cast, even Elizabeth, when the gray light catches her correctly. Sometimes I think that it's simply the quality of light which causes this cast, if—were the sun to appear—it would cause many changes, not just in the cast of skin. Perhaps the winds would cease. Perhaps the air would grow warm. Perhaps rain would come. And perhaps, when all of these things happened, the others here would begin the slow but inexorable processes which would take them from me, and back to the earth, forever.

I'd miss them. Elizabeth may have been right; in some strange way, I may think of them as ornaments. As bric-a-brac, perhaps. Knick-knacks. It's a grisly idea. But it's entertaining.

What does one do with a missing wife? More correctly, what *can* one do with a missing wife? Encounter her living ghost on the stairway? Conjure up memories at bedtime? Prepare tea and scones and leave them on the table always?

But then, I don't know what I want to do with her, or what I'd do with her if I found her, or if she found me, or if we came across one another on the island, or in that other house.

Of course I've looked everywhere. I'm sure that I've found her footprints in the dunes, and it occurs to me that she may have simply walked into the ocean, sick to death of the life that has been provided her here, on this grotesque and lovely island. But I've found no evidence of footprints on the ocean side of the dunes, which suggests little, because such footprints would last only half a day or so in this wind.

I've called to her, too. But, again, the wind covers much, and I'm all but certain she cannot hear me.

I think, however, that she has never heard me. She has her gaudy, Technicolor world. And I have my world. So I've lost little.

The creature which once may have been human warbled beneath the bedroom window before daylight. There was no hint, in the sound it made, of the bark which heralded its first appearances. Only that warble, which is so close to song, and which is almost soothing in its strange atonality, as if—like so many; like myself—it is simply trying hard to find its place in a universe that is a friend to no one. And so it warbles off-key, in various keys, trying to find the tone which resonates in its miserable gut and heart in the air and earth around it.

I went to the window and peered down at the creature. I couldn't see its face. I saw a rough texture to the darkness, nothing more. But I believe it was peering back at me. I believe that its eyes, which may have been green, or blue-green, or blue, locked on mine, and that when I spoke to it, it spoke back, though I heard nothing except its atonal warbling.

I am arranging the others as I feel they should have been arranged when I came to this island. I am arranging them as they no doubt want to be arranged, as *I* would want to be arranged were I in their shoes. But it is no small chore to arrange them. I'm as old or older than any of them, and they offer me no help whatsoever. Of course, I know that they're beyond helping themselves, or helping me, but when one sees arms, and legs looking fit, and strong backs, one naturally hopes for help.

The arrangement I found for Joanne was simple enough. I sent her off in her rowboat. I pushed the thing out as far as I could into the choppy ocean, perhaps fifty yards, and I let the currents grab her. In no time, she was gone.

And I put the black-haired man back in the tide pool. Face down.

And I've put Jane back on her exercise bike, though she seems angry again.

And I've put a young man named Henry on his back on a blanket, on a dune near the ocean. I've covered his midsection with a towel. He used to be taking a bath in one of the bathrooms in the other house. He used to have one arm up, so he could use a scrub brush (absent) on his back. I didn't like this. His genitals were huge, all too apparent, blue and ugly.

And one I've named Rebecca is writing her first novel here in the dining room of my little house. She's using an old Remington Rand Noiseless typewriter. Her fingers are poised above the keys, her head is lowered slightly over the platen, and she's reading what she's written—which is absolutely nothing, to date, and which will remain nothing forever. Rebecca used to be washing dishes at the other house.

I've seen Elizabeth as a silhouette against the horizon, at dusk. I'm sure it was Elizabeth. It could have been no one else. She has a distinctive figure. An hourglass figure. And she walks slowly, gracefully. I saw her from my bedroom window. She was a hundred yards away, walking toward the ocean, over a dune. I called to her, "Elizabeth, what are you doing?"

Then sunlight grabbed her and, in a moment, both she and the sunlight were gone.

It is the first sunlight I've seen here.

I must admit that it scares me.

The others do not stay as I've arranged them. As if they have minds to command them, and hands that grasp, and legs that can make them walk, they have all gone off into other arrangements—the black-suited man is again in his high-backed chair on the dune, and Jane is now washing dishes at the other house, and the man named Henry is fishing, rod and reel poised, and Joanne is sunbathing under a gray sky, and Rebecca is standing just outside the house with an artist's brush in hand, as if at an easel.

This makes me very angry, very angry. I can feel it in my ears and behind my eyes. These people are at the mercy of the wind's intentions, the winter's intentions, *my* intentions. They are beyond their own intentions. They have no memories, no needs, no wants, no lusts. They are organs, flesh, hair, and blood as thick as pudding. They are bric-a-brac, adornments; they serve the ambulatory, they serve *me*.

The sun made a brief appearance today. It changed the wind and changed the temperature. It is changing the others, too. It's corrupting them, however slightly. The pale blue cast of their skin is becoming blemished by small irregular patches of white, and green. This is most apparent in those who remain outside.

I pray for cold, and wind, and cloud.

Quite early this morning, I awoke suddenly, without knowing why, made my way downstairs, and saw that the front door was open, that Elizabeth was standing on the front porch looking in at me. I saw her face well, despite the darkness. I think it was illuminated from above by light coming out of my bedroom window.

I said, "Elizabeth." It wasn't a question. I was merely mouthing her name.

She closed her eyes briefly and sighed.

"Elizabeth," I said, "I'm very lonely here. I'm very lonely here. Come inside."

She shook her head slightly, as if the gesture gave her sorrow.

I was half a room away; I did not move toward her.

Eventually, she turned and walked off.

The sun's brief appearances have grown less and less brief. It rises each day, and it sets. And the others have become corruptible. Skin sloughs off. Breasts wrinkle. Eyes descend.

This makes me very angry. I can feel it everywhere.

And all the while, Elizabeth watches—from a distance, on the dunes, at the windows, too. But never here, inside my little house.

I cried to her, this morning, about loneliness, again. I felt foolish and vulnerable, but I babbled and blubbered at her nonetheless, until she simply wasn't there anymore.

She could not hear me.

She has never heard me.

So I've lost little.

But how can I be lonely, now, with the others all about, arranged so prettily in the positions of life, and protected, here—inside this little house—from the lingering and awful sunlight?

I keep them away from the windows, where the sunlight insinuates itself and causes skin and hands and noses and eyes and necks to decay.

I speak to them. They do not speak back, or change their attitudes of life. I think I would jump out of my shoes if they did.

It's a bit close here, now, in this small house. I have barely room to sit in my chair. Elbows and breasts and thighs, knees and feet and chins and hair are arrayed around me like shadows at dusk.

I don't turn to the windows anymore. The sunlight is there. And I know Elizabeth is there, too, looking in at me, doubtless with pity, always with pity. And the creature which may have once been human is at a different window—one shaded from sunlight—and it is warbling its atonal song. That song is constant, now. As the wind was. It's a beautiful song, one I know I've always heard, even in childhood, and one which I think I understand, at last.

ALL AT THE END OF MID-EVENING

Now what? Fluff the pillow? Open the window, let the cold air in? Turn off the TV? Turn on the radio? Listen to what? Beethoven, Vaughan Williams? Turn off the radio? Read? Read what? Who? Weldon Kees? Sharon Olds? Who? Billy Collins? John Grisham? Stephen King? So many questions.

Do what? Dream? Dream what? I saw two men lug a fishing shack out onto the lake this morning. Dream what?—Dream of reading Weldon Kees in a fishing shack on the ice? Dream what?

Yesterday, on a long drive, I saw twelve wild turkeys in a field moving fast toward the road, their shiny necks thrust straight out. What a strange thing that was. Almost beautiful. Almost surreal. I'd never seen twelve wild turkeys all at the same time before.

I'd seen only one, or two. But there they were. Twelve. Moving as one. And while I watched them, as I drove by, I wondered what the proper word would be—Flock? A flock of wild turkeys? After all, it's a "murder of crows," and a "bevy" of quail, a "murmuration" of starlings. I thought

I should look it up when I got home. I thought I should know for sure.

Dream what? Dream of twelve wild turkeys on a suicide run toward the road? I dreamt something else last night. I don't remember what, with certainty. Something about sex.

And there, now, is the night, in earnest. A few lights on the tall hill, and the night, and the snow, which has been swallowed by the night. And, because I've turned off the TV, and turned on the radio, music, too. Shostakovich. One of his lesser pieces. Better to hear Creedence Clearwater Revival. Better to hear Bob Dylan, AC/DC. I turn off the radio, am intimidated by the sudden silence, turn the radio on again, turn it off, listen to the damned hum of the computer, listen to the whine of the furnace. Dream what? Dream what?

If I hear a slow snuffle beyond the window in the darkness (as I did in summer) I'll dream of bears tonight, early. And sex later.

It is, in fact, "flock." A flock of wild turkeys on a suicide run toward the highway in winter under an ashen sky.

CLOCKING THE MOMENT

Shadows and sun on the Buddha. I got him at T.K. Maxx, along with some Christmas doo-dads; he's comforting. He looks tranquil. He's good with sun or shadow. He's good with both.

All this anger.

"Put your shoes away, dammit!" she says, and here I am—an adult, a grandfather, for Christ's sake.

"Yes, I will. Sorry," I tell her, and do as she asks. I put them away. I tuck them into the closet, so only their tips are visible. They're new, but they're scuffed. I think she's upset about that, too.

I can't help it. I can't help anything. I know that sounds convenient, but it's true. The Buddha sits quietly, neither smiling, nor frowning, simply . . . accepting. That's a good thing. The Buddha accepts everything. The snow, the sun, shadow, anger, regret, forgiveness. It's all the same to him. All the moments. Lasso the moment. Don't let it go.

I think she should accept, too, in the same way as the Buddha. Leave my shoes alone. I do nothing else that's inconvenient, nothing else that's inappropriate.

I wanted to slap her, once. We were on a picnic. She told me there was mustard on my face, then she pointed and laughed. I wanted to slap her, but I let it go, I let it pass. It's what the Buddha would have done. Let that discomforting moment pass into another, meld with another, and another, meld with the moment that is a day—sun and shadow, wind, dusk, and midnight.

I'm leading into nothing, here. I have held her and loved her, put my tongue deep into her mouth, stepped up quietly behind her to give her a tickle, made coffee for her, and trimmed Christmas trees with her. We've laughed together, loved, too, and snickered at passersby who were worth snickering at.

And now there she is, in her moment of anger, delivering my dirty underwear to my door. Hanging it on the knob. Knocking. "Surprise for you," she says.

I center on the Buddha, who's sitting partially in shadow, partially in sunlight, who's neither smiling, nor frowning, who accepts her, who accepts me, accepts his place on the windowsill, next to nothing at all. He does not suppose that he's alone. He knows it.

So much anger in this house. In this tiny village. On this blue planet.

WELDON KEES

My grandmother named the spiders that lived in her cottage—they were as big as clocks and she talked to them while she washed dishes; they dangled over her sink and she told them they were welcome because they were doing a wonderful job at catching flies.

I called her "Nana." She called her spiders Thomas and Ojibwah, and other names, too—Robinson and Little Boy and Greta Van Buren. In the attic room, where I slept, the spiders were nameless. They stole into my bed in the deep hours and bit, and went away.

I secretly thought my Nana was crazy for naming spiders.

Weldon Kees jumped from a bridge into anonymity, except among people who cared, people who didn't want to follow him into a languid eternity, who needed his poetry, only. Such a tidy little man; shirtsleeves rolled into square folds, thinning black hair angular with control, eyes as dark as the anarchic moments before sleep—if he named spiders, he must have named them after nightmares. I think he enjoyed the dinners

of the civilized, nothing that might drip and stain, and he must have
always kept his napkin on his lap, always kept his elbows off the table,
always complimented the eager chef (because tidy men who eat hungrily
gladden the hearts of chefs), and then, finished, he must have pushed his
chair gently, almost without sound, away from the table, and stood, and
swiped delicately at his pants, and touched his shirt buttons, and quickly
fingered his neat mustache, and then he must have gone off to contem-
plate the naming of spiders, and the awful chaos and coercion of words.
I want to believe there's a Kees ghost loose on that Kees bridge or in the
water beneath, or somewhere downstream—slipping, slipping, slipping
in his wingtips on the wet stones, in the mud, in the tall grass, trying for
a toehold on the earth, again, believing himself able to cope, at last, with
the untidiness that breathing brings.

TOWER MAN

The first time I saw him, he was a hundred feet up the great smoky gray shaft of the tower. He was hunched over, like a spider, and his head was lifted a bit, as if he were looking where he was going—up. He was wearing a brown suit, and I thought at the time that this was very odd, indeed.

He moved first one hand, then the opposite leg, then the other hand, then the opposite leg. These movements were accomplished with clear purpose, but without much apparent speed or urgency. I couldn't take my eyes off him until my wife called out, "For God's sake, Thomas!" and I snapped my gaze to the road again. I hit the brake pedal hard. I was closing in on the rear end of a Corolla wagon. We came to an abrupt, jarring halt, and I said, gesturing with my chin, "Look at that man, there."

My wife leaned over to peer out my window. "What man?" she asked. "Where?"

"There," I told her. "On the tower." I looked again. He'd vanished.

My wife suggested that he had probably been doing some kind of maintenance work. I asked her what sort of maintenance a seventeen-hundred-foot-tall concrete tower required.

"Maybe he was changing light bulbs, or something?" she said.

"Light bulbs?" I said. "I've never seen any light bulbs on the side of the tower."

"Well there has to be some kind of illumination, doesn't there?" she said. "Otherwise, planes would hit it."

"It's lighted from below," I told her. "They've got a bank of spotlights on the ground. Besides, the airplane warning lights are at the tip of the tower, not a hundred feet up."

She guffawed. "Think you know everything, don't you?"

"No," I said.

"Well, there's a hell of a lot you *don't* know," she said.

I said nothing. I thought she was wrong, of course.

I must have passed the tower several thousand times, on my way to and from my office, and I had never seen the man before. He did not seem to be very large or very small, though he did appear to be quite thin. His clothes flapped around his body like a flag in a brisk wind.

It is, of course, the CN Tower that I'm talking about here. No other seventeen-hundred-foot concrete tower exists anywhere else on earth, and when I thought about it, then, I was surprised that no one else, to my knowledge, had ever tried to scale it. People ride over Niagara Falls in a barrel, and they jump from various high places on bungee cords, or with parachutes, so why hadn't anyone tried to scale the CN Tower?

I asked my wife this and she said, "First of all, it would be a stupid thing to do, and, secondly, how can you be sure that no one *has* tried it?"

"But the mere fact that something is stupid, *per se*," I told her, "has never been much of an impediment to those truly desperate for notoriety."

"Well put, as usual," she said, with a little smile. "But I repeat, how do you know it hasn't been done before?"

I said nothing. It wasn't worth an argument. Life is too short for argument, of course; it is only long enough for certainties. And my life was full of certainties, then. Career, wife, home; the easy and steadfast rituals of daily living—coffee with cream upon waking, weather reports on the radio, oatmeal on cold mornings, Grape Nuts on warm mornings, a brisk good-bye and a well-placed kiss on my wife's cheek, followed by a quick but orderly drive to my office, and, there, numbers, numbers, numbers. The certainty of numbers. The reality of numbers. The security of numbers, home, and wife, and the easy, comforting and necessary rituals of daily life.

I saw the man again several days later. He was a bit further up the tower this time and moving in the same spidery way that I had seen him move before. I pulled my car to the curb to watch him. He was perhaps five hundred feet from me, then, and, after I had been watching him for half a minute, he turned his head and looked my way. I cannot say that he actually looked *at* me, I can only say that he looked *toward* me, because I could not see his face clearly, of course—the distance was too great. How could I see him and know his intentions unless he was at arm's length? I saw only a pale pink oval fringed by a mane of slightly darker hair. And I saw, too, the suggestion of eyes and mouth—three dissimilar dark ovals in the larger oval of his face.

I heard a car horn blare behind me and when I turned my head briefly to look, and then looked back, the man on the tower had vanished yet again.

"I'm going up there," I declared to my wife that night. "I've been giving it a lot of thought, and I'm convinced that there's something very . . . wrong."

"With what?" she asked.

"With that man climbing the tower," I answered.

"I didn't see him," she said. "I don't think he exists." She grinned. "You've cooked him up from your imagination, Thomas."

"Why would I do that? I don't have an imagination."

"You do now."

"That's preposterous. Why in heaven's name would I dream up a man in a brown suit scaling the CN Tower? And why, at my age, would I suddenly be cursed with an imagination? I'm not a child."

"How can I answer that, Thomas?"

"He's real, dammit!" I declared. "For God's sake, I can see him. He's as real as the hairs on my head. He could be a . . . maintenance worker."

"Maintaining what?" my wife asked, and I realized at once that it was a question I had asked her only several days earlier.

"Oh hell, forget it," I said. "What do you know? What do you deal with day upon day? Reality? Of course not. I *do*. And so I certainly know about it."

I don't like heights. It's not that they make me queasy; they make me feel mortal, small, and fragile. It is not a way any living creature likes to feel. And that is why I had never before—during all my fifteen years in Toronto—gone up in the tower. My wife has, several times, and she's enjoyed it. She says the view is "exhilarating and humbling."

"I don't like feeling humble," I told her.

"No kidding?" she said.

"No adult should be made to feel humbled by anything. What is the distinction in it?"

She had no answer.

But the thin man in the brown suit was actively trying to draw me up into the tower. I was sure of it. I believed he knew me, or knew of me. I did not believe no one but I could see him. That was stupidity.

"Don't you think there would be spotlights and helicopters and police everywhere if other people could see him?" my wife asked.

I told her she was engaging in speculation. "And speculation," I said, "is for fools."

She bristled. "I'm not a fool, Thomas."

"Of course you're not," I said. "But you *are* engaging in speculation."

She said nothing.

I went to the base of the tower, bought my ticket—$2.00—and made my way to the exterior elevator. I hesitated there, outside the elevator. Several people were already inside it, and the elevator attendant—a young Chinese woman dressed in a blue and white CN Tower uniform—was giving me a questioning smile. I said to her, "I'm not sure I can do this."

"Yes, sir," she said.

"Can you give me a moment?" I said. "I'm having some small difficulty here."

"I'll be back down in a few minutes," she said. And the doors began to close.

I stepped forward quickly and boarded the elevator.

My discomfort increased with altitude. I had closed my eyes, of course, but it hardly mattered. I believe that some internal barometer senses changes in altitude and that information is given unfiltered to our rational minds. So I knew, then, that with each passing second, whole yards of distance were being put between me and the base of the tower. I must stress again that this is not a fear of heights I'm talking about. It is not the idea of falling that upsets me, it's the idea of separation from the good and constant earth, the idea of smallness and powerlessness that gives me discomfort, and which is the very sub-stance of mortality.

I opened my eyes, at last, of course. If it didn't matter that I had them closed or open, then why should I go to the effort of keeping them closed?

And when I opened them, I could see him, twenty feet beyond the elevator—which had stopped and was discharging its passengers. He was near the edge of the tower, where it curves. He was looking up, and moving slowly, but with clear purpose. And, only a moment after I saw him, he turned his head and looked in my direction. His eyes were large and pale, but rimmed by an amazing darkness, as if he had not slept in decades, and his gaze was . . . beyond me, an inch to the right of my eyes, an inch to the left, or above, or below. I knew that he saw me, but our eyes did not meet. And I did not know if it was he who was avoiding my gaze, or if it was I who was avoiding his.

I said to the elevator attendant, without looking away from the man on the tower, "Do you see him?"

"See who, sir?" she said.

"That man there?"

I believe she looked where I was looking; "No, sir," she said. "I don't see anyone."

The man—his gaze was still generally in my direction—moved sideways on the tower. Then, employing the same exaggerated hand and arm motions I had seen him use before, in moments, he was gone.

The elevator attendant said we had arrived at the skypod level—twelve hundred feet up—and if I wanted to go further, I had to get on an interior elevator.

"No," I said. "I'll go back down."

I told my wife about the encounter. She said again, "Thomas, it is simply your imagination."

"That has never been a phrase I have much liked," I told her.

She smiled. She is forever smiling at me. I do not much like the sort of smile she employs; it speaks of secrets and judgement and unshared amusement.

"I have never much liked that phrase," I explained, "because the parameters of the imagination are unpredictable, anarchic, and chaotic."

"Are they indeed?" she said.

I nodded vigorously. "Yes. Only the mad and the very young can have room or time for them."

We live on the first floor of a squat apartment building a few miles from the tower. We sleep with the windows uncovered because it's less confining for both of us (and is a rare point of compatibility between us). I sleep on the side of the bed nearest the window; I always have. My wife's side is close to the wall and, on some mornings, she has no small difficulty wending her way between the bed and the wall on her way to the bathroom, which adjoins our bedroom, except if I have already left the bed, when she merely rolls over to my side, and off. But she has not been able to do that for a very long time because I have been in this bed for a very long time.

I do not like the wall side. I've tried it, and since I'm much larger than my wife, I stumbled quite a lot moving between the wall and the bed. I do not like to stumble. It's embarrassing; it is not the way I want to begin my mornings.

I have a wonderful view out my window, which is only six or seven feet from my bed. I have the tower there, and it is beautifully framed by the window itself. I often use the tower as a point of reference and focus, especially when I have trouble sleeping, or when I've awakened in the wee hours with some business problem chasing me from sleep.

I know the tower. I know the equation it sets up with the earth and sky. I know the spray of light the moon describes on it, and the harsher, transient light the city casts. I know the tower's peak, and geometry. I know its skin.

So, through my window, and even at that distance, the man on the tower was clear to me that first dawn I saw him from my bed. He was a tiny imperfection against the deep blue sky that framed the tower—he was a mote of dust on the tight skin of the tower. He had no form, but I knew that he was hunched over, like a spider, as always, on his climb, and I knew that his head was turned toward me, and that his amazing vision was somewhere in my direction.

After what must have been many minutes, I nudged my wife. She does not awaken easily, and so I got no more than a quick soprano noise from her. I said anyway, "Look there. Can you see him now?" And when I received no response, I repeated my question. Then I fell silent.

I went to the base of the tower that day and saw him. He was halfway to the skypod level. From beneath, I could see his suit jacket flapping in the wind, constant at that height.

I called to him, "What do you require of me?" I wanted him to look back, in my direction, although I knew this would have been precarious for him. "What do you require of me?" I called again. He moved one hand very slowly forward, caught a grip of the tower with it, paused, moved the other hand slowly forward, caught another grip. "Look at me!" I screamed. "Talk to me. Look at me! Who are you? What is it that you require?"

I sensed that people had gathered around me. They were like a dark degeneration of my vision to my right and left as I looked up the tower.

Someone said, "He thinks there's someone up there. He believes there's someone on the tower."

"Does he?" said someone else. "Is there?"

But I knew that their vision could not be nearly as acute as mine, so I did not argue. Life is too short for argument; it is only long enough for certainties.

I called to the man for a very long time. I watched him make his way up the tower as slowly as the progress of minutes ticking away the span of a life. I repeated myself many times because, surely, endless repetition is a thing undeniable by any creature.

But the man never looked back.

I went to the tower a dozen times, in the weeks that followed, in my search for him. I wanted to see him at arm's length again. I wanted to catch his eye, or to have him catch mine. I wanted to speak with him, if only to the extent that I could read his lips. For I knew so well that he had something to say to me; and I grew to understand that I had nothing whatever to say to him.

But after that first early dawn, and that first distant glimpse of him against the side of the tower and the deep blue sky, and after my endless entreaties to him from the base of the tower to acknowledge me, I did not see him from the windows or elevators of the tower itself again. I saw him only from my own window. I saw him as a mote of dust on the tight skin of the tower, and I grew to be able to see him in my mind's eye from the distance that is punctuated and framed by my window. I saw him in the mornings, and afternoons, and during the early evenings, and after midnight. And I decided at some point that he was making headway up that tower, but that it was achingly slow, as slow as the progress of a life.

"Look there," I have said to my wife more times than I can count, "do you see him, now?" And, each time I've said it, she's flashed me a quick and pleasant smile, and answered, "Yes, I can." But I know she does not see him in the way that I do. I know that no one can see him in the way that I do. And that no one can know him or his intentions as I do.

His place on the tower changes so subtly from day to day and hour to hour and minute to minute, but it does change, and it is my place here, in my bed. It is my place on the tower, too.

And on some morning—this morning, tomorrow morning, a morning far in the future—his eyes will find mine. And that is when I will leave this bed, and join him.

TOMORROW, 25 YEARS FROM NOW

I'm listening to music on a little radio; Vaughan Williams, I think—and you're there, close by, listening too, moving about and enjoying the music in your own way; glancing now and again at the radio and smiling, then at me and smiling as if to say, *Look, we have perfection yet again.* But I know from this vantage point in this space and in this time that you're there with me. That's so important. It's tomorrow, twenty-five years from now and we have all that we wanted, or, at any rate, all that we knew we could have—finding ourselves lost together (for the ten-thousandth time) in the sublime simplicity of needing little, the music of genius, separateness that dissipates for entire hours, a holy kiss and a holy kiss and a holy kiss—I give up nothing for all of that, except my sorrow.

THE SCREAMERS AT THE WINDOW

"Such an unrepentant chair in which to work. Full of lumps and faulty movement. How could he work in such a chair? And at such a table. In such a house. So much noise. So much of the real."

Magnificence, a one-eyed Boston terrier, told Daniel it was a stupid title—"derivative, exploitative, sensationalistic." But Daniel chuckled low in his chest and said, "What do you know about titles? You're only a dog," though he knew it was the wrong thing to say.

Magnificence shrugged. He was sitting on a tall stool near Daniel's computer. When he shrugged, his front paws lifted from the stool briefly, which made Daniel chuckle again. "You look foolish when you do that," he said, though, again, he knew it was the wrong thing to say.

"Do what?" said Magnificence, and cocked his head.

"Shrug," Daniel said, and nodded as if to indicate the shrug itself. "Your feet lift off the ground."

Magnificence glanced at his paws, which were now firmly planted on the foot stool. He looked at Daniel, cocked his head again: "You're just

175

trying to change the subject. You know you have to throw that title in the crapper."

"Listen," Daniel said, and leaned over so his face was only a few inches from Magnificence's face, "you don't devise the titles around here. *I* do!"

Magnificence stepped back and cocked his head again. "Jesus, lay off the ham and eggs!"

Daniel sighed and sat back in his chair. "Now look who's changing the subject."

Magnificence jumped from the stool, started for the kitchen doorway, to the right of the table Daniel worked at, stopped, looked back. "You'd be nowhere without me, Daniel. You'd be slinging hash at Denny's. You'd be selling pencils on Front Street, repairing light bulbs, selling your own plasma."

Daniel sighed again, then nodded sullenly. Jesus, why did he always say the wrong things?

Magnificence continued, "I may be just a big-headed Boston Terrier whose years are numbered—as are any dog's—but I can still see and hear and smell a shitload more of what's going on in this intoxicated universe than you."

Daniel nodded again, with reluctance. "Yes, I know," he admitted. "I'm sorry." His tone said he was sorry indeed.

"Yeah," said Magnificence, "well, I've heard it all before. You have these little temper tantrums because you can't stand the fact that a Boston terrier with a ridiculous name and freckles on his little pink belly is your better when it comes to the literary arts."

Daniel shook his head. "I just want the titles to be mine, at least. I think I'm pretty good at titles."

Magnificence said, "Now you're whining. Don't whine." And he toddled off, into the darkness that was the adjoining room.

A couple of minutes later, Maureen came in and said, "Who were you talking to?"

Daniel gave her a surprised look. "Talking to?"

"I heard you talking to someone. Were you talking to that dog, again?"

Daniel shrugged. Sometimes she made him nervous because she knew him so very well—better, even, than he knew himself. But that was all right. Hell, it was more than all right. He *needed* her to know him well because he knew himself so poorly, and because it was abundantly clear she loved him, and because—all that being true—she would sooner or later become precisely the help-mate and lover and lifelong companion he had always wanted and needed.

"Don't shrug," she said. "It makes you look foolish," then she bent over and looked at his computer monitor: "Good title," she said.

He gave her a smile. "Yes, it is, isn't it," he said. And, from the other room, he heard, "Jesus H. Christ on a yellow moped!"

It was a half-hour later and Daniel needed to talk to Magnificence, but the dog was nowhere in sight. Daniel didn't call to him (Magnificence hated being called to: "It's such a doggy thing," he maintained), he simply looked through all the house's many bedrooms, its several bathrooms, its closets, made his way to the cavernous attic, then to the equally cavernous basement, then back to his computer, jiggled the mouse to shut off the screen saver, stared at his title, and knew (as he had known for the past hour) that he had offended Magnificence, yet again, and that the only way he was going to be able to continue working on his story was to apologize and *mean it* (because the dog's ability to sniff out lies was almost supernatural).

He read the title aloud, liked it, thought for a moment that he could write the story without Magnificence's help, thought it was long past time the dog became, simply, a dog again, instead of a one-eyed critic and cynic with pointed ears.

Which is when he became aware that Magnificence was sitting on the tall stool again. Daniel glanced at him. Magnificence stared back, round, brown eyes alive with recrimination.

Daniel said, "Jesus, I looked everywhere for you."

"What's 'everywhere'?" said Magnificence.

"The whole house," Daniel said. "The whole Goddamned house. Everywhere."

"Uh-huh," Magnificence said in a long-suffering tone.

Daniel said, "Listen, about this morning. I'm sorry. Really."

Magnificence said, "Yeah, and I'm the Queen of France."

"I'm *really* sorry," Daniel said.

"Ain't *that* the truth," said Magnificence.

Daniel sighed, read the title again, silently, then said, his eyes on the monitor, "But I actually think it's a good title. You heard Maureen. She thinks it's good, too." He looked at Magnificence, who said, "Yeah, I heard her. What a piece of work *she* is. You've got her programmed better than you've got *me* programmed, my friend." He nodded to indicate the computer monitor. "Listen, that title's got precious little to do with what I told you. It's merely designed to make people read the damned story."

Daniel shrugged. "And what's wrong with that?"

Magnificence rolled his eyes. "You're as predictable as a politician with one hand extended and the other in his pocket." He stood, craned his big, square head a bit to get a look at the computer monitor, sat down. "If that title had more to do with what I told you, then it would be a good title. But it's got about as much to do with what I told you as frozen spinach has to do with Jack Kerouac."

Daniel smiled. "That's a strained analogy if ever I heard one."

Magnificence grimaced. "A lot you know. And it's not even an analogy, thick head."

Daniel frowned. "Listen, you said you heard someone screaming. Isn't that true?"

Magnificence nodded. "Yes." He paused, went on, "And, as a matter of fact, I hear someone screaming even as we speak. I hear *several* people screaming, in fact. Perhaps more than several. Perhaps half a dozen."

"So, *there* you go . . ." Daniel said.

And Magnificence cut in, "I can smell them, too. They smell like Spam."

Daniel cringed. "Spam?"

Magnificence nodded. "Uh-huh. And onions." He sniffed the air. "And . . . what's that? What's that?" He sniffed more conspicuously, then added, "Yes. Stale ranch dressing, mushroom gravy, and . . . yes, yes . . ." He cocked his head. "Blood!"

"Jesus H. Christ!" Daniel breathed.

"On a yellow moped," said Magnificence.

Daniel gave him a suspicious look. "You're not shittin' me, are you?"

What passed for a smile flitted across the dog's flat face: "Appropriate though it may be," he said, "—because shitting is, after all, a major part of any dog's daily activities—I am not shitting *you*, no." He paused, clearly for effect. "Yes—Spam, onions, ranch dressing, mushroom gravy, screams. And blood." He heaved a big, Boston terrier sigh. "At the very least, it's most unpleasant. As always."

Maureen came into the room, then. She was sweating, had apparently been on her daily jog. She wiped her brow and her cheeks with a dish towel, gave Daniel a hard stare. "Daniel," she said, "you're a crazy man."

He nodded slowly and whispered, "Yes, I know."

She looked about the room, then at Daniel again, smiled; Daniel couldn't read the smile. Perhaps, he thought, it was meant to be forgiving, though he could think of nothing for which he needed forgiveness. "How's the story?" she said.

Daniel said, low in his throat, as if he were talking about a death, "Spam, screams, blood."

Maureen sighed. "Yes, well that's nothing new, is it, my love." She reached out, touched his shoulder. "Perhaps it's time to start another one."

Daniel shook his head quickly. "I can't do that. I always begin stories and never finish them. And they're always about the same thing, no matter what the title."

"It's a huge universe," Maureen said.

"A huge universe?" said Daniel.

"Huge and multifaceted and full of possibilities." She smiled. "Think outside the box in which you've caged yourself."

"Good Lord," muttered Magnificence.

"Forget the dog," Maureen said. "You don't need him. Just open your eyes. Shit, open *everything!*"

He gave her a questioning look. "Huh?"

"You heard me," she said, and left the room for the darkness that was the adjoining room.

Daniel looked at Magnificence and said, "How does 'The Walkers on the Road' strike you?"

Magnificence sighed.

It was late evening and Daniel was in bed, the stunning and naked Maureen to his left, Magnificence to his right: a nightlight in the shape of a green squirrel bathed the room in a soft, green glow. Magnificence hated it: "Who can sleep with all that light?" he grumbled.

"I need it," Daniel said, not for the first time.

"Yeah, yeah, I know. You need the Goddamned nightlight. What in the name of greasy grimy gopher guts are you afraid of?" He'd asked the question—in those same words—many, many times, but had never gotten an answer.

"Are you talking to that dog again?" Maureen said. "Criminey, Daniel, it's late. Go to sleep. Everyone needs to sleep. Even you. Even that dog. Even me." She paused. "And all the others."

Daniel stiffened.

"That bothers you?" Maureen asked. Daniel thought he heard amusement in her tone.

"No," he said.

She chuckled. "Well then, if it doesn't bother you, it doesn't bother me."

"Bitch!" Magnificence whispered (in his doggy way).

Daniel said, "*Should* it bother me? Were you *trying* to bother me?"

"You *need* bothering," she said.

"Do I?"

"Yes," said Magnificence.

"Yes," said Maureen. "You need bothering as much any man who's drowning in his own slowly rising bath water."

"I was thinking about 'The Walkers on the Road,'" Daniel said. He felt Maureen turn toward him:

"Another story?"

"I don't know. Maybe the same story."

"It's *all* the same story," she said.

Daniel hesitated a long moment, then said, "It seems that way, doesn't it."

Within minutes, all three fell into a deep, deep sleep until morning.

A breakfast of buttermilk pancakes, maple syrup, Jimmy Dean's Pure Pork sausage, home fries, orange juice, and freshly ground coffee was just what he needed this morning, Daniel thought, but he'd settled for white toast (one piece, from a heel, because that's all the bread box offered), half a grapefruit, which had been sitting in the fridge (wrapped in waxed paper) for several days, and instant coffee. Maureen was apparently still puttering about in the bathroom; she'd been in there for what seemed like a year or more, he thought, and Magnificence was still involved in his "morning constitutional" (as Magnificence liked to call it); he'd been outside for nearly twenty minutes, and had yet to scratch at the door to be let in.

Daniel felt very alone in that kitchen, with his shitty meal, his clogged "morning nose," the silence.

He sipped the instant coffee, grimaced, nibbled on the heel of toast, set it down. He needed Magnificence. He needed Maureen. Jesus H. Christ, where were they? Did it really take that long for a Boston terrier to empty its bowels? Did it really take that long for a woman to scrub her cuticles, or pee, or do whatever in the name of heaven she was doing? It was always this way? Shit, he was *always* alone!

"Self-pitying blubberhead!" he heard, and turned his gaze toward the source of the voice; Magnificence sat on the tall stool near the stove.

"How'd you get in?" Daniel asked.

"You let me in fifteen minutes ago." The dog's tone betrayed surprise and annoyance. "You don't remember?"

Maureen breezed into the kitchen, then; Daniel looked wide-eyed at her: she was dressed beautifully in white and looked as marvelous as a deep-winter landscape. "I don't like what you're eating, Daniel," she announced, came over, scooped up his plate, his cup, his not-very-tangy grapefruit. "I'm going to make you something that's fit to be eaten," she added, and put his dishes in the sink, his grapefruit in the garbage disposal (which she let run for a bit longer than Daniel thought necessary, until Magnificence shouted, "Jesus H. Christ, shut that thing off," and she, as if in response, shut the thing off).

Then she turned to Daniel—her smile as broad as the ocean, which transformed her, Daniel thought, into a thing as marvelous as deep summer—and gushed, "Thank you so very, very much for last night, my love!" and she swept across the kitchen to him, threw her long bare arms around his neck, so her ample breasts cupped his face, planted a kiss on top of his head (where the hair was very thin indeed), stepped back, said, "Well then, what will it be? Will it be your usual? Will it be your sausage and eggs? Home fries? Ground coffee?"

"Somebody ram a sock into her mouth!" Magnificence cried, jumped down from the tall stool, crossed the kitchen, hopped into Daniel's lap, and looked pleading up at him. "Please, please, tell her to shut up."

"How can I do that?" Daniel said. "I need her this way. She's . . . enthusiastic."

"Yeah, well, that's not *all* she is," Magnificence said.

She came into the kitchen, then. She wore a faded blue terry cloth bathrobe and pink bunny slippers. She rubbed her eyes, glanced at Daniel, said, "Christ, how can you eat at a time like this?" then crossed the kitchen to a far cupboard, opened it, rummaged about in it for a few seconds, shut the cupboard door, came to the table, sat across from Daniel, put her head in her hands: her eyes were bloodshot; he thought she looked like hell. "Hey," she said, "we ever going to screw again?"

"Don't beat around the bush," Magnificence muttered.

She went on, "Now *there's* a title you could work with. 'The Couple Who Screwed Each Other Only Twice in a Century.' There's a fucking good title."

"But I thought we made love just last night," Daniel said.

She pursed her lips. "Oh yeah," she said. "I remember. It was unforgettable."

She appeared in the kitchen doorway, then, paused, looked appraisingly at Daniel: she was dressed in jeans and a loose white blouse. She looked good. She almost always looked good. Often, she looked much better than good. "What are you eating?" she said.

Daniel shrugged. "Nothing."

She eyed his coffee cup. "What's that? Instant?"

"How'd you know?"

"Because I don't see the percolator anywhere." He kept the percolator in a cupboard.

"Quite the detective, isn't she?" said Magnificence, who was still in Daniel's lap.

"And," she said, "I think you're talking to that stupid dog again; am I right?"

Of course she was right. She was almost always right. He'd grown used to it. He needed it.

"I have another title," he said.

She pursed her lips; clearly, she didn't like the ham-handed way he'd changed the subject. She took a few steps into the kitchen, stopped, looked about, looked at Daniel. "You don't need that dog, you know." She paused, then added, "You don't even need me, though you're not yet aware of it."

He looked pleadingly at her, but said nothing. He hoped his pleading look said what he could not say in words.

She sighed. "Listen, if I make some real coffee, do you want some?"

He nodded. "Yes. Thanks." She went to the cupboard where he kept the percolator, opened it, took the percolator out.

Daniel said, "The new title is 'The Inhabitants of the House.'"

She glanced at him. "And?"

"And what? That's it. 'The Inhabitants of the House.' Do you like it?"

"I like all your titles, Daniel. They're all good. But that one's very sad."

"Sad? Why?"

"Because it . . . pertains."

"And?"

"Thick head," said Magnificence.

"And nothing else," said Maureen. "It pertains. It pertains . . . sadly."

"Very cryptic," said Magnificence.

"I don't understand," said Daniel.

Maureen threw open a cupboard door. "Shit, no coffee!"

Daniel said, "Please tell me what you're talking about. I need to know what *you* know, Maureen."

She looked at him.

Magnificence looked at him.

"It pertains to what *is*," Maureen said, then added, "I can't start the day without coffee. I'm going out."

"Such an unrepentant chair in which to work. Full of lumps and faulty movement. How could he work in such a chair? And at such a table. In such a house. So much noise. So much of the real."

Daniel couldn't write because he was very bothered by her remark, so he put on a Creedence Clearwater CD, listened a few minutes, decided it didn't fit his mood, put on a Mahler CD, listened for half a minute, put on an Enya CD, grimaced, turned off the CD player and went outside to mow his vast lawn.

"Where are you going?" Magnificence asked, as Daniel ambled toward his five-car garage.

"I'm going to mow the lawn," Daniel said.

"Again? You mowed it two days ago."

"I like to mow it. It helps me think. It's almost like meditation."

Magnificence guffawed.

Daniel glanced at him. "I meditate. You don't think so? I meditate a lot."

"Shit," said Magnificence, "you meditate the way a one-eyed man uses a stereopticon."

Daniel glanced confusedly at him. "Huh?"

"Think about it."

"Do I have to?"

Magnificence said nothing.

Daniel was in the garage, looking at his behemoth TORO riding mower—fifty horsepower, twin thirty-six inch blades, a super-smooth dark green finish that seemed to magnify sunlight. He'd even tweaked the mammoth engine so it had the same *potato-potato-potato* growl as a Harley.

"Overkill," Magnificence said.

"It's a huge lawn," said Daniel.

"You think so?"

"Well, look at it." He nodded to indicate the lawn.

Magnificence looked at the lawn, then at Daniel again, then quickly at the lawn, then back at Daniel. "We look, we see," he said, "we don't see, we look again, the universe changes, we see."

Daniel glanced confusedly at him. "Jesus, you're as cryptic as a goose in a nightgown."

Magnificence rolled his eyes.

Daniel hopped on the TORO, adjusted the seat, turned on the ignition. Nothing. He scowled.

"I guess it's not the day for meditation," said Magnificence.

Daniel tried the ignition again, without success.

"It's a big universe," said Magnificence. "You can't hope to mow all of it."

"Huh?" said Daniel.

"I'm hungry," said Magnificence.

"Then I'll feed you," said Daniel.

Maureen was playing Solitaire at the coffee table in Daniel's expansive lower parlor when he came in; she looked up at him, squinted a little, looked at her cards.

Daniel said, "Something's wrong with the TORO."

She said nothing. She moved a king so it was under a queen.

"That's an illegal move," Daniel said.

"It's *my* game," she said, and moved a ten so it was under a nine.

"You're playing it backwards."

"And?"

"Let her be," said Magnificence.

"Yeah," said Maureen, and Daniel thought it sounded like a question, so he said, "Yeah, what?"

She moved an eight so it was under a six. "Yeah, like you know *anything*," she said.

"I know as much as anyone," Daniel protested.

"Yeah," said Maureen. "We all do."

"That's as obvious as a hissing cockroach at a clambake," said Magnificence.

"Huh?" said Daniel.

"I'm hungry," said Magnificence.

They went into the kitchen.

"'An Unsatisfactory Meal,'" said Daniel, as Magnificence chowed down on turkey slices.

Magnificence looked up at him. "No. It's quite satisfactory."

"You misunderstand. It's another title."

"Is it?"

Daniel nodded sagely. "It's a metaphor."

Magnificence swallowed a slice of turkey without chewing, and said, "All your titles are metaphors."

"Of course they are," Daniel said.

"'The Screamers at the Window,' 'The Walkers on the Road,' 'The Inhabitants of the House,' 'An Unsatisfactory Meal'—all metaphors."

"Good, huh?" said Daniel.

"And the Spam and blood and onions—all the gritty stuff?"

Daniel didn't like being quizzed about his metaphors by a wise-cracking, one-eyed Boston terrier, but what was he to do? He shrugged.

"Stop shrugging?" said Magnificence, who was finished with his turkey slices, but still looked hungry.

Maureen came into the kitchen, then. She was scruffy looking in white bib overalls and a faded blue blouse, and she had dirt on her hands. "I've been gardening," she said. 'Oh I just love gardening. It gets a body all involved with the world as it is, don't you think? It makes you one with all the *stuff* that created *us*." She smiled as if she'd just invented the smile.

Daniel said, "No. You were playing Solitaire. And you were playing it backwards."

She looked confusedly at him. "Was I?" she said, still smiling.

"Yes," said Daniel.

She stopped smiling and left the room for the darkness that was the adjoining room.

Magnificence said, "This is no lawn. This is a small, dreary space."

Daniel, atop his TORO (Magnificence sat between his legs), said, "No. It's vast. It's formidable. It's on the top-ten list of vast and formidable things, like tidal waves, earthquakes, breathing out and breathing in."

"And love, and wind, and messy sex on hot afternoons," said Magnificence.

"What would you know about such things?" said Daniel.

The dog shrugged. His front legs lifted from the mower's seat. "Only as much as you," he said. "Which is apparently not much."

"Well, of course," said Daniel, started the TORO—*potato, potato, potato*—and attacked his vast lawn.

He was finished before twelve, when he realized he was famished and parched. He needed homemade lemonade. Ham on rye with Swiss. Maureen's startling macaroni salad. Pringles neatly stacked potato chips.

"You know what?" Daniel said to Magnificence, who was once again on the tall stool near the table Daniel worked at. "I think I could tell an entire and meaningful story with titles alone. I think it's a damn good possibility. It is also possible that I've actually started such a story."

Magnificence looked very skeptical.

Daniel went on, expansively, arms flailing, "I mean, look at all we have to work with. Maureen herself said it. And you, too. 'The vast universe full of possibilities.' We can't *deal* with and *comprehend* any of it, really. We can't get down to the bone and gristle, really. We may try, but we can only deal in murky generalities. We can only deal with *titles*." He smiled a smile as broad as the great ocean. "All the gritty details add up to only that, after all. Generalities. Titles. Certainly, you agree."

Magnificence looked bored.

Maureen breezed into the kitchen. She carried a plate filled with macaroni salad, potato chips, and ham and Swiss on rye, which she set down between Daniel's computer keyboard and his monitor. "Oh," she said, "it's just as you desire," then breezed from the room, though not before reaching around and lifting her skirt to give Daniel a brief but very satisfying glimpse of her naked rear end.

Daniel smiled. He thought he could fashion a title out of that—her rear end. Perhaps he'd think about it.

He looked at the plate.

Magnificence said, "All but empty, my friend?"

Daniel continued looking at the plate.

Magnificence said, "You're a sad and foolish man, Daniel."

Daniel took the plate to the sink, ran water on it, cleaned it with a ragged dish cloth.

"You should use detergent," said Magnificence. "Bacteria abound."

"None to use," said Daniel, and rinsed the plate, put it in the dish drainer, went back to his computer, looked at the screen, read aloud from it, sat back, looked down, between his legs, at the scarred, gray linoleum.

Magnificence said, "So?"

Daniel looked at him. "I miss her."

Magnificence looked at the entrance to the kitchen, then at Daniel. He sighed.

Daniel looked at his keyboard.

Magnificence jumped from the tall stool, came over to Daniel, sat on the linoleum, looked up at him.

"Yes?" Daniel said.

Magnificence shrugged. His feet lifted from the floor.

"Yes?" Daniel said again.

Magnificence looked at the kitchen doorway once more, back at Daniel, at the doorway again, stood, ambled to it, stopped with his back to Daniel.

"Yes?" said Daniel.

Magnificence moved through the doorway and was lost in the darkness that was the adjoining room.

Daniel got out of his chair, crossed the small kitchen, stood in the entranceway to the room beyond. "Yes?" he called.

The little house said nothing.

"Yes?" Daniel called again. "Yes?" he screamed. "Yes? Yes? For God's sake, *yes?*"

He got silence.

He stood in the doorway a few moments, then went back to the table, sat in his chair, put his fingers on his keyboard. He sat like this for many minutes, until his wrists began to ache, when he sat back, folded his hands on his lap, looked at the entrance to the kitchen, saw nothing in the room beyond.

He thought of calling out, again. Names. Entreaties. Pleas. It had always been effective.

He shook his head. No. He'd work. He needed to work. He needed to *know*.

He put his fingers on the keyboard. Thought a moment.

"The Dancing Undead," he typed, then read the title aloud: "The Dancing Undead."

He smiled. It was a terrific title.

"Entreaties to the Mute," he typed. "Living, Loving, Laughing, Lying," he typed. "Groping the Air," he typed. *Terrific!* He read all the titles aloud. Once. Twice. Three times.

He sat back in his chair. Grinned.

From the tall stool near the stove, Magnificence said, "Read me a story, Daniel."

Daniel looked at him. Smiled. Nodded. Looked at his computer monitor:

"Such an unrepentant chair in which to work," he read aloud. "Full of lumps and faulty movement. How could he work in such a chair? And at such a table. In such a house. So much noise. So much of the real."

BREAKDOWN

Even when he's caught in the tall grasses, great wings flapping in a truncated and ineffectual way, the red-tailed hawk looks noble. It's that hawk face. It's capable only of nobility. It's frozen in nobility. It's trapped in nobility forever. Even its denuded skull is noble.

He could be pushing madly on a door that says "Pull" and still he'd look noble. He could be blind stumbling drunk and blubbering about Kierkegaard, trying to buy drinks for the house with a Sears card, and still he'd look noble. What a responsibility! All that hawk angst and no way to let it show. He sees green and shadow all around him in the tall grasses, and it's beautiful, it's his world, this place, this green and shadow, where the mice run, and high above, a swath of gray-blue, and it's beautiful, it's his world, too, and he flaps his great wings, and flaps his great wings, and flaps, and flaps, and it's all ineffectual—that flapping—and there he is, in his world, with the running mice, the green and shadow, and he's hoping (I know this) for the winsome, worried, resigned mask of the dreamer—*Oh hell, caught in the tall grasses, again! Will my troubles never cease?*

TOMATO AS METAPHOR

Georgeorge Bloom couldn't believe he was eating tomatoes for breakfast. He didn't like tomatoes, except on toast, with mayonnaise, and, for God's sake, he hardly ever ate breakfast, anyway, and, when he did, it was almost always one poached egg and an English muffin, half of which he usually gave to Chef Brody, his bull dog.

Chef Brody was looking questioningly at George, now, and George was thinking, *This is a very strange morning*. First, no sun, only sleet, which poured from a deep red sky, then his wife left early for work (and she was more-often-than-not late for work, bless her heart), then the mail came at eight, and it usually came at ten-thirty, then his mother called to say, "Oh, I'm so terribly sorry, George," and when he asked what she was sorry about, she said, "Well, you know. Everybody knows," and hung up. When he called back, her phone simply rang and rang.

But he had to admit that he liked these tomatoes. They tasted very different than tomatoes usually did—they were tangier, tastier, meatier, as if he weren't eating tomatoes at all, but a unique new species of vegetable (was it a fruit?) that masked itself as a tomato. Good Lord, he didn't even need to put anything on the tomato to make it palatable—no salt and pepper, no mayonnaise, no honey dijon dressing . . . Was this how tomatoes had always tasted? What a revelation!

Chef Brody barked at him, once; it was a quick, low-pitched bark, but because Chef Brody was barrel-chested and healthy, it was also very intimidating, though not to George, who had raised the dog from a puppy. "What do you want?" George said, and gave Chef Brody a questioning look. "You can't have my tomato. Dogs don't eat tomatoes."

Chef Brody barked again, in the same way he had barked a moment earlier, and George realized he was asking to be let out. This pleased George because it was a part of his morning routine that hadn't changed on this otherwise very strange morning. He reached and gave Chef Brody a pat on the head, then stood, went to the side door, and put his hand on the knob. When he looked back, he saw that Chef Brody hadn't followed him, as he'd expected. "C'mon now," George said, and slapped his thigh.

Chef Brody looked questioningly at him.

"C'mon, dog!" George said, and slapped his thigh once more. But Chef Brody still looked questioningly at him, as if, George thought now, the dog didn't recognize him. How very odd. How perturbing.

He went back to his seat at the table, back to his (half-eaten) tomato, and said to Chef Brody, "I'm *George*. You've known me for years."

Chef Brody looked questioningly at him.

George looked at the back door again.

Chef Brody looked at the back door.

Someone knocked softly at it. *Who could that be?* George wondered, and Chef Brody barked.

"Who's there?" George called, but got no answer, only another soft knock, and another deep-throated bark from Chef Brody, who usually ran to the door when someone knocked at it. George looked at him: "Well, go ahead!"

Chef Brody stayed put.

George sighed, got up, went to the door, opened it.

A short balding man, in a crisp gray suit and dark gray bow tie, smiled flatly at George and extended his hand, which George took: the man's grip was soft and cool. The man said, "Do you like the tomato?"

George let go of the man's hand. What was this? Why would this man appear at his back door and ask about a tomato? This was more than perturbing or odd, this was . . . *disturbing.*

George said, "I'm sorry; did you ask about the tomato?"

The man nodded. "Do you like it?"

"How in hell did you know I was eating a tomato?"

The man nodded to indicate the kitchen table. "Well, I can see it there. Half a tomato." He grinned in a friendly, playful way. "It's an odd thing to have in the morning. A tomato."

Chef Brody barked.

George looked back, said, "Quiet, dog!" and Chef Brody barked again.

The short balding man said, "I represent The Terminal Company of East St. Louis and Other Points East." He grinned again.

"You're a salesman?" George asked.

The man shook his head. "Oh, no. I'm selling nothing. I'm here on behalf of my client."

"Who is?"

"Why, you, of course, Mr. Bloom."

George sighed. He'd had enough. First his wife had left so early in the morning that he hadn't even had a chance to say goodbye, then his mother had called with strange, unnamed regrets, then the sky had poured hailstones all over his lawn, then he'd chosen something utterly unusual for breakfast (though, yes, it had turned out to be an appealing choice).

He closed the door in the balding man's face and waited, expecting the man to knock again. After a minute, and no knock, he opened the door again, but the man wasn't there. He looked at his lawn: it was green.

He worked hard at that lawn and it was always green, except in winter. He looked at the sky; it was red. He craned his head out the door. Jesus, where was the sun? What was this perpetual sunrise? He closed the door, went back to the kitchen table.

His tomato was there. Still half-eaten. And, next to his plate, the mail. *Field and Stream,* a bill from the cable company, a letter in a pale blue envelope that didn't have a return address. This caught his attention. He picked it up, looked at the handwriting on the envelope: it seemed to be a woman's handwriting. How odd. Why would a woman be writing to him? He sniffed the envelope. It smelled of nothing at all. He put it down, glanced at Chef Brody, who glanced back, then glanced at the back door, then at George again, who said, "A woman is writing to me, dog. Why is that, do you think?"

Chef Brody barked, which gave George a start. "Jesus, dog!" he said.

He opened the envelope and took out the letter. It read:

Dear George,

Delete one thing.

Your good friend,

Greta

"Huh?" George said. He reread the letter silently, then aloud:

"Dear George," he said, "Delete one thing. Your good friend, Greta."

He furrowed his brow, read the letter yet again, said, "Huh?" once more, glanced at Chef Brody (who merely glanced back), glanced at the letter, at Chef Brody, put the letter on the table, next to *Field and Stream,* looked at it, picked it up again, put it down. "Jesus, dog," he said.

He knew no one named Greta. The only Greta he knew of was Greta Van Sustern, the Fox News commentator who'd changed her face to please her public. But the change hadn't taken well. She'd begun to look unattractive, again, after only six months.

And why would *she* tell him to "Delete one thing," anyway?

So it was another Greta, of course. A Greta he couldn't remember.

Christ, there had to be hundreds of thousands of Gretas extant, so it would be easy for him to forget just one of those Gretas, right?

What *was* he thinking? There were no Gretas in his life. There was a Sandy, a Cecile, a Berenice, two Carols, a Reneé, a Sally (his wife), a Vivian, and three Nancys. But there were absolutely no *Gretas*!

He looked over at his tomato, thought it looked a bit paler than it had only minutes earlier, glanced at the back door, expecting another knock, glanced at the letter, thought of picking it up again, didn't.

"Delete one thing?" he said. What for? For God's sake, *what for?* And *what* thing? A channel on the TV, a CD from his CD collection, a can of soup from the larder, a friend from his very short list of friends, a pet (but Chef Brody was his only pet, and he wasn't about to delete *him*), a meal from his daily meals, a hat, a coat, a pair of gloves, a painting, a book, a memory . . . A memory? A *memory?*

A memory?

What memory?

And only *one?* How was that possible? How could you go into your head and delete a memory? How could you reach into your gray matter, pick out a memory—say, the memory of your first kiss—and *delete it?* How would you know you'd deleted it if you'd *actually* deleted it? Would there still be a label attached—"Memory of First Kiss"—but when you tried to peer beneath the label, you'd see nothing?

He looked at his tomato, again. It was very pale, now. Too pale for eating. Why had it grown so pale so quickly? He glanced at the back door. Night. Hadn't it just been morning? He couldn't remember. He glanced at the letter, at Chef Brody—sitting by with a look of anticipation, Lord knew why—at the back door again. Day. Early. Yes. Of course it was day, early. It was morning.

He looked at the letter, picked it up, put it down, cocked his head at it, looked at Chef Brody, who was still sitting by with an anticipatory expression, said, "What do you want?"

Chef Brody kept silence.

George said again, "What do you want?" and added, after a moment, "Dog."

Chef Brody looked obliquely to his left, as if in response to a noise, though George had heard no noise, then back at George, and barked once, quickly.

"Stop that!" George said. "What are you doing here?"

Chef Brody made no response.

George glanced at the table. It was empty. Of course it was empty, he thought. He hadn't eaten. He needed to eat. It was morning. He should have breakfast—first meal of the day. He glanced at the back door. Night. It was night. Not morning. Night. He shrugged. Dinner, then.

He looked at the cupboards, wondered what he'd eat. Thin spaghetti with marinara? Mushrooms and salad greens? Cornflakes? Weetabix? Veal scallopini?

Chef Brody barked.

George looked at him, said, "What?" and Chef Brody barked again, a good, deep, rumble-up bark that, because he was sitting, made his front paws lift from the floor.

A knock sounded at the back door. George snapped his gaze to it, muttered, "Yes?" thought whoever knocked hadn't heard him and said, louder, "Yes?" but got no answer, so he went to the back door and opened it, found only sleet and red sky and dark green lawn, so he closed the door, turned, looked at Chef Brody, said, "What are you doing here?"

Chef Brody kept silent.

George muttered, "Well . . . oh . . . " saw the pale green letter, went over and picked it up, read, "Delete one thing," put the letter down, said, "What thing?" looked at the empty kitchen, the red windows, thought, "Delete what? Delete what?" heard a knock at the back door, looked at the door, called, "Yes?" got no answer, set the letter down, went to the back door, opened it, saw light blue sky, pale green lawn, closed the door gently, turned to the empty kitchen, wondered briefly why it was so empty, thought it had always been empty, of course, thought *Delete what? Delete what?* turned to the clear blue sky, saw no sun, saw no clouds.

Heard nothing at all.

SALLY PINUP

ONE

My name is Denver Whitehouse and I'm as real as the potatoes on my plate.

My universe is exquisite. Incomplete, but exquisite. Hellish, at times, but exquisite.

The telephone rings. I pick up the receiver: "Hello?" I say. There's no answer. "Hello?" I say again. Still no answer.

"Dammit, who's calling?" I say (though I'm beginning to believe I know who's calling). No answer.

I hang up.

The telephone rings again.

I ignore it.

The telephone stops ringing.

My universe is a place where telephones ring.

———

My father's third wife, Irene, once told me, "Robert, you must always keep in mind that the great creation which is life gives us only what we really and truly *want* it to give us."

"My name isn't Robert," I said.

She put her forefinger to her pretty mouth, lowered her hand a little, said, "Oh, I'm so very sorry," and glanced quickly right, then left, as if looking for something. Her gaze settled on me again. "But, shit, if you're not Robert," she said, "then who the hell *are* you?"

My exquisite universe is full of questions that seem to have no answers.

My name is Denver Whitehouse and I'm as real as your imaginings, your dreams, your pain, as real as your orgasms and your fantasies, as real as your memories, regrets and your hunger.

And this . . . *place* . . . is where I live:

Fifteen Meadow Drive; a gray bungalow built decades ago. Small kitchen, small appliances, and a small, red-linoleum-topped table with three matching chairs; two small bedrooms, one with a double bed in cherry, the other—smaller—with a black-iron twin bed; I have one and a half baths, a small attic room for storage, and a plain red-brick fireplace, not in use, a front porch room with screens (storm windows are kept in the basement during spring, summer and early autumn; it's mid-spring, I believe, as I write); the oak floors throughout the house are mostly in good repair.

And beyond this house, in the city beyond this house, in the universe beyond this house, there is the overwhelming presence of what has come to be called *dark energy*, just as that other universe—the one *you* live in—possesses.

It's always much like an evening in late autumn in this city. People move about quickly, shoulders up, arms hard to their sides as a fitful wind plays with the city's sparse trees. Small animals—some feral, some let out to prowl—move about the pitiful landscape like dark slices of failing vision.

It's a likely place for murder, which happens only now and again, as in almost any city.

My universe exists in many places and many times all at once.

But I do not.

I cannot.

Though I know, now, that there are others, probably many, many others, who do.

She calls herself Sally Pinup, though it was not her real name, which, she said, was "Charlene Gary," and went on to explain it was a name she'd always hated: "A given name that's feminine wedded to a male surname," she said. "And so I eventually became known as Sally Pinup. And you can see why." She looked briefly down at herself, smiled coquettishly, and then, in a heartbeat, returned to her universe and left me alone in mine.

But, I realize as I write, that that's not true. In whatever universe we find ourselves, we are never alone. I can't prove it, though I *know* it as well as I know when the mailman's at the door.

In all times and in all places, murder is murder.

"I've been murdered," she told me. She was no more visible than last evening's erotic dream. "I've been murdered," she told me again: in my universe it was merely a brief whisper at my ear; in hers it was a trembling scream: I heard both.

They're like rivers that intertwine—our separate universes, her universe, *my* universe. All the *stuff*, all the flotsam and jetsam flow together for seconds, minutes, hours, whole days and weeks. I can't explain it, but I know it happens because I've been there; I *am* there. Shit, I *am* there.

I love my universe, my bungalow, my street, my neighborhood, my city. There's peace to be had here, if I don't stray too far. I can turn up the radio a bit, I can listen to a CD—Rachmaninoff, David Bowie, The Chieftains. My universe, her universe, our universe—it's all music, sad and powerful, happy and terrifying, quiet and seductive. In any universe, music is music, murder is murder, and, wherever you suddenly find yourself, magic is magic.

Sally Pinup is magic. Or what brought her here, from her universe to this bungalow, this city, this universe, was magic. Forget that *rivers intertwining* stuff; it was only a metaphor. Magic isn't metaphor. Magic is the way everything works. I can't prove otherwise, so it must be true.

"I want you to find my murderer," she said (that whisper at my ear, that trembling scream) "and I want you to kill the bastard."

"My God!" I breathed.

"I can't really see you," she said. "You're a muddle of spiky bits and pieces."

"I don't understand that," I said.

"Of course you don't," she said. "I don't either."

I knew next to nothing about murder, then. I knew that it happened often in my universe. I read about it a couple of times a week, saw news about it on television: I even knew someone who knew someone who'd been murdered, and he seemed to feel it was a great topic for conversation. He told me, "Yeah, he tried to call this woman, you know—this woman who'd been murdered—and someone picked up the phone and said, 'Who's calling?' and this guy, this friend, said the voice was so . . . *cop*-like he simply gave his name, and then the guy asked for an address . . . " He smiled a little, as if he'd just had a lick of his favorite ice cream.

It's true, you know—murder makes some of us smile. Especially when it's murder that's distant and complex and even a little clumsy.

Sally Pinup's murder was all those things, I believe, though Sally Pinup herself isn't distant, and she isn't clumsy.

The phone rings; I pick it up, say, "Hello," hear nothing. It's the way my universe works, now. The telephone rings and, almost always, it's as if no one's calling.

"It's like you're made entirely of puzzle pieces," Sally Pinup said.

"But I see *you* just fine," I said.

"Maybe I need glasses, Mr. Whitehouse."

I almost said, "Call me 'Denver.'"

"Will you find him, Mr. Whitehouse? Will you find the bastard who killed me?"

I sighed. She was standing near the plain red-brick fireplace and I was sitting not far from her in my orange wing-back chair. She looked incredible. Almost real. I wanted to reach for her, decided, instead, that she'd find the gesture threatening (and reminded myself that she saw me only as "spiky bits and pieces," a "jigsaw puzzle").

"Did you know him?" I said. "The man who murdered you."

"Yes," she said.

"By name?"

"Yes. His name is Bill. He has a surname, of course, but I've lost it."

"Lost it?"

"Yes, it's left me. That memory of his surname. It's left me. Much has left me. Much has left me. It happens to all of us. We lose memories, and other memories, real or not so real, take their place."

And then, as she'd done before, she returned to whatever served as her universe and left me alone in mine.

She owned a kitten and its name was Abigail. I know this because she told me, "I have a kitten named Abigail. It wasn't I who named her. My boyfriend named her and then gave her to me as a Christmas present. *Abigail* is such an awful name but how could I rename her? I couldn't." A brief silence, and then, "She stayed near me after my murder. She snuggled close and stayed with me for a long, long time. She's devoted to me, as I am to her. How could it be otherwise, murder or not, death or not."

Abigail the kitten is here, now, in my bungalow. I see her from time to time, and I hear her, too—she possesses a very pleasant, very melodic and plaintive meow. I believe, from the momentary glimpses I have of her, that she's a small calico with no tail.

"Did you know him well?" I said to Sally on a mid-spring night.

"I think I did," she answered. "Yes. I think I did." She was standing close to me as I stood at a window in my living room and watched a soft evening rain fall. I could feel her presence as strongly as I could hear her words, though, oddly, I could see her only out of the corner of my eye: when I turned my head toward her, she vanished, though her words remained.

I asked her, my gaze on the soft evening rain, "Why did he kill you?"

"Why does anyone kill anyone?" she said. "Because, in that moment of the kill, they feel it's necessary. They feel it's the only thing they can do and *survive*. And so, they say, they can be forgiven for whatever murder they commit."

"I don't understand that," I said, and turned to look at her, saw my orange wing-back chair, my floor-standing lamp, the gray wall, a print of Edward Hopper's *Nighthawks* on the wall, near a print of van Gogh's *Starry Night*.

I sighed.

She said, "Oh, I think you do, Mr. Whitehouse. But, if not, you'll understand when it's time for you to understand."

I thought then, as I had before, *There's a lot more to her than her name reveals.*

"Hey," she said, and chuckled a little, "don't judge a book by its cover art."

Her killer, whom she calls Bill, is here too. Just like Abigail the kitten. Both are in this bungalow with me. But he—her killer—has never spoken to me, has only made his presence obvious in odd ways, as if he's being coy. For instance, I can *smell* him now and again and, you know, it's not a terribly off-putting smell, it's a smell Sally described as "a little like Jasmine tea. A sort of sickly sweet smell. I think he drinks lots of it. Jasmine tea. As I do. As I did. As I still do. In my way. In some of the places I spend time." She laughed and then said, "When our future is behind us, we have so very much time on our hands, don't you think?"

And there he is, now and again—wrapped up in the passing odor of Jasmine tea.

"Kill the bastard," Sally Pinup said, "and his smell will dissipate. It will be replaced by other smells." She chuckled. "You won't enjoy that, I'm sure."

I said, "But isn't he already dead?"

"Not in any way that matters," she said. "And don't get smug, Mr. Whitehouse. In our separate and intertwined universes my killer is not at all dead. And I'll tell you, too—he stalks me. It happens while I sleep. While I dream."

I thought, *The dead who dream?*

She said, "That's the purpose of dreaming, of course—to take us beyond the need or the desire to exhale and inhale, the desire to sweat again, to digest food, to make love."

And there's this: he, her killer, weeps: I hear it, his weeping, wherever corners meet—doorways, windows, walls . . . it's not the kind of weeping you'd expect from a killer. There's nothing demonic in it. It's as gentle as a purr.

Sally Pinup said, "He weeps constantly. He even wept while he was murdering me. It burbled out of his thin lips. It still does. It's everywhere.

"Kill him, Mr. Whitehouse, *kill* the bastard and his weeping will end."

I often encounter doorways in my bungalow I wasn't aware existed, and when I walk through them, I feel that something has changed—in the bungalow itself, in the way it's lit, maybe, and in myself and the time frame in which I live. Which brings up another reality: I can't remember when Sally Pinup came into my life, whether it was last week, last month, or last year, and I don't know if anything that needed resolution regarding her appearance here has been resolved. Except when I dream. Because we can make memories when we dream. I've done it often. But there's this, too: I'm not sure *when* I dream, or *if* I dream. I think it's possible that I'm dreaming now, as I write, though if that was true, for whom would I be writing? Myself?

Sally Pinup told me, "He's vicious and malicious and he has powers I cannot describe. I don't believe you can describe them, either.

"After he killed me, Mr. Whitehouse, after he killed me, he shaved all my body hair off with an electric razor. Then he collected the hair—from my arms and legs and . . . other areas, though not from my head, though he said my head hair was gorgeous, delicious—and he put it into a little dark wood container, walnut, maybe; yes, I believe it was walnut. And he did this because, he said, 'Body hair holds a person's *sum*.' And he said he wanted my *sum* . . . "

I burst into her monologue with, "That's simply insane!"

And she said, nonplussed, "No. It isn't. It's true. It's reality. You know that, Mr. Whitehouse." She paused a moment and then added, "It's as real as the odor of Jasmine tea."

And then she went off to whatever universe it is that separates us, in whatever way we are ever actually separate.

I found myself in her apartment recently. I believed, in my first minute there, that she'd been taken away. Yellow police tape—*Crime Scene, Do Not Pass*—lay across the outside of the front door; I knew this because I opened the door from the inside, and there it was, the yellow police tape. I shut the door quietly.

I have little idea how I came to be in her apartment except that I passed through one of the increasingly abundant, unfamiliar doorways in my bungalow and saw, first, a photograph of her with what I assumed were her parents, on a small, dark-orange bookcase, and next to that, a tiny gun-metal blue television on a short, bright-green wooden table; the television's rabbit ears were completely extended and pointed straight up. The apartment's front door, bookcase, photograph, and tiny TV were, at that point, the only items in the apartment.

"Good Lord!" I whispered, because it's more than jarring to find yourself, suddenly, within a given moment, in an unfamiliar room.

"Look around," I heard. It was Sally Pinup, at my ear. I turned my head quickly left, right: nothing; I looked behind me, saw only the bungalow's living room, bathed in an odd, wan light beyond the doorway that had led me there. I lurched. "I can't see you," I said.

"You don't need to see me," she said. "You need to look around. You really need to look around the place where I lived. The place where I *live*. Know *me*, Mr. Whitehouse, and know my *killer*." And she laughed quickly; under other circumstances it would have been charming.

"Look around *what?*" I said. "There's nothing here."

"Only because you're standing still. Stand still and go nowhere." She laughed again.

I nodded to indicate the framed photograph on the bookcase. "Those are your parents?" I said.

She said nothing.

"Are you still here?" I said.

"More than you believe," she said.

"I asked if those were—"

"My parents?"

"Yes."

"Yes."

"Those are your parents?"

"Yes. Almost without hesitation, I would say those are my parents, Mr. Whitehouse. And they, too, like me, are . . . hmmm—not-too-much dead." She laughed again, at my ear. It was as loud as a scream, and I lurched once more.

"But, Mr. Whitehouse," she said, as if in apology, "there are many who have told me that my laugh is . . . charming."

"Was Bill one of those people?" I said, and thought, in so many words, *One of your more lucid moments, Whitehouse.*

And she said, "He was simply my murderer. He knew me only well enough to take my life. There is no great insight involved in that."

So true! I thought.

"True?" she said. "Maybe, maybe not. I knew him well or poorly; I have
little idea." Then, after a quick silence, she added, again at my ear, "Hell,
we might have been lovers. I don't know. Or maybe we were married.
I don't know. My past . . . seeing *into* my past is pretty much the way I
see *you*, in puzzle pieces, small puzzle pieces, damned spiky little puzzle
pieces; and who can put them together?" Another brief silence and then,
"Bill wasn't my lover, he wasn't my husband, he wasn't anything, just my
murderer, just my murderer! That makes him nothing! Look around,
Mr. Whitehouse. Find what you can here, in this place almost no one
inhabits."

And I realized, without knowing how I realized it, that she was gone.

I took her advice. I looked around her tiny apartment.

It's damned difficult finding nothing at all. You have to look a long, long
time. And, as far as I know, I'm not a detective. Hell, I didn't know *what* I
was looking for. Letters, photographs, canceled checks? Who knew?

And making my way around the apartment was all but impossible.
When I moved a few yards right or left, the part of the apartment where
I'd just been—walls, floors, ceiling, furnishings, et cetera—disappeared,
so I found myself partially in the bungalow and partially in a very small
part of Sally Pinup's apartment—an arm's-span of wall, a bit of floor, a
whisper of ceiling, some furniture, a radio here, a music box there. At one
point, I called out, "Sally, can you give me a little guidance?" and when I
got no response, I repeated myself and heard, at my ear, "It's up to you
alone, Mr. Whitehouse!" and I answered, "Why? Why is it up to me
alone, for God's sake? *You're* the murder victim!" And, again at my ear,
I heard, "That's just so cruel, Mr. Whitehouse. So cruel!" followed by a
quick laugh.

———————

Bill. So many people with that name, then and now and all the decades in between. *Bill.* Fat man, thin man, average man? None of the above? Why in the hell did he exist? Simply to become Sally Pinup's murderer? Simply to shave off her body hair after he murdered her because it equaled her "sum"? Did such people actually exist? Of course they did. And do. And will. They exist to murder. Was Bill such a man? And if so, was there *more* to him? Or did that question matter? When a soul is focused, during its earthly existence, on its moment(s) of murder, does the fact that he (or she) is, otherwise, an artist or a prize fighter or a master chef really matter?

I asked myself these questions one night not too long ago, when Sally Pinup was elsewhere, I supposed, and Abigail, her kitten, appeared, in its other-worldly way, again and again, in my living room doorway, where it meowed once, twice, three times, as if to proclaim its existence, then, *poof,* vanished.

Bill. What if he was a character in a novel? What if he was someone who killed for bizarre reasons that no one would be able to truly under-stand, reasons that, once explained—for instance, "I killed her so I could shave off all her body hair because it equaled her *sum.*"—would elicit only an incredulous glance, followed by "Huh?" What would someone like that *do*, otherwise, when he wasn't murdering someone, or thinking about murdering someone, or remembering it? What was his *focus*, oth-erwise? Hell, did he ever really have any focus but murder, an *otherwise* that wasn't murder?

Damn! I heard at my ear. What a steaming pile of horse shit. You think I got murder on my mind every fucking second of every fucking day? What are you—stupid? I have a mother, just like you, and she needs looking after, just like your mother does. And I got rent to pay and a job to go to, and food to buy, just like you. And I cheat at Solitaire, too. Just like you.

"Bill?" I said.

Bill? I heard.

"Did you kill Sally Pinup?" I said.

Sure, I heard.

"Sure?" I said. "Just like that?"

You want it some other way? I heard. *You want reasons for what I do? Maybe you wanna know why I spit on the street or eat blueberry pancakes or pick my nose. Shit, there ain't no reasons. It's who I am, that's all. Just fucking who I am! Don't tell me that's too fucking hard for you to understand.*

"No," I said. "It isn't." I got no reply. "Bill," I asked, "are you dead?"

I heard at once, *You mean really dead? You mean like dead-dead? Oh, hell, Mr. Whitehouse, sometimes I really wish I was. Don't you?*

Abigail the kitten appeared in the doorway, meowed three times, as if declaring its existence, and, *poof!* vanished.

I have been wondering lately about my Uncle Cyrus.

My name is Denver Whitehouse, I'm as real as the potatoes on my plate, as real as Dirty Harry's pajamas, and I believe I live in a dozen universes at once. Or, maybe I live in only one universe and it's a lot more damned different from the one I previously thought I lived in. Like so many things (I've learned), it could be that it doesn't matter.

Not long ago, perhaps only moments ago, I found this on my desk top: it's written in blue ink in a tight, spiky hand: I have no idea how it came to be on my desktop, though I have a pretty good idea.

Sally P.,
Who the hell knows me? Not you. Not you. But you will.
You will!

And you'll find that I'm
unforgettable!
                    —Bill

TWO

She told me, "My mother used to serve us mashed potatoes and yellow
squash for breakfast every morning, along with something she called
'turkey twirls,' strips of dark-meat turkey that she twirled into little ring-
lets. That's a good memory. It's good because she served us this very odd
breakfast every morning with gusto and sunny smiles, even though we
told her over and over that the mashed potatoes were all right, and even
the turkey twirls, but not the yellow squash. And she said it was okay,
that the yellow squash was simply serving its purpose for being and that
should make us happy. What's the come-back for that, Mr. Whitehouse?
Even if you're a kid. As we both were. Kids, I mean. My brother Kyle
and I. One time he said, 'Aw, gee, Mom, you know I'm not gonna eat that
stuff,' meaning the yellow squash. And she said, 'Which will be something
you'll remember until your last days—not that you *should* have eaten the
yellow squash, Kyle, but that you *didn't* eat it. We remember, I think, only
such things, the things we *didn't* do, wouldn't you say that's true?' And
she gave Kyle her huge, loving smile and Kyle said, 'Yeah, I guess.' But he
didn't know what the hell she was talking about, and neither did I, and I
still don't."

   She was sitting on my sofa when she told me this story. She looked
animated, even happy, sharing the story with me, sharing her past with
me. She grinned nearly the entire time she talked. And, oh, what a grin!

   "It was to give us memories, my mother said. She was like that; and it
was good of her to be concerned about the memories we'd carry into adulthood and beyond. The mashed potato, yellow-squash-and-turkey-twirl-

breakfast memory, for instance. She was great. She was beautiful and she was great and she was loving and she was a lot strange." Sally paused very briefly and went on, still grinning, "She was murdered, too, Mr. Whitehouse. My father did it. He used a sharp fish bone and slit her throat. Then he undressed her and put her in the bathtub and bathed her; took extra time with her long auburn hair, made it even more beautiful, I remember, than it was in life." Another pause and then she went on, "Now *that's* a memory."

Yes, I, too, saw the connection between her mother's murder and her own, the hair connection. What did I make of it? Only that there was a connection, in style, apparently, between the two murders. But what the hell do I know? I'm not a detective. I've never even read a detective novel, not even Sherlock Holmes. I have no interest in being a detective, no interest in solving crimes, bringing the bad guys to justice, throwing my weight around for the sake of good versus evil (and I should tell you that I have considerable weight to throw around because of my weakness for foods that mean to do me harm).

What do I know, indeed?

I see you in bits and pieces, Mr. Whitehouse, she said. *I see you as if you're made of spiky puzzle pieces.* Hell, maybe we'd see everyone that way if we had perfect vision.

My name is Denver Whitehouse and I'm not the fat detective.

The phone rings; I pick it up, say, "Hello," hear nothing. "Hello," I say again, with an edge in my voice. Mindless repetition, of course, can upset our normally pleasant natures. Still I hear nothing. No breathing or whispering or background music. Nothing. "Shit," I say, and hang up. It's the way my universe works, now. The telephone rings and, almost always, it's as if no one's calling. But someone is indeed calling. I know that much at least.

My Uncle Cyrus visited early last night. He doesn't visit often. The last time was the day Bill Clinton was sworn into office, many years ago. Uncle Cyrus told me he was visiting because it was "past time, as the poet said, to enter that cottage of darkness" and he wanted to say his goodbyes to everyone who deserved a goodbye, which, he said, "Includes lots of people, even you, Denver, if only because you always knew how to listen when someone was talking to you."

I didn't recognize him. I remembered him as very thin, almost gaunt, his skin nearly yellow, his hair thin and prematurely gray. But the man who visited me was not that man. The man who visited me was fit and happy looking, and he moved as if he was ready to dance, not "enter that cottage of darkness."

He sat on the same couch Sally Pinup had sat on only a couple days earlier, put his elbows on his knees, looked down at himself briefly, and said, "I'm wearing this getup" (what looked like a new and expensive gray suit with an orange tie and white button-down shirt) "because it's what men are supposed to wear when death's about to make its move."

"But you look great, Uncle Cyrus," I said.

He smiled thinly. "I do, don't I? Hell, it's because I gave up lots of stuff, lots of the bad stuff people get involved with, you know what kind of stuff—devil's food cake and whiskey sours with cheese dumplings and sleeping late and smoking too much and exercising only enough to make it to the bathroom, then to the Barcalounger, and giving up all that stuff did my body good, but, shit, life wasn't *fun* anymore." His smile broadened. "But that was all right. I felt okay. I felt good, in fact. So to hell with *fun*, I thought. And then, not too long ago, and without meaning to—as close as I can judge these things: our memories are often not very reliable, are they, Denver?—I walked out in front of some great big boxy thing on wheels, some noisy, red thing on wheels that was going too damned fast, and I guess, you know, that did the trick."

"You *guess* it did the trick?"

"Well, yeah: here I am, right?" He gave me a huge, toothy grin.

"I don't understand," I said.

"Of course you do. You're a good listener, like I said. So of course you understand." He reached into the breast pocket of his suit, withdrew what looked like a small greeting card, and held it out to me.

"What's that?" I said.

"It's what it looks like," he said. "It's a greeting card. It's for you from me." He thrust his hand out further. "Take it, just take it, okay."

I took it, glanced at it, read these words aloud:

"*Life comes and life goes,*

But hey, death is forever!"

It was printed in white on a black background, and at the bottom of the card was a dancing stick figure in a top hat. Below that, were these words:

Ta ta for now!

When I looked up, Uncle Cyrus was nodding and grinning; he said, "Your new friends aren't part of the world I inhabit, Denver."

"The world you inhabit?"

"The several billion of us. The World of the Death Dancers." He grinned again. "A little whimsicality. You don't mind."

"Are you talking about Sally Pinup?"

He cocked his head. "You never know until you know, do you? And maybe not even then."

The universe in the streets beyond my bungalow, in the city beyond my bungalow, may well be as I remember it, a place of consuming darkness where darkness is likely on any street, in any city; a place where people walk slowly or quickly, alone or in pairs or more, in silence or with noise attached; a place where breezes are fitful and turn corners like cats at play, move with great deliberation through open doors, up skirts and into unbuttoned jackets; a place where sunlight is a compassionate or brutal stranger. I believe I haven't been part of that universe for some time. Weeks, perhaps.

Your new friends aren't part of the world I inhabit! Uncle Cyrus said.

If that was true (and why would Uncle Cyrus lie?) then what kind of world, what kind of universe, did Sally Pinup inhabit? What kind of universe did *I* inhabit, and did it make any sense even to ask such questions? Or was it (is it) like holding a hand up to stop a hurricane?

As Uncle Cyrus said, *You never know until you know. And maybe not even then.*

I found this note on the seat of my orange wing-back chair, the handwriting was spiky and small, almost illegible:

Hey there, hi there, ho there,

You got a tall order to fill, my friend. Tall as moon dust. Boy, she's got you going, doesn't she? That's her way. It's always been her way. She won't change. She can't. Poor pitiful thing. But you gotta love her. I know I did. How about you?

I like your chair.

Bill

I put it with his previous note, in the middle drawer of my roll-top desk.

And that's when Sally Pinup made an appearance.

She sat in the orange wing-back chair. Fetchingly.

She said, "As far as I can tell, Mr. Whitehouse, you're not at all fat."

"Thanks," I said, "but you can't see me, can you?"

"Only in bits and pieces; they float in the air like moths. Or bats." She smiled. Great teeth. Great lips. Great everything! Then she continued. "I don't know about this Uncle Cyrus, Mr. Whitehouse. I don't believe in him. I don't believe he exists. I think he's straight out of your gray matter. I think *you* believe in him. Maybe because of necessity." She glanced about until her gaze settled on my roll-top desk. "I believe in *Bill*. I believe in the notes he's written. But I don't believe in Uncle Cyrus. Watch out for him. Watch out for that . . . man. Like the foods you're addicted to, he means you harm." Another fetching grin. "And *I* mean you no harm at all. How could I?"

Shit. Now, oddly, I'm exhausted, the kind of exhaustion that results from a great, long-lasting orgasm.

Later, then. Later.

Time to dream.

                   .

The phone wakes me. I stare at it a few moments. It sits on a three-foot-tall, dark-cherry phone table near my bed. It's an old-style phone with a dial, though there are buttons with numbers beneath each hole on the dial. My second wife bought it for me; "It's a retro phone," she said. "I thought you'd enjoy it." It was the only gift she bought me, during seven years of marriage, that I liked. Her name is Lucy, and I named the phone after her. Lucy the Phone.

I pick up the receiver on the fourth ring, say, "You woke me," and hear, "I wasn't trying to." It's a woman's voice. I recognize it only after a few moments. It's Sally Pinup's voice. "I couldn't know you were sleeping," she says. "It's the middle of the afternoon, after all."

"How can you call me on the telephone?" I ask. "How can a ghost call someone on the telephone?"

"Ghost?" she says. "Who's a ghost? I called you about Tuesday."

"Tuesday?"

"Evening. Tuesday evening. Don't tell me you don't remember?"

"That's precisely what I'm telling you."

"Our dinner date. At Gregio's. You've forgotten, haven't you?"

"*Who* is this?"

"Oh, c'mon, Michael, you know who it is. Are you just having fun with me?"

"Michael? Who in the name of Lila Pratt is *Michael?*"

"Oh, good grief," she says. "Is this Beechwood 4-5789?"

"Huh?"

She hangs up.

I hear a dial tone.

I look at Lucy the Phone. There are no buttons with numbers beneath its dial holes.

"Oh, for the love of three oranges," I say.

I get out of bed, go into the kitchen, peer out a west-facing window, see my universe of familiar narrow streets, sturdy houses, people walking slowly against a brisk wind, and, in the distance, a cell phone tower.

I hear at my ear, *Understand one thing, my friend; she makes no mistakes. She'll have your head on a platter soon enough for what you've done. I tell you all this for the sake of your welfare, believe me. Believe me. Believe me.*

I don't recognize the voice. Strangely, it sounds like the voice of a five- or six-year-old child.

It's a stinging cold day early in April as I write. And this small city where I pay taxes, and buy groceries, and where I used to take my little Schnauzer Eliot for daily walks (he died two years ago; old age, the vet said) is in central New York State, and sits on a vast plateau that foments extremes of weather year round—blizzards in winter; foundation-rocking thunderstorms in spring, summer and fall; and even an occasional tornado, though they're usually almost benign.

I realize all at once that I need this city, that I need its realities, its light and shadow, its hard edges, its extremes of weather, its small, green hardware stores and massive supermarkets, its cell phone towers and ubiquitous fast food restaurants, its veterinary offices, aging bowling alleys and home-based hair salons sporting pink and yellow shutters.

I need to know I'm part of this city, if only because I breathe its air.

I need to know that I can die.

"Of course you can die," she says. "Everything that lives can die, and usually does, given the right circumstances." She chuckles. "Mr. Whitehouse, Mr. Whitehouse—may I call you 'Denver'? I've so wanted, ever since we got together—"

"Got together?"

"Oh yes, you remember, I'm sure. How could you not? You were having cake, I was having a frappe . . . But none of that matters anymore. We have moved on, you and I. We have moved on." She cocks her head fetchingly. "You continue to breathe the air, and I pretend." She chuckles again. It's like song.

I decide I may be dreaming.

But I realize quickly I'm not dreaming, that I only wish I was dreaming. Nightmare or otherwise, we can almost always wake from a dream.

I found myself in her apartment again, which was piecemeal (again), much as she sees *me*, though the pieces were longer, wider, taller this time—ten feet of wall (sporting blue-flowered wallpaper) left and right, a dark-wood floor with enchanting oriental throw rugs here and there; it was a larger apartment than I had thought on my original encounter, and

I found, this time, that she paints (painted), portraits mostly, and mostly what looks like her immediate family, her mom and dad, someone a bit older who may be a brother, and herself, several of herself, nude, half-nude: these are portraits she has signed—Sally P.—in the lower right corner.

And there's a portrait of a tall, thin man in a gray suit, red tie, and blue fedora. He's smiling but it's a false smile, and I asked myself, "Could this be Bill?" and heard, in a voice I didn't recognize, as a whisper at my ear, "It *could be* no one, my friend. It *is* who it *is*. You asked the wrong fucking question."

I said, "And what question should I have asked?" I got no answer.

I was in her kitchen, then.

So was she.

At the refrigerator.

She wore tight, light-green short pants, green high-heeled shoes, and a green blouse tied just above her navel—lots of skin. Wonderful skin.

She said, her gaze on the inside of the refrigerator, "My apartment is haunted." She looked at me, grinned an almost impossibly wide grin, added, "Perhaps you've noticed," let her gaze return to the inside of the refrigerator, and muttered, "People always whispering at your ear. Don't you hate it, Mr. Whitehouse? Don't you just fucking hate it?" She brought her finger to her mouth, tapped her lips a few times, and added, "Where's the fucking picante sauce?"

And, my voice trembling a little, I said, "I saw your paintings," and gestured a little toward the hallway.

She nodded without turning her head in my direction, said, "Fucking picante," and then looked at me and went on, "Don't you hate picante sauce, Mr. Whitehouse? Don't you simply hate it?" She looked confusedly at me. "Oh for the love of Mother's broad hips, Mr. Whitehouse—what *are* you doing here? It's too early, it's too *fucking early*."

"Early?" I said.

"Yes. Too *fucking* early, as a matter of fact. I haven't been *murdered* yet! Dammit, I haven't been *murdered* yet!"

She grinned again; it froze on her face.

I backed out of her kitchen, found myself again in my apartment, heard, in the same voice I'd heard minutes earlier, "*This* is what you *should* have asked, Mr. Whitehouse: You *should* have asked, 'Is that Bill?' Because if you *had* asked *that* question, of *her*, she would have answered, she *could* have answered. Do you understand *now?*"

Abigail the kitten meowed at my heels. Three meows. Each one a snippet of feline music. Each a melodic declaration of her existence.

THREE
Growing Old Backwards

My name is Denver Whitehouse. I don't much care for my middle name, so I don't use it, except when I'm signing a contract, when I use the initial, which is B. So I'm actually *Denver B. Whitehouse*. I have signed many contracts in my forty-five years on the planet. Contracts for the purchase of cars and houses, contracts for credit cards and bank accounts, contracts for marriage. I have been married three times, and now I'm single. I loved all my wives, and I still love them; it was they who left me, for reasons I will never understand.

All three exist in their own universes now. They almost never call or write. They leave my universe alone.

"You're like a wolverine, sometimes," my first wife Doris said. I had no idea what she was talking about. I'm never like a wolverine; I am almost always as gentle as a ladybug.

And I'm not the fat detective. I'm not a detective at all. I'm a man growing old backwards.

What makes us grow old? I wonder. *Genetics, tension, fate?*

My universe is a place where what has come to be called "dark energy," as the predominate force in nature . . . predominates. So my assumption, you understand, is that dark energy—which we cannot see or sense—causes us to grow old. The continuous presence of that *other*, that thing called *dark energy*, which we somehow *know* exists, but cannot touch or taste or experience in any normal way, is like a disease that overcomes us throughout the time we have been granted by whatever or whomever grants such things (perhaps it's the *dark energy* itself that grants us whatever time we have been allotted).

I believe firmly in all that I believe.

I shared some of my beliefs with my third wife, Constance, and she was skeptical. "Denver, you know I'm skeptical of such ideas," she said.

And now there's Sally Pinup relaxing toward me in my universe, cohabiting with me in our separate universes, beseeching me to *kill the bastard* who murdered her, setting loose her demons in my comfortable bungalow.

And if you're thinking, now (this just occurred to me) that the B in *Denver B. Whitehouse* stands for "Bill," you're wrong: who the hell uses a nickname (for instance, "Bill" for "William") as a middle name, first of all, and, secondly, the B stands for Bowman; just so you understand.

Would you want to be called *Bowman?*

There you go.

"Why does anyone kill anyone?" she said. *"Because, in that moment of the kill, they feel it's necessary. They feel it's the only thing they can do and survive."*

Very intelligent lady.

What are the landscapes of death? The cities of death? Its streets and avenues, towns and villages? Surely they exist.

And if they do,
　　Mr. Whitehouse,
　　　　they amount to no
　　　more than endless
　　and awful
　　　　chaos.

I once knew someone named Sally, though she wasn't quite as delightful
to look at as Sally Pinup. We went to the same high school and we hung
out together—in the cafeteria, at baseball and basketball games, stuff like
that. She was blonde, unlike Sally Pinup, and not as playful and quick.
I can't recall her last name, hard as I try, though I know she wore glasses
that weren't at all right for her face, and she smiled only when there was
reason to smile.

She died on her seventeenth birthday. I had been to her birthday party,
was just about the only one there (very sad), and barely an hour after I
gave her a goodbye buddy hug, she was dead. I don't recall how and I
don't know why.

Early April as I write; cold and forbidding beyond the windows: a strong
and steady north wind moans like the lost.

Sally is here as I write. I can sense her, not see her. She likes to play
with my senses, I think: *I am here, I am here, I am nowhere!* she tells me.

And, just now, at my ear, *Have you found him?* It's her voice, there's even
a hint of her breath on my cheek, the odor of lipstick.

And just a moment ago, she told me, *I once wore glasses.*

"Please let me see you," I say.

You like the way I look, don't you? How cheerful that makes me.

"It's disturbing to talk with you this way."

She laughed softly. *Bill is here. He's in your house at this very moment. He's in your house, your comfortable bungalow. Bill, my murderer. The man who knew me not well enough.*

"I don't know what that means," I said.

Of course you don't. How could you? Could you understand a pelican spouting gothic poetry?

"I don't know what that means, either."

Feel happy you don't, because when you do, your world will come apart, along with our separate and cohabiting universes.

Her name is Sally Pinup and she's as real as she pretends to be.

I'm beginning to feel uncomfortable in my bungalow, in my city, in my universe, in my skin itself, as if there's really no place for me to lie down and rest, to exist peacefully with myself. Ask me to tell you what I'm talking about and I'll answer, *I don't know, I really don't know. Shit! I don't know!* But again, after some time, I can hear him, Bill, where corners meet, where right angles are formed, I can hear him weeping, and it sounds like a purr, like a ragged purr.

My name is Denver B. Whitehouse, and I'm as real as I pretend to be.

FOUR
In the Belly of the Pelican

I believe my memories haunt me.

It feels good to say that, to present it as a possibility, along with all the other possibilities that give me great comfort—for instance, someday, we'll fly to the stars, we'll live a thousand years, create diamonds using advanced technologies, and we'll finally defeat all disease, heartache, loneliness, boredom, and evil completely.

But here's the thing: I *believe* in Sally Pinup, I *believe* in Bill, and I believe he murdered her, shaved off all her body hair and saved it in a dark walnut box because it was her "sum," and I *believe* in Uncle Cyrus, too, and Abigail the kitten, and cohabiting universes, dark energy, paranormal sex in the afternoon, et cetera, et cetera.

Will I find the bastard who killed Sally Pinup? Will I find Bill? Or will it be like trying to find a wisp of smoke which, half a century ago, rose from a cigarette? A wisp of smoke that has long since dissipated

>Yes, Mr. Whitehouse.
>   That's exactly what it
> will be like.   You're
>   an intelligent man.

Where was I? Oh yes, yes . . . moving stealthily about in what suddenly appears to me of Sally Pinup's small apartment: the gaily painted walls; the small dark-pine bookshelves; the Felix the Cat wall clocks, long black tails moving slowly, almost elegantly, back and forth, like pendulums—so many of these clocks here, so many—the spotless kitchen and its blue linoleum-topped table with stainless steel legs and two matching chairs; the red metal toaster and pastel green refrigerator—a *Tappan*—and, from time to time (here in this moment, gone in the same moment) Sally herself looking on, smiling an enigmatic smile, as if she knows my secrets.

But if I do have secrets, they are mostly unknown to me.

We sat close to one another and had a charming conversation: it was in her bedroom, as small as her living room, as small as her kitchen: I sat in a white rocking chair that threatened to give under my weight; Sally sat on her well-made bed, looking elegant and available, as she always has. She was the first to speak.

"I see you only as a moving mass of spiky puzzle pieces, Mr. White-house; it's as I've always seen you, as if you don't quite exist."

"I exist," I told her, "as surely as you do." I tried to rock the chair; it moaned ominously.

"It's not meant for visitors," Sally told me, "only for wraiths such as I," and she crossed her legs, uncrossed them, hurriedly crossed them the other way. "It doesn't know your intentions." She laughed a little. It was a soft laugh, melodic, appealing.

"Oh, I think it knows my intentions completely," I said.

Sally put her hand primly to her marvelous lips. "Mr. Whitehouse, that sounded so . . . forward." She glanced toward the door, which was closed. "Someone's here," she said. "Someone's here who shouldn't be. Do you know his name, Mr. Whitehouse? I'm sure you do. You must know it, of course, otherwise I wouldn't be asking you."

I rose quickly from the rocking chair, went to the door, opened it, peered out. "I can't hear anything," I told her.

"Please close the door," she said. "Please close the door, Mr. Whitehouse."

I closed the door.

She asked if I wanted some tea. "Do you want me to make you some of that tea you love?" she said. I wondered aloud if she should leave the room, considering the other person in the apartment.

She answered, "Yes, I should leave the room, *especially* considering the other person in the apartment."

Our conversation ended.

And so the odor of Jasmine persists in my comfortable bungalow: I have grown to expect it, to search for it, and am disappointed when

I do not find it—behind a door, for instance, or under the bed, in a dresser drawer.

I even speak to the odor (because I know it's *his* odor, *Bill's* odor, not that I at all expect it will speak to *me*):

"You have invaded my universe, just as *she* has," I say. "But *she* is welcome here."

The odor is silent, sharply appealing; it moves about the bungalow with me.

Beyond the bungalow, beyond the universe that is the bungalow, there is more darkness than love tonight: but that's true of any universe—those as small as small kitchens, and those as large as the space between stars.

The phone rings.

I answer it. I hear an incoherent whisper, as if steam is beginning to erupt from a radiator.

I say, "Hello," get silence. "Damn you!" I say. "Damn you to hell."

You know who I am, Mr. Whitehouse.

I hang up.

Sometimes we're haunted. Sometimes we haunt, my Aunt Winifred told me long ago, when I was just beginning to eat food that "meant to do me harm." I looked at her a few moments and then confessed I didn't know what the hell she was talking about.

Hell, she said, *has nothing whatever to do with it. Not, at least, the hell we've been spoon fed at St. Thomas's.*

I still don't understand, I said. And she leaned over and whispered in my ear, *Sometimes we haunt* ourselves, *Denver.*

Why do I bring that up? I can't say for sure. Perhaps because the quickest way to solve a mystery is to fit ourselves snugly into the mystery itself. To *become* the mystery. Not that I've suddenly morphed into being a detective. I haven't. I am still what I've always been—a man who does his best work quite beautifully.

But here's why I thought of Aunt Winifred and her quotable quotes: her last name was *Sally*. And, by God, since these episodes with Sally Pinup started, it almost never occurred to me—my Aunt Winifred talked much about ghosts; they fascinated her: she claimed to see them everywhere, felt their presence everywhere, communicated with them in odd and not-so-odd places—in restaurants, on buses, at street corners; and she said, now that I think about it (and I believe this is an exact quote), *Denver, I tell you I see them, but I don't believe I do. I think, perhaps, that I'd like very much to see them, and so my small lie is no more than a fantasy. Nor do I hear them. But there's this, and it's very important: I feel them, as if they're crowding me—usually in a very loving way—in many of the places I go to, and even while I'm going there.*

And her name was Winifred *Sally*.

What a happy coincidence that is, don't you think?

I believe she's still alive. I haven't seen her in a very long time, but I always enjoyed her company. She was animated, friendly, agreeable to look at, her dark hair long and elegant, and she smelled good.

Sometimes we haunt ourselves, Denver. What a fanciful idea.

I was in Sally's kitchen, hoping to see her, when a man appeared from the other room. He was dressed in a sharkskin suit, white shirt, yellow tie and gray fedora: I could see the hard bulge of a gun just above his waist, beneath the suit. He had a thin mustache and his lips were also thin, his eyes small and dark.

He said, "And who the hell are you, bub?"

I said, "I could ask you the same question," and heard my voice tremble, thought I sounded foolish, so I repeated, "I could ask you the same question," and added, after a moment, "Mister," and my voice still trembled.

He smiled as if he'd caught a rat in a cage. "Okay, bub," he said, and, after unbuttoning his suit coat quickly, and not without an odd grace, pulled his gun out, pointed it at me from his hip, and added, "you got three seconds to get your hands up or it's tootles for you!"

I tilted my head a bit, confused. "Tootles?" I said.

"*What* was that?" he growled, as if I had really wondrous balls to say anything at all.

"You said," I told him, "'or it's tootles for you,' meaning me."

"I never said that! I *never* say '*tootles*.'" He cocked the gun, and then, though he still held it at his waist, angled it so its barrel was pointing at my head. "What I *said* was, 'or it's *curtains* for you!' That's what in the Sam Hill I said."

"Actually, no," I told him. "What you actually said was . . ."

He fired. The bullet tore into the pink cupboard behind me. I heard glass shatter. He looked in great confusion at his gun; "For the love'a Pete," he muttered, "I missed."

I threw my hands in the air.

He lifted the gun and straightened his arm so the gun's barrel was only a couple of inches from my nose.

"You don't need to kill me!" I said, my voice trembling again. "There's really no need for you to kill me."

"Yeah," he said, "I know." He grinned a grin so big his gray Fedora moved up half an inch. "I know I don't *need* to kill ya," he growled. "But it would sure make my day."

I attempted a smile: "Dirty Harry's pajamas," I said.

"Huh?" he said.

Then I did something I'd never have guessed I had the balls to do: I quickly stepped a couple of feet to my left, hands still in the air. And he, along with his part of the kitchen—doorway, countertop, floor, the right-hand section of the pink cupboards—vanished.

It's midafternoon, three days later, and bright sunlight floods through the bungalow's tall, narrow windows. I have gone nowhere, have seen no one, am, I'll admit, a bit too flummoxed to do much of anything; I hesitate even to move about here, in the small universe that is my bungalow. I've been to the bathroom a couple of times, the kitchen, the front hall closet, the living room. I move very slowly, very cautiously wherever I go. I've seen no one.

(*Good Golly Miss Molly, Your Strange Son is in very Strange Circumstances*)

I have so little—my bungalow, my small, fenced yard and its much smaller vegetable garden, where I grow a little corn, some tomatoes, squash; and peaches, and I have my elegant Stickley and Mission Oak furniture, collected from various obscure antique shops over the years; I have my music, too, and my literature; my small and large secrets, which give me great enjoyment at night, when I'm nearing sleep; I take them out and peer at them, find them titillating (some of them) or comforting (a few of them), or vexing (one or two of them, which I try valiantly to expel from my mind, which, of course, is never really possible).

Yes, my mother's name was Molly, and she hated it. "Good Golly, Miss Molly," she heard throughout her life as a greeting from friends and acquaintances and other members of her family.

"I'm glad you never say it," she told me. "You're a fine son, Denver."

But I was actually not her son; she was my stepmother, and so—this is one of those secrets I mentioned above—it was all right that I harbored very strong feelings for her long past her untimely and quite unexpected death at forty-three, following a skiing accident in Colorado.

We gather so many secrets in the span of a life. Some of them comfort us, some of them vex us, and some of them titillate us, as I've said. And I think that if most people sat down and listed their many secrets, it would appall them what kind of people they were. I mean no judgement by that; it's merely an observation. I make the same observation of myself from time to time.

Good Lord, *Bill* has returned.

He stands quietly near doorways, wherever I go. He wears no particular expression, does not stare: his mood seems almost contemplative—a tall, thin man in a gray suit who smells of Jasmine tea.

I have tried to speak with him several times. I addressed him by name—"Bill?" I said, "I believe in you. I actually believe in you"—but I received no answer, not even a glance. He has nearly the countenance of the dead, as if, had he once possessed a soul, it has left him.

He doesn't block my way, doesn't turn his head to follow my movements, doesn't seem ill-at-ease.

This is the first time I've seen him so completely; have, before, simply smelled him; heard him *purring* at all the bungalow's right angles, as if he was part of the wood and plaster itself, part of the bungalow itself.

Perhaps I should be afraid of him. I'm not. He seems less like another man than a *representation* of a man, someone conjured up by someone with a very active imagination.

I believe he'll speak to me eventually.

Have I thought of killing him? It's what I told Sally Pinup I'd do, after all. And I asked myself, before his appearance, "*Will* you kill the bastard?"

I don't know. I know only that I believe in him, that he's in my bungalow, wherever I go, and that, now, at this moment, as I write, killing him may be just an exercise in melodrama.

———————————

FIVE
Sally in the Garden, all Smiles

April is too early to expect a bounty from one's backyard garden, but she was eating a peach when I went out there.

"You grow magnificent peaches," she said, and gave me a very friendly smile: she looked at the once-bitten peach she held close to her mouth. "Not many people know the best way to grow peaches," she said, and took her second bite, chewing slowly, savoring it, eyes closed.

The sun was bright, almost overpowering, and she was dressed in green, as usual—a color that her red hair demanded.

"My mother taught me how to grow peaches," I said, and I glanced at my two peach trees, which were bare.

She took another slow bite of her peach, savored it, let the rest drop to the ground, and said, "It's not a peach your mother grew." She cocked her head fetchingly at me. "It is *you* your mother grew, Denver B. White-house." She nodded at the bungalow, a dozen feet away. "Kill him, then. Kill the bastard! As you said you would."

"I did say that, yes. And I will. Perhaps sooner than either of us imagine," I said.

"Believe in *yourself* most," she said. "Believe in the will of your arms and gut." She smiled again, broadly, fetchingly. "That's something my father used to say."

"He was a wise man," I said.

She scowled. "Nah. Just a man. He put ketchup on his eggs, farted everywhere, spit on the sidewalk. That's what men do. And they spout platitudes, too." She looked at the remains of the peach on the ground, and then at me again. "Did you see my paintings? Did you see what I painted? I have talent, don't you think? A good, appealing face, a great body, and talent."

I looked at her a moment, then said, "Why have you come to me to find your murderer?"

She grinned. "Why? Because of the once-in-a-lifetime intimacy we shared, of course. Such world-shattering intimacy, Mr. Whitehouse. Don't you remember?"

I shook my head, began to answer, but she cut in, and with a glance at the bungalow, said "Look at my paintings again. I think that's something you must do." She paused. "Then *kill* the bastard who has brought us both so much pain."

I talk with the mailman quite a lot. I know when he's at the door. He's not quiet about what he does; he opens and closes the mailbox with great gusto, as if he's proud of being a mailman. And why not?

"Hello, Mr. Whitehouse," he said. "Beautiful day, wouldn't you say?"

"Yes, so it is. What do you have for me on this beautiful day, Howard?"

"From the looks of it, just bills, Mr. Whitehouse. Just bills." He opened the mailbox and handed me my mail; I saw that he was right.

"Good day, now, Mr. Whitehouse," he said.

"Good day, Howard," I said. "Good day, and thank you." He's a kind man and deserves many thanks.

All mailmen should be named Howard, don't you think? And all pinup girls should be named Sally. That's one of the many rules that help the universe work well.

Bill spoke to me, at last. He looked me directly in the eye—his gaze like the gaze of a viper—and said, in a voice shallower and less powerful than I had imagined it would be, almost a hoarse whisper, though there was *voice* in it, something left over from his obviously absent soul,

"I was delicate and very cautious with her skin, Mr. Whitehouse." And he turned his head away and became what he had been moments before— an opaque and motionless *representation* of a man.

"You bastard!" I snarled, my face very close to his, so the odor of Jasmine tea nearly overwhelmed me. "You filthy bastard!" And I stepped back, so I was an arm's length from him. "Bastard!" I said again, though at a whisper, and I slapped him across the face; it was the first time in my life that I'd struck anyone and it made me feel oddly exhilarated, so I slapped him again, with the other hand, although the first blow seemed to have no effect on him. The second had no effect, either. My exhilaration should have lessened, I realized, but it hadn't. I felt even more exhilarated, as if I were on the verge of the most terrific orgasm of my life. I balled my right hand into a fist, planted the fist hard into his midsection, though again without effect. No matter; I hit his solar plexus hard with my left fist, again with no effect. It was all right. Somehow I knew he wasn't going to respond to a beating. Somehow I knew he was beyond pain. I might as well have been striking out at a dream figure, though, with each blow, I felt his skin or muscle give way slightly, which told me he was no dream figure, he was flesh and blood, right in front of me, in my bungalow. He was my damned *punching bag!*

So I hit him, harder and harder, in the face, the side of his head, his chest, stomach, groin, neck, all to no effect. But it was okay. It was more than okay. It was beautiful: I *felt* beautiful, powerful, *real*—a man doling out retribution! A man, despite everything, who was valiantly, even hero-ically, trying to right a wrong!

Then I felt an incredible, searing pain in my hands. I held them out, palms down, at waist level. Looked at them. Winced hard at what I saw, gasped, and cried out, "Blood!" though I strung the word out to a couple of seconds, "Blooooood!" and heard, at my ear, Sally Pinup's sweet voice, "No shit, Sherlock. It certainly isn't olive oil, and Bill, there, isn't *cottage cheese!*"

"What a fool I am!" I cried out. "What a Goddamned fool I am!"

"Stop beating yourself up," she said at my ear. And she laughed.

It has been weeks since I've been able to do much of anything with my hands; but they've healed at last. I had to leave the bungalow and see my doctor, Estelle McCurdy, whose first question wsas, "For the love of Pete, what did you do, Denver, use your walls as a punching bag?" As it turns out, that's precisely what I'd done. Odd what the brain tells us is real in times of stress, even a brain as devoid of imagination as mine.

But Uncle Cyrus has come by again; he just left, in fact, and he was full of advice, as usual: "Stop whatever it is you're doing, for God's sake! For some odd, or not-so-odd reason, you've built yourself a little fantasy world and you're not up to dealing with it because you can't admit why you built it in the first place. Good God, Denver, you're not Peter Pan."

"Huh?" I said.

"Well you're not," he said. "*His* fantasy world was at least real. And he knew what he was doing in it."

"He did?"

"Of course, he was fighting Captain Hook. That was the villain's name, right? I'm sure it was." I'd given him some tea, Earl Gray, which he enjoys. He sipped it and went on, "But you're no more Peter Pan than I'm Shirley Temple. So just get back to whatever it is you *do* and forget what's her name."

"Sally Pinup, Uncle Cyrus. Her name's Sally Pinup."

"That's no one's real name," he said with a sniff.

"You're right. It's not her real name, but it's the name she goes by, and that makes it real, sort of."

"Sure it does. But it doesn't make *her* real," he said.

I shrugged a little: he was right, of course, as far as it went.

He sipped his tea, nodded, said, "Good stuff!" took another sip and added, "Like I told you before, Denver, she exists in a universe different from mine, or yours, and she exists there for reasons I can't get hold of." He raised an eyebrow. "But she's right; don't go beating up on yourself anymore."

Moments later, he left the house in his black '68 Lincoln.

Abigail the kitten just appeared in a doorway and meowed three times, as if reminding me she exists. Then she went away again; to where, I have no idea.

> Sometimes, Denver,
>   we haunt ourselves
>   and sometimes
>   we don't.
>   Here's the deal:
>   Is it really important to
>   know the difference?

I'm slow-roasting a chicken in a small white porcelain roasting oven that sits on one of the kitchen counters. I drizzle some yogurt on the chicken every once in a while for added flavor. It's a six-pound chicken and will take several hours to cook, but, when it's done, I'll enjoy it with some coleslaw and French fries, followed by blueberry pie and Breyer's vanilla ice cream..

Sally Pinup has promised to join me.

"You *must* kill him!" she said, and wiped a drop of ice cream from the

corner of her mouth with a flowered napkin I'd provided. "You must kill
the bastard!"

"I don't see how," I said. "He's not made of cottage cheese, as you
reminded me . . ." She smiled. I continued, " . . . but neither is he made
of flesh and bone. I don't know how I'll do this thing."

I should point out that Bill is here, in the bungalow with me, only now
and then (he's very like Abigail the kitten in that respect), though his
countenance and bearing haven't changed at all.

I popped a forkful of blueberry pie into my mouth. It's made locally, at
a bakery called "Hinson's Bake and Eat," and it's to die for.

Sally pointed at my chin. "Blueberry," she said, and I wiped it off with
my own napkin.

"If you don't kill him," she said, "I don't know *what* I'm going to do,
Mr. Whitehouse." There was no anger in her voice, only frustration. She
added, "Do you know that your spiky puzzle pieces are slowly, oh so
slowly coming together? Perhaps at last I'll see the real you."

We were seated at my small kitchen table—walnut with inlaid white
tiles—and I reached across it, took her hand, which, at first, seemed to
frighten her, though, after a moment, she smiled a little, and I said, "That
would be a good thing; it would be a very good thing, Sally."

"Perhaps you're right," she said. "Have you looked at my paintings and
photographs, again, as I asked?" She took another bite of her vanilla ice
cream.

"No," I said, "but I will. It's precarious, moving about in your apartment." I didn't tell her that I was a little reluctant to look at the paintings
and photographs again: I wasn't at all sure why.

"Of course it's a precarious thing," she said. "It's a wholly different universe, isn't it, than your bungalow?"

———————

SIX

Beliefs in Training

I believe Bill possesses this house, this bungalow, my universe: and so, over the past few months or weeks, may have become part of me. Am I saying he possesses me? No. And I can't explain what I'm talking about, why I *know* I'm not possessed by him.

I'm trying so hard to be rational. I'm trying hard not to speak in riddles, which is often what I do. I reread this narrative and it befuddles me, sometimes. I ask myself, "Who in hell *is* the person who's telling this tale?" Because, of course, from time to time, I don't recognize him, or his memories.

It's so baffling not to recognize memories; the phrase itself seems oxymoronic: a memory is a memory, after all—of course it's recognizable: for instance, the memory I have of my father's voice, my mother's smell, or my memory of a house we lived in when I was young, its color, size and architecture. But, since Sally Pinup came into my life, my memories, some of them, are baffling and unrecognizable.

And there's a new one, now; here it is, fully fleshed:

I own a car, although, years ago, it sat all but unused in the garage because I preferred walking; it was easier to get to know the neighborhoods all around me that way. I walked many miles each week through the neighborhoods and into the city itself, night and day. I talked with many people on these walks, especially during daylight; sometimes, people will talk with a non-threatening stranger, such as I, sometimes they won't; but often the people who did talk to me revealed themselves subtly, and sometimes not so subtly—their predilections and their confidences and secrets.

I'm a tall man, though I was much thinner in the years I walked so much, and I dress well. My face has a soft, benign look, and I've been told my voice is pleasantly low-pitched, almost caressing; I suppose you could call me avuncular, which may explain why people found me easy to talk with.

One early spring day—a Tuesday, midafternoon—I was walking several blocks over, on Sycamore Street, comprised of comfortable one and one-and-a-half-story homes that sport bright green lawns and, many of them, in-ground swimming pools, when a stocky man of forty-five or so, hair thin but dark, stopped me as he picked up his mail and asked what I was doing.

"I'm getting some much-needed exercise," I told him.

He looked quickly around, as if someone might be watching. "Have you got a moment?" he said.

"A moment?" I said. "Sure."

He smiled a little, as if in apology, and said, "It's just that you look like someone who can keep a secret. I had an uncle like that. You look like him."

"Thank you," I said. "And yes, I can keep a secret."

"Perhaps if we could talk up there," he said, and gestured at his enclosed front porch. "I can offer you some iced tea. It's a warm morning for early spring, wouldn't you say?"

"Yes," I answered, "it is indeed a warm morning. And yes, I'd love some iced tea."

And so, the unrecognizable memory continues:

he led me to his enclosed porch and offered me a chair at a small, round, white metal table. I sat.

"I'll get our tea," he said, and disappeared into his house, a white clapboard ranch with a red roof. Moments later, he reappeared with two plastic glasses and a pitcher of dark iced tea in hand; he poured a glass for me, then one for himself, and sat, took a sip of the tea, and announced, without preamble, "I've been cheating on my wife." He inhaled deeply, exhaled slowly. "There, I've come clean, at least to you." He took another sip of his iced tea and added, "You have no idea how relieved I feel."

"I can only imagine," I said with an avuncular smile.

"It's so good to unload myself of that heavy burden," he said, "even to a stranger. Maybe *especially* to a stranger."

Of course, that conversation may not have occurred exactly as I've recalled it here (if it occurred at all), though I'd say it's pretty close. And this is the point: my (*unrecognizable*) memories tell me that same sort of conversation—involving secrets and revelations and confessions— occurred dozens of times during the several years I walked the city and its neighborhoods. People told me not simply about adultery but confessed to petty theft, to beating their dog, stealing a car, even, once, to murder, which, as I recall now, was not a confession by the murderer himself, but only that the man talking said he was "pretty sure" his "friend" had been involved in "a death," as he put it. "In college. After a sorority dance." Naturally, according to my unrecognizable memory, I quickly excused myself from that conversation and walked straight home, where I found myself reaching for the phone, to call the police, perhaps two dozen times, though I never made that phone call.

Except, I hasten to add, that it was the only time someone confessed to me any knowledge of a murder, and the words he used, as I recall them now, are little more than approximations of what may have been the actual, almost hour-long conversation; for instance, "Yes, I believe it was during a sorority dance that this death took place," and, "His name escapes me, though I remember it was quite an unusual name," and, "His victim was left in a comfortable position. He was very gentle with her."

What can I say about these "unrecognizable memories"? As I wrote before, memories are memories, meaning they exist continuously in the gray matter, and to call them "unrecognizable" is like saying "the rain is dry." I think sometimes it's as if my ongoing *connection* to these memories, and perhaps others, has been cut, somehow. I'm not sure what that means, only that the memories may, indeed, be real, but their ongoing, continuous presence in my head is another matter entirely. Whole months or years may have passed without my knowing when some of my memories may simply have become inaccessible. I have no idea why.

Something very grim and tenacious has gotten hold of you, my friend.

SEVEN
Hesitating toward me from a Doorway

I used Sally's bathroom. It was joyfully painted in yellow and blue; several Van Gogh prints hung from the walls beside a Picasso self-portrait on the back of the door; a Dali print sat below it with one of Sally's ubiquitous Felix the Cat clocks beside a small window. And for me, I'd found, there was simply nowhere else to go. The need, when I'd stepped through the open doorway, was sudden and urgent, so I quickly crossed the room to the toilet, flipped up the seat (it was pink), and peed there, in her bathroom, in her apartment, in her universe. I felt like I was invading her privacy, even though she was, apparently, nowhere in the place.

And so, done, I put myself away and heard from behind me, at the door, "You should have asked first, don't you think?" It was her voice; I was mortally embarrassed.

"I should have, yes," I said. "But you weren't here."

"It's all right," she said. "I'm here always, I'm here not at all; take your pick."

I turned around, faced her, saw that she was standing with her back against the doorjamb, one leg straight, at a diagonal to the jamb, the other leg bent, bare foot pointed at the floor; her wonderful arms hanging at her sides. I got the impression she was posing.

"You like my taste in bathroom art, Mr. Whitehouse?"

"Your taste is wonderful," I said. "Some of my favorite artists."

"Yes, I know." She gestured a little to indicate the toilet. "Are you finished in here, or is there more work to do?" She gave me a little smile.

"No," I said, embarrassment flooding through me again, "there's no more work to do."

"Good," she said with a small nod. "So wash your hands and join me." And with that, she turned and exited to her right, toward, I'd learned after a few visits to the place, the small living room.

I washed my hands, dried them on a light green towel, left the room, looked right, left, saw no one. "Sally?" I called.

"In here," she called back. I looked in the direction of her voice, saw her walls merge with walls in my bungalow—different colors, different heights, different flooring: I'd gotten used to this. "Where?" I called.

"Oh, Mr. Whitehouse, you *know* where."

I said nothing.

She chuckled; I'd no idea why. I followed the sound of that chuckle, found her where I'd expected to find her, in her living room; she sat, legs crossed, in a small Queen Anne chair, her arms on the chair's dark wood arms. She said, "I hear you met Detective Quatrain."

"Was that what he was? A detective. 'Quatrain,' huh? Quite a name."

"He's bonkers," she said. "He'll shoot you just for looking cross-eyed at him. I never trusted him to find Bill. He's a maniac."

"Just like Bill?"

"Do you think Bill's a maniac, Mr. Whitehouse?"

"Call me Denver. Okay?"

"Sure." She gave me a once-over. "But from what I can see of you now, which is more than when we met, but not much more, I'd say you don't look at all like a 'Denver,' though you do look like a 'Whitehouse.'"

"Are you talking about my girth?" I said.

"You seem to have it." She uncrossed her legs, crossed them the other way, went on. "So, do you think Bill's a maniac? Why? Because he murdered me? Because he didn't know me, and still he murdered me? Because

he murdered me in the *way* he murdered me?" She seemed, in those few
questions, to have moved from distracted, unremarkable conversation to
anguish.

"You're weeping," I said. "Good Lord, I'm so sorry."

"You don't know me, Mr. Whitehouse; not as you think you do. I've
come to realize that. I . . . cry a lot, even now."

"I'm so sorry," I said again.

"I hate crying. I absolutely despise it. It's a sign of weakness. It's something weak *women* do. And I'm not a weak woman."

"Everyone cries . . ." I began.

"Not everyone, Mr. Whitehouse. Not everyone. The men in my life
never cried. My *father*, the bastard, never cried. My brothers never cried."

"I understand . . ."

"You actually understand very little." She wiped her tears away with
her fingers.

A ghost who cries! I thought.

"Bullshit!" she said.

"Bullshit?"

"Your thoughts are so often simply bullshit! The gray matter slips out
and coils around what's easiest to believe, what's most *easily grasped*." She
shook her head a little. "But everyone's thoughts are like that, aren't they?
Even mine." She laughed; it was short, brittle. "Even considering the state
I'm in, meaning, hell, I don't *have* any actual gray matter anymore, and my
thoughts are still bullshit."

"How did Bill murder you?" I said, and launched immediately into
an apology: "I'm sorry. Again, I'm so sorry. I don't know where that
came from. You said something about 'the way' Bill murdered you, and
I don't . . ."

"It's no big thing," she said, "how he murdered me; I'm talking about
how he murdered me. It's no big thing. He murdered me in the way men
murder women; as if we're beautiful but otherwise worthless. That's how

he murdered me, with that absurd idea moving about inside him, moving his hands, his moist hands. His weak hands." She looked away, looked back, went on. "He was a weak man, Mr. Whitehouse. He murdered me only to prove he wasn't weak. He thought I was beautiful and he knew he was weak, so he murdered me with his weak hands. It's nothing to murder in that way, to make your weak hands strong with anger and self-hatred."

"Sally, I . . ."

She shook her head: "Please, oh please don't tell me how *sorry* you are, again. It makes no difference: my murder is done. My murder is done."

Abigail the kitten appeared in the doorway, meowed once, went away.

"Bill is here," Sally told me.

"In this apartment?"

"Yes. In this apartment. My apartment. And in your bungalow. In our . . ."—she smiled a little—"shared universe. Bill is here. He claims both of us."

"I don't understand."

"Oh, but you do," she said, "you actually do," and she was gone, along with her apartment.

The bungalow seemed very dark at that moment, as if my vision was failing.

Bill said, in a soft, clear voice, from everywhere in the place, "I was very careful with her skin. Such beautiful skin, don't you agree, Mr. Whitehouse? Such beautiful skin. Even in death. Skin should be beautiful in death, I think. Bodies should be beautiful in death. *Hair* should be beautiful in death."

"Oh, please, "I whispered tightly, "will you just, dammit, shut the fuck *up*!"

And he did.

Our separate universes, Sally Pinup's universe and my universe, are like rivers that intertwine. All the *stuff*, all the flotsam and jetsam flow together for seconds, minutes, hours, whole days, and weeks. Perhaps forever.

I wrote that, or something close to it, much earlier in this narrative. I realize now, though I didn't then, that Bill is part of the "flotsam and jetsam" I was talking about.

Abigail the kitten, too.

And Sally Pinup herself.

Maybe even her mom and dad, whose photographs adorn her walls. And Sally's paintings, too. And the man there, in some of those paintings and photographs—the man who makes me look away, close my eyes, will myself elsewhere. Elsewhere.

And then there's Uncle Cyrus, too, who might actually be what he appears to be.

All of which leaves me with one overwhelming question: am *I* completely what I appear to be? There is no question about my name: it is what I have said it is; I couldn't have made it up. What would be the point? And it—my name—isn't one of those "unrecognizable" memories I've been writing about these past few pages. My name, as I look into my past, into my young adulthood, my teenage years, my early childhood, has always been with me, and I have always hated it. Wouldn't you? *Denver Bowman Whitehouse.* What in the hell was my father thinking?

But that is neither here nor there (unlike Sally Pinup, who, she's as much as said, is neither here nor there and, as well, is *both* here and there).

And the bungalow I live in is as actual as the air I breathe. I have injured myself on its walls.

And here I am—Denver Bowman Whitehouse (a name which, I'm certain, no one else on Earth possesses), living in a bungalow somewhere in upstate New York, and trying to find the killer of a beautiful apparition who calls herself Sally Pinup, and who tells me that her killer is named Bill, and that he inhabits her apartment and my bungalow all at the same time.

I've seen him. Bill. I've heard him speak. And I've tried to give him a good beating—succeeded in beating myself up instead. Both hands bear the beginnings of scars that will be with me forever.

Are these, now, my lucid moments? And if I had moments, perhaps many, that weren't lucid, would I remember them? Would I want to remember them?

Do the "unrecognizable memories" I've written about hint, perhaps broadly, that there's an "unrecognizable person" dwelling inside me? Someone who leads a life I'm not aware of?

And who the hell is it that, from time to time, whispers in my ear?

I have seen it reproduced like this. Have not questioned it. Perhaps I should. Yes, perhaps you should.

I'm a well-intentioned, somewhat overweight, fairly intelligent, though not at all imaginative person living what used to be a quiet life in a mid-size city in northern New York State.

The phone rings, once, twice—I answer on the third ring, say, "Hello, this is Denver Whitehouse," hear nothing. "Hello," I repeat, "this is Denver Whitehouse." Nothing. I hang up. Moments later, the phone rings again and I pick up the receiver on the first ring, though I say nothing.

After a few moments, I hear, "Hello?" It's a child's voice, a boy or girl of five or six or seven. "Hello?" it repeats.

"Hello," I say, "who is this? Why are you calling?"

"Because," the child says. "Just because."

"Because why?"

"Because I can. So I do."

I begin to believe, again, that I recognize the voice of this child, that I've heard it a million times.

"What's your name?" I ask.

"My name?" the child says. "You want to know my name?" He sounds surprised.

"Yes," I tell him, "I want to know your name."

"Skinky!" the child shouts. "My name is Skinky!"

"The *hell* it is," I shout back, and I hang up the phone.

EIGHT
Too many Worlds, too many Damned Worlds!

I know this, now: each of us owns a continuously expanding world full of memories. And sometimes, when we open the correct window, or go through the correct damned door, and then go through it again, the memories trickle back, in metamorphosis, and play chaotic hopscotch in our heads, in our universe, our world, our bungalow, our pastel apartment.

What do we see and hear, then, that our poor eyes and ears simply can't reveal to us?

I have been wondering a lot about my Uncle Cyrus, about what he called "The World of the Death Dancers." I let the phrase pass too easily, I think. I don't know why. Perhaps because it seemed so grimly whimsical (" . . . a little whimsicality," he said), perhaps because, with my not very active imagination, I couldn't simply see it as a very odd metaphor, could see it merely as what he called it, and, since that image was preposterous and grim, I couldn't deal with it: I needed, simply, to move away from it.

I wish Uncle Cyrus was here, at this moment. I wish he'd drive up in his monstrous Lincoln, park the damned anachronism in my driveway, get out, trudge up the walk to the porch, and knock on my door. His were always (always) four knocks, (a true memory): one soft, a pause, then three hard.

I know the questions I'd ask him.

I have been a week alone in the bungalow. In that week, a thousand unrecognizable memories have passed through my brain—a noisy parade of people and events that I recall, now, only enough to say that those people and events were here, behind my eyes, and that they have now blessedly departed.

Sally Pinup has been elsewhere. Bill, too. And even Abigail the kitten (who gave me strange comfort—her simple and musical meows that announced her existence: I actually called to her a couple of times several days ago).

I've searched the bungalow, in vain, for a hint of Sally's apartment, as if its past appearances left brittle bits and pieces behind.

And I've spoken to Sally, in her absence. Little bits of nothing, which is probably what can be expected from a man she sees only as "spiky puzzle pieces." For instance, "I'm not a bad person, Sally." Followed by, "I don't know why I said that; I've always believed that it's only people who are *actually* 'bad' who make such a childish proclamation. My brother, Thomas, was fond of killing small animals—squirrels and feral cats were his favorite targets. He said more than once, 'Well, why so squeamish, Denver? The fact that I kill these animals doesn't mean I'm a bad person.'"

And, "I don't know what Uncle Cyrus is all about. I don't think I actually remember him."

Sally, who was not here, but who may, I thought, have been listening, made no response.

Just now, I heard at the front door one soft knock, a pause, and three hard knocks.

It's several minutes later. The knocks at the door have been repeated a couple of times.

Machinations of the Unknown Holy

I did not answer his knocks. I simply turned around in my chair to find him at the center of the arched doorway that separates the living room from the dining room. "My God!" I muttered.

I was sitting at my desk, some fifteen feet from him.

"Don't be afraid of me," he said. "So many are; but it is unnecessary." He was taller than I remembered, and his bright white hair was very full, uncombed, almost wild; he wore a beautifully tailored gray suit and shiny black Oxfords, though, oddly, he wore no shirt beneath the suit, and he stood very still as he spoke, his gaze unnervingly steady and unblinking.

"Don't be afraid of me," he repeated. "So many are, but it is unnecessary."

He already said that, I thought.

"And you want to know why," he said; it wasn't a question. His gaze remained steady, unblinking, unnerving. "I'll tell you why."

I said, "I don't believe in you, Uncle Cyrus."

He said, "Don't be afraid of me. So many are, but it is unnecessary."

"You said that," I told him. "You said that already."

He repeated, "And you want to know why." It wasn't a question. "I'll tell you why."

His gaze remained steady and unblinking. He shoved his hands hard into his pants pockets, made his hands into fists in his pockets, looked quickly left, right, and then at me again. "So many are afraid—" he began.

"*I'm* not afraid of you," I interrupted.

"And I'll tell you why," he said. "Because *we* are the Death Dancers." He did a quick two-step, *click, clack, click, clack* on the oak floor, glanced at his shiny black Oxfords, clearly as if surprised, and looked at me again. "We are the Death Dancers," he proclaimed, "and many are afraid of us. I'll tell you why."

I realized, all at once, as if it was a revelation, that Uncle Cyrus had been dead for some time, had worked as an aluminum siding salesman in Hackensack, New Jersey, and had been painfully thin, not very bright, quick to laugh, especially at bad jokes, and slow to anger. A forgettable man. And the man standing beneath the archway that led to my dining room was *not* Uncle Cyrus.

"Who are you?" I asked.

"Who are *you?*" he said.

"That's an evasion," I said.

He did another quick *clickety-clack* two-step, hands still balled into fists in his pants pockets, looked with clear confusion at his black Oxfords, and then at me again: "I am one of a billion Dancers of Death," he declared with solemnity. "Many are fearful of us, but it's unnecessary."

"I'm not fearful of you," I said, as if I actually believed it.

"How do you know?" he said, his gaze steady and unblinking. "Do you believe I'm unreal? I'm not. I'm as real as the potatoes on your plate."

I looked steadily at him a moment, as if letting him know I was sizing him up, and then said, "Who is Sally Pinup?"

"*She,*" he said, "is the *potatoes* on your *plate*. The hellish potatoes on your plate." He did another two-step, looked confusedly at his Oxfords, and then at me. "The hellish potatoes on your damned plate."

He did another quick two-step.

I stood.

He cocked his head. "I am one of a billion or more Dancers of Death," he said. "Many are afraid of us, but it is unnecessary." Then, for the first time, he gave me a little grin. "Good Lord," he said, "have they no *mirrors?*"

He turned around, shrugged a little, glanced back at me with another small grin, did another quick two-step, made his way to the front door, and was gone.

You are very fearful of the Death Dancers, Whitehouse, whether you realize it, or not.

I cannot listen to the voice at my ear without becoming angry. It speaks to me in riddles that I'm sure are truths I cannot understand.

But, you see (as you've seen), I have no imagination at all and it's driving me bat-shit crazy.

NINE
Who can Believe the Pelican?

Not too long ago, Abigail the kitten appeared in the same archway where the *faux* Uncle Cyrus appeared, meowed quite musically three times, clearly to signal her existence, then trotted off and, like the *faux* Uncle Cyrus, was gone.

Sally Pinup was with me for a while after that: she was very much at my ear, if not in person (though she was never really here "in person," was she?).

"We are all chameleons, Denver," she whispered. "We are all Death Dancers and we are all chameleons—both the living and the . . . otherwise." She chuckled grimly.

"And what about me?"

Another chuckle. "None of this is about *you*, Denver, and none of it is about me (our particular world-shattering intimacy has been completed, hasn't it?), and none of it is about Bill, or Detective Quatrain, or Uncle Cyrus, or my mother and father. It is, all of it, every word of it, about Abigail the kitten, because her existence is undeniable. She has made sure of that."

"You're joking."

Another chuckle. "No," she said. "No, I'm not joking." Brief pause. "Ask yourself, 'What do I remember most clearly of all that has happened to me in the past months?' And your answer, of course, would have to be Abigail the kitten and her musical meows—her proclamations that she exists. Here she is, there she goes. Little Abigail the kitten. No fussy philosophizing for her. Just snippets of beautiful feline melody."

I said nothing. She chuckled once more. "You'll see me again. And I'll see you—mostly as spiky puzzle pieces, I'm sure. You're the greatest chameleon of us all, my friend. You're so good at it you even believe the fairy tales you tell *yourself!*" Brief pause, a quick, humorless chuckle, and then she added, "Oh, about my murderer—about Bill, Mr. Denver B. White-house"—she said my name with teasing playfulness—"when you get the chance, please, oh please, just, you know—kill the bastard!" Her voice became a hard whisper: "*Just* kill *the bastard for me!*"

OTTO'S CONUNDRUM

*I*t's a hell of a town, this crazy damned town! Winslow Homer thought, and scratched his nose hard, then his cheek, his chin, his nose again. Itches everywhere, always—on the impoverished skin, through the muscle, then into the bone and, at last, into what remained of his soul!

He studied his fingers in the awful light, pursed his paper-pale lips. Blood! A leak! *Shit!* Always these leaks—large and small, everywhere. Who knew why? What a bloody damned existence, this existence, though he loved it so, especially tonight, because tonight had been such high-screeching pleasure and deep-red romance.

He adored his mouth on nights such as this. He almost forgot the aches and the itches and the leaks on nights such as this.

And she lay so quiet and sultry, now, so exquisite, perfect, and attainable in her silent ignorance, her first and final taste of a new and glorious existence that he could not let her keep (without paying *the price*).

Pity. Pity.

Pity.

John Ortne loved *The Eatin' Hole*, especially just before dawn, when the
sky was the color of aluminum and the black silhouettes of the creatures
of the pitch-dark disappeared slowly beyond the western horizon, and he
could safely watch them from behind the diner's thick, narrow windows,
hot black coffee in a yellow cup warming his hands, the pungent odors of
eggs and bacon, sausage and home fries filling the place like smoke.

"Some people think they should be allowed to kill more," he said to red-
haired Donna J., seated across from him in the green booth and holding
her own cup of coffee (which she drank with lots of cream and three
sugars) in her long, graceful hands. He nodded at the hulking shapes of
the receding silhouettes.

She said, "They tried that, remember?" and lifted her coffee cup; she
was especially delectable, he thought, when she brought coffee, or Coke,
or eggs, or practically anything to her mouth and opened her lips. "Two,
three years ago," she added. "It didn't work."

He nodded. "Yeah, you told me."

"Too many ended up dead," she said.

He nodded again, brought his coffee to his mouth, hesitated, enjoyed
the moment that her coffee passed between her lips and onto her bright
red tongue. She noticed, said, "You're so predictable."

"I know," he said, and added, "It's because you're so *un*predictable." He
smiled, sipped his coffee.

She smiled, too. She really liked his sense of humor: it made up for
his nose. She reached into her voluminous bright yellow purse, retrieved
a couple of nickels, popped them into the miniature jukebox under the
window, said, "Whatchoo wanna hear?"

"Anything," he said, thought a moment and added, "How 'bout *Town
Without Pity*." He nodded at the miniature jukebox. "They got that?"

She flipped through the selections, said, "Yeah, they got it," and keyed in A-05.

The waitress, a dark-haired, gum-chewing dumpling of a woman named Sally, came over: "You got a call, Johnny," she told him, and inclined her head backward to indicate a black payphone on the wall near the cash register. "It's Otto."

The miraculous voice of Gene Pitney washed over them—" . . . *Why do people hurt us so/Only those in love would know/What a town without pity can do!*"—but John realized he wouldn't be able to enjoy it:

Otto was calling.

Otto hated phones. He couldn't see a man's eyes through them, and the man's voice was always just a strangled electrical squawk; it was never a voice capable of being judged, considered and evaluated. "Otto?" he heard.

"Yeah, sure, this is Otto," he said.

"What's kickin'?" Otto heard.

"*Kickin'*?" he said. "*Kickin'*! And what is that—another unremarkable colloquialism, my friend?"

"Sorry," he heard, then, after a moment, "What's up?"

He sighed, got a faint whiff of his own malodorous breath as it wafted over him from the telephone's transmitter, crinkled his nose, said, "Now there is yet another one with which to somehow deal!"

"You mean there's another body?"

"Yes, my limpid friend," Otto said. "Another body. Dead and gone, in my judgement. And one very much in its prime."

"It's someone who's young, you mean?"

"And delectable, yes, he has said to me, in his way."

"*Who* has said to you, Otto?"

"One of our chief malefactors; Winslow Homer, of course."

"I'll be right over," Otto heard.

"No, no, not that," he said, "please, for it is unnecessary, now. Go straight away to his home, the home of Winslow Homer."

"Gotcha!"

Winslow Homer was seated—oddly and uncomfortably, John thought—on an overstuffed, dark green footstool near an ornate, blazing fireplace; he had his long thin back turned, was wearing a dark red great coat, and, with a stiff wave of his hand, when John entered the huge, poorly lighted room, made it clear he wasn't going to turn around and that John should stay put. "State your business, please, Mr. Ortne," he said in a very deep and melodious *basso profundo* that sounded very strange coming from his reed-thin body.

John said, "We've gotten a complaint."

"Really?" Winslow Homer said. "How not-at-all unique: it's what makes the world go around."

"Huh?"

"*Complaints*, Mr. Ortne. They make the world go around. Without them, nothing would get accomplished, don't you agree? The trains wouldn't run on time and everyone's breakfast eggs would end up runny."

"That's not the kind of complaint I'm talking about," John said.

A small, unnerving chuckle came from Winslow Homer. Beneath his dark red great coat, his body shook. "Indeed," he intoned. "Indeed." Another stiff wave of the hand clearly signified what the previous wave had signified.

John said, "I'll stay right where I am."

"Indeed, "Winslow Homer said again. "Indeed."

John said, "We received a complaint that there's a dead woman here."

Winslow Homer said, "Oh piffle, Mr. Ortne. The world is overrun by dead women. If there were one here, it would be no great matter."

"Then you're admitting it?"

Another unnerving chuckle: John wanted to say, *Oh, stop that!* but said nothing. Winslow Homer said, "I admit *everything*, Mr. Ortne. I admit and confess all the sins of man and beast—even those sins I have yet to commit. I happily confess all the sins of creation." Pause. "No, stay where you are!"

"I am," John said.

Winslow Homer said, "No, Mr. Ortne, you were contemplating the myriad possibilities."

"Huh?"

"You were thinking you could rush me and subdue me."

"No I wasn't!"

Chuckle. "Do you have any *idea* who you're talking to, Mr. Ortne?"

"You're changing the subject," John said.

"Indeed," Winslow Homer said.

John took a deep, preparatory breath, then said, "Can you show me where you've put this dead woman?"

Winslow Homer shook his head, chuckled again, lifted his hand, lowered it, chuckled yet again: "She has followed off," he said.

"Followed off?"

"Yes. Followed off. She is, Mr. Ortne, no more now as never."

"Shit," John said. "I don't understand that."

"Of course you don't," said Winslow Homer. "You understand it no better than a galloping badger understands Easter eggs."

John pursed his lips. He didn't know how to respond. This creature followed all of his words—John's words—with gibberish.

Winslow Homer went on, "Go and find another dead woman, Mr. Ortne. Whoever it is, she will do you just as well."

"But I'm not looking for just *any* dead woman, Mr. Homer."

"Oh, but surely that's not true. How could you *not* be looking for just *any* dead woman? You have, I think you'll admit, no name for the dead woman you seek, and no description, either. Nor do you have the proximate cause of her death, its time, or the probable location of her alluring body."

"Oh, but I gotcha there, Mr. Homer—"

"By all the repellent saints," Winslow Homer cut in, "you are as dim-witted as a geriatric house fly."

John took another deep breath. He was getting nowhere. This man was sucking him in with doubletalk and gibberish. John said, "I won't allow this discussion to continue at this . . . this . . . " He was stuck.

"Yes, Mr. Ortne?"

"At this level."

Winslow Homer shook his head and raised his hand once more; but now, he beckoned to John with his forefinger.

"Huh?" John said.

"I want you to come over here," Winslow Homer said. The fire in the fireplace flickered brightly.

"Why?" John said.

Winslow Homer said, "Because I want to see your face."

"Well, maybe," John said, "you could just, you know . . . turn around and look at it."

Winslow Homer shook his head again. "I need this warmth." He held his hands out toward the fireplace. "Come here, please."

John said, "I see no need . . . "

"She," Winslow Homer cut in, "this comely dead woman you seek, though for only the devil knows what purposes, is somewhere in the cellar." He nodded to indicate the floor: the fire flickered brightly again, and he continued, "Oh, I don't remember *where*. That's hardly my concern, is it?" Short pause. "So go and find her. She is, after all, your stated reason for coming to this house. I certainly didn't *invite* you."

John shook his head, though Winslow Homer wasn't looking at him, and said, with a little catch in his voice, "Not entirely."

Winslow Homer shot back, "Oh, be specific, Mr. Ortne. Don't

throw terse, meaningless sentences at me as if I were some kind of dart board."

John nodded once more. "I came here, Mr. Homer," he said, again with a little catch in his voice, "because I'm the law in this town."

A deep, gut-wrenching chuckle erupted from Winslow Homer.

"And you," John added, "are a lawbreaker."

Winslow Homer's deep chuckle grew quickly to a high, harsh, screeching rattle: his emaciated body shook beneath his dark red great coat: his right arm flew up, then down, up again, then down, and, at last, slapped his knee.

John closed his eyes a moment. *Now what?* he wondered. Then he shouted, so Winslow Homer could hear him above his rattling laughter and knee slaps, "Do I need a key for the cellar door?"

He had to pee. The need had crept up quickly on him as he descended the cellar stairs in the nearly pitch-dark, and held tight to the scarred wooden railing, which was as cold as Winslow Homer's laughter ("Have you got a flashlight, Mr. Homer?" . . . "And to what possible use, Mr. Ortne, would I put such a device?").

What in the name of heaven was he doing here? This was no place for Mama Ortne's fair-haired boy. And what good was the silver badge he carried when no one in this Godforsaken town respected it? ("What I mean, Mr. Ortne, is that once you're in the cellar you will have no need of artificial light.")

Shit, too! John thought. *Skinny damned vampire suck-bomb!* Always speaking in riddles and gibberish, and only because (it was as obvious as Jimmy Durante's nose) he so very much needed to sound . . . needed to sound . . . What was the word?

He took a couple of careful, graceless steps down the cellar stairs, hand tight on the railing.

What was the fucking word? Oh yes—*erudite!* That was the word. Skinny damned vampire suck-bomb always needed to sound *erudite!* And what was more pathetic than that? Nothing! Only fools, or the dead, or, for God's sake, *dead fools* needed to sound *erudite.*

He took another step down the cellar stairs, then another, and another, hand tight on the railing all the while.

Suddenly, a sliver the size of a hefty sewing needle pushed sharply through the edge of his palm and made him scream.

And when the scream was done, he heard from above, "Oh quiet down, would you!"

He looked up, wanted to shout a rebuke, an epithet, something rude and coarse, and he wanted to shout it with finality and authority, but he gave a long, trembling sigh, instead, because of the pain, he told himself, grabbed hold of the quarter-inch of sliver poking from his hand and, after a deep breath, yanked the entire sliver out and screamed again. And when it was done, he heard only silence from above.

The cavernous cellar was a place of surreal, dim light, soft-edged shadows, and the stinging odor of skunk.

John crinkled up his nose. *Jesus Hopping Christ! Skunk! In Winslow Homer's fucking cellar! Skunk!* He hadn't expected it, had expected the overwhelming stench of decay, the breath-stopping smell of corruption, the fetid miasma of death, not simply the stinging odor of skunk. It seemed odd, anticlimactic, inappropriate, especially to this place. And it made his eyes water. He rubbed them, to no avail, put his hand lightly over his mouth and nose, looked about. *Whatever it is,* he told himself, *it has to be dead, anyway.*

He saw formless shapes in the surreal, dim light. It was a surreal light because it had no apparent source, and because it was a sickly combination of various shades of green—lime green, olive green, olive drab, fungus green, leprous green, soylent green. It moved lazily, like a fog, although the place was as warm as a summer attic, and that, in itself, was odd.

Something grows here, he realized, and became aware, for the first time, that the cellar floor was made of dirt. "Jesus," he said, "dirt," and bent over, fingered some of it, found it greasy, almost hot, threw it down, straightened quickly.

He heard from above, in Winslow Homer's melodious *basso profundo,* "Don't go poking around in the dirt, my friend! You'll find it very, very familiar and, therefore, very, very unpleasant!" and John sighed again, shook his head slowly, miserably, wanted to respond with finality and authority, wanted to run from the place, drive all night back to Pittsburgh and spend the rest of his life around steel mills and pleasantly ordinary people. But here he was—in the city of Nyxon, among creatures he told himself he did not understand, creatures that merely tolerated him (he knew), or found him vaguely entertaining, perhaps—creatures that, in a moment of anger or futility or, hell, simple amusement, could tear his head clean off and shove it up his ass.

Creatures like Winslow Homer, the all-but-human entity above, who, at that very moment, John realized, was peering at him through the wooden floor. Who could possibly say what was happening in what remained of that creature's brain, other than the unending need for murder, which was its greatest pleasure, followed by something the creature called "sleep"?

John lifted his head and called toward the cellar ceiling, "You've got a skunk loose down here!"

He got no answer. He lowered his head.

("Did the woman you murdered have a name, Mr. Homer?"

"I didn't ask.")

Shit, he didn't ask!

("Why *would* I ask, Mr. Ortne?")

Skunk smell and pale green fog and greasy hot floor. What in the name of all that might be holy was he *doing* here?

He lowered his head and saw her, then, not far off, lying naked, half-in and half-out of the hot earth, and swathed in the hellish, moving fog:

She took his breath away, made him forget the stinging, suffocating odor of skunk, the fog.

After a long, long moment, he whispered, "Jesus!" but stayed put; from where he stood, she was more a beautiful illusion than reality; she was a wonderful passing moment he could hold onto forever if he merely stayed where he was; if he moved closer, she would be transformed into something hideous. Because she *was* something hideous. Because, in truth, he was seeing only what she *wanted* him to see.

"Christ!" he breathed. This place, he thought—the cellar, the house, Nyxon itself—was the locus of nightmare posing, for some of its inhabitants, as a land of dreams.

He heard from above, "You may be sure of *that*, my friend."

He sighed and took a step forward.

And, swiftly as a cat, the alluring, naked woman lying supine in the earth, sat bolt upright—an act which pushed John backward a step, then two, then, as she rose, wearing a smile no living thing could possibly accomplish, pushed him back another step, and then another.

She said, in a tight soprano that bore within it the soft, insistent and grinding warble of death, "This is no great matter, Mr. Ortne. I am only *late!*"

And he heard, from above, "She is someone to be reckoned with, my friend." Maniacal laughter followed, then, "I'd suggest you run long and hard!"

And so he did.

Donna J., a cup of coffee with cream and two sugars at her lips, said, "You take it all too seriously, John. Though I suppose you can't help it."

"Huh?" he said.

"Never mind," she said, smiled a little, as if, oddly, in reassurance, and sipped her coffee.

He was seated opposite her at *The Eatin' Hole* and was desultorily pushing a plateful of French fries around with his fork: he wasn't looking at her—he had his eyes on the fries, and he didn't like what he was seeing: "Of course I take it seriously," he said, and jabbed a fry with his fork, looked at it a moment, popped it into his mouth, and made a face. "Jesus," he said, "it tastes like tar!"

"Like tar?" Donna J. said, though if she were merely repeating his words.

He nodded and pushed the plate toward the center of the table. "Yeah. Tar."

Donna J. smiled again and nodded at the counter to indicate a very tall and painfully thin man dressed in a white T-shirt, baggy jeans, and a white, grease-spattered apron (it had the words "Nifty Dead Poodle" emblazoned across it in red): he was gathering plates at the counter. "See him?"

"Uh-huh," John said.

Donna J. turned her head to look at John again, "Well that's Gandor. He's the Thursday cook. Everything he makes is fantastic, except the French fries. No one knows why, but they always taste like tar."

"Well, shit, why didn't you say something when I ordered them, for Christ's sake. I wasted a buck-fifty."

She shook her head, leaned forward and said, voice low, as if sharing a secret, "I didn't say anything because he's Sally's brother, and if I'd said anything, she would'a bopped me with her order pad."

"You're kidding!"

She shook her head again, said, "Nope," straightened, and nodded at his strawberry milkshake, which he hadn't touched. "You can drink that. I guarantee it's fantastic. Gandor really knows his way around milkshakes. Ham on rye, too. And mashed potatoes. Best damned cook in the city, except when it comes to French fries."

John answered directly to no one, although he had been hired by the man named Otto to "oversee events in our little city," a phrase which, when John asked for an explanation, Otto explained meant, "Your presence and, after a fashion, your diligence, will remind the citizenry of Nyxon that a tiny semblance of order, or even its *illusion*, is always better than toying with the chaos created by the complete lack of order. Do you understand?"

John shook his head and said, "I'm not sure. Probably not."

Otto said, "Of course," paused and added, "Well now, let me put it more simply." His large head nodded quickly a few times and he went on, "John, I'm sure you agree that anarchy and chaos are dandy. In fact, they're delightful. They remind us that there really is no God, only pretenders." He cocked his large head. "Do you understand *that?*"

John said, "Yes, I actually think I do."

"Good," Otto said, lit a cigarette, withdrew it from between his wide, impossibly thin lips, held it near his cheek, and continued, "But when there is absolutely no structure whatsoever, only chaos, we put ourselves at the mercy of the great and uncompromising universe, and so, into the maelstrom we must toss a tin cup."

"Or a tin badge?"

Otto smiled, a gesture which, on his flat face, seemed to mean nothing. "Or a tin badge, yes."

John didn't much care for Otto; probably, John realized, because Otto was so clearly aware of his superiority in all things—especially things of the intellect—and also because Otto, though completely human, showed about as much emotion and humanness as a Jello mold.

"Are you going back to Winslow Homer's house?" Donna J. asked at *The Eatin' Hole.*

John shook his head. "Not on your life. I mean, I did what Otto wanted—what I was hired to do. I went there. I asked questions, I made a pest of myself. So maybe next time, if Mr. Homer thinks he can just . . ." He shook his head again, in clear frustration, then swiped one hand across the table. "Next time, if he thinks he can just do *that*—what he did, I mean—then maybe he'll think twice."

"But probably not?" said Donna J.

John nodded dismally. "Yeah. Probably not."

He lay un-quietly in his double bed, in his two-story white colonial, in what he'd been assured was Nyxon's "safe zone" (a mile and a half from the city proper), without lights or music or distraction, other than his large, marmalade cat, whom he'd named "Stuff," who, he thought, had acquired *him* rather than vice versa, and who, at that moment, was not-very silently stalking some night creature in the bedroom across the hall. The bedroom's door was open and John could see movement in the room, though he wasn't at all sure it was Stuff he was seeing; it could easily be Stuff's prey, he realized, because the prey of cats in Nyxon often reached alarming proportions.

"Stuff?" he called. The thing he was looking at in the nearly pitch dark stopped moving and, a second later, John could see its eyes shining dimly. "Good," John said. "Sorry. Didn't mean to disturb you. Continue."

The eyes vanished.

John put his hands behind his head and looked at the ceiling: he saw little, the suggestion of a light fixture, and something very dark and small near it, which John didn't recognize (although he'd grown accustomed, day or night, to seeing things in the house that he didn't recognize).

He wondered what year this was and found himself very depressed that he couldn't remember—did the year end in a seven or an eight? Neither?

He heard a sudden screech, terse and very high-pitched, from the other bedroom. It wasn't the screech of a cat, he knew. He closed his eyes a moment, whispered, "Good Lord, why in the *hell* do I live here?" then said aloud, "You're a fine hunter, Stuff."

"I want to stay with you for a while," said Donna J., at The Eatin' Hole, a half-hour before sunrise the following morning, as they ate breakfast— she, a tall stack of French toast, real maple syrup, home fries, ham slices, and a large, freshly squeezed orange juice, and he eggs over easy, white toast and black coffee. He liked most of the food at The Eatin' Hole, but wasn't up to eating much this morning—though he didn't know why— and she had once told him that the food was "edible, though barely," but, considering the alternatives, it was the best place to eat in the entire tri-county area.

He said, as he diddled with his eggs, and watched the runny yolks move in a desultory fashion around his deep-red plate, "You know you can't do that, Donna. You know you can't do that." His tone was full of resignation and sadness. "It's not allowed, it's just not allowed, and we both know why." He focused on his desultory egg yolks, wanted to add, "At least I *think* we both know why," but said, instead, "*Do* we know why?"

"Of course we do," she said, and popped a piece of French toast into her mouth. "Oh, hell, John," she continued, and reached across the table to touch his hand, which made him look up at her. "I *like* this place. I *like*

Nyxon. And I'll tell you something else—I like you, too. A whole lot." She cocked her head in a comely way, and added, "My God, I may even *love* you! So how on earth"—quick smile—"could I do anything to *harm* you?"

She's so damned pale, he thought, looked down at her long, thin, very white hand, light blue veins, and blood-red nail polish. Then he looked at her again and said, "You're really quite beautiful."

"Lucky, too," she said, and squeezed his hand "And so are you," she added. "Lucky, I mean."

"I am?"

"Yes." She popped another piece of French toast into her mouth, and continued, "To have *me* in your"—she chewed, swallowed—"life, of course!" She gave him her biggest, broadest smile, open-mouthed, full of deep-red tongue and bright white teeth. And how very sad, he thought, not for the first time, that her eyes did not seem to participate in that smile.

"Yes," he said, and patted her hand a little, "I'm very lucky indeed to have you in my life."

"Eat more!" she exclaimed, changing the subject abruptly; she nodded briskly at his plate. "And not that slop. Get something hearty. Get some meat, John. Here"—she withdrew her hand and picked up a ham slice, held it between her thumb and forefinger—"eat one of these. You really should, you know. Eating the way you do just isn't natural." She dropped the ham slice in his plate, so it all but covered his runny eggs, then bent over the table a little, stared a moment at the ham slice, the bits of viscous egg yolk at its edges, said, "Now *that's* food!" sat back, looked out of the window at the rust-red horizon, declared, "Gotta go!" stood quickly, and left the diner nearly at a run.

John watched the door close slowly on its bright hydraulics, saw, out of the corner of his eye, Sally the waitress sigh a little, looked at her, shrugged, then, after staring at the ham slice in his plate for a minute, decided he wasn't very hungry and went home.

Otto almost always called between four and five in the afternoon, whether or not he had anything to say, and today was no exception: it was four thirty-five when the phone rang. John picked up the receiver, said, "Hello, Otto," and Otto said, "Yes, of course," and, after what seemed like a long moment, added, "There's been talk about your girlfriend, John. People have overheard you making plans. You know the rules."

"Shit, Otto, we haven't made any *plans*. Whoever told you that was lying."

"The only liars here in Nyxon," Otto declared, "are those to whom it matters to lie. My source was not one of those souls."

"Uh-huh," John said, "whatever that means," and could think of nothing to add.

"But that's not why I called, of course," Otto went on. "I called because we have a matter that requires your urgent attention."

"Me and my tin cup, you mean?"

"Tin cup?"

"Forget it."

"Surely," Otto said, and finished with, "Meet me at Desolation Hall at six thirty, please. Don't be late."

"I'm never late," John said.

"Indeed," Otto said, and hung up.

Stuff came over as John hung up the phone, looked into John's face, gave him one of his quick, questioning meows, cocked his head, and John said soothingly, "Everything's all right. It's just Otto's way. Nothing to worry about, my friend."

Stuff blinked a few times, hesitated a moment, then moved off quickly, gracefully, and low to the floor, as if in anticipation of prey.

John drove a Ford. Everyone in his family drove a Ford. His father, rest his soul, had driven a Ford, and so had his mother (though she was no longer allowed to drive), all four of his grandparents, as well, his brothers and sister, too, and most of his cousins. His was a Ford family through and through.

The Ford he drove in Nyxon was a dark brown coupe; it boasted sturdy running boards, a two-part rear window and windshield, *Flo-through* ventilation, push-button AM tube radio (though reception in Nyxon was iffy at best), an on-the-column, three-speed shift, and a manual choke that never failed.

He loved that Ford. It was, he told Donna J. once, "simple, serviceable, and sexy."

But it was also underpowered, and, at certain hours of the night, in and around Nyxon, that was unfortunate and reckless, at times even suicidal.

And John thought, as he drove the winding, narrow road—Desolation Road—toward what had come to be known as Desolation Hall, past huge, decrepit houses that some would believe had been abandoned— though they were anything but empty—and down apparently endless stretches bordered on both sides by nothing but wide, dead oaks, past hitchhikers with thumbs stuck too far out, and grins too impossibly wide, he decided he would have to replace the Ford soon, because tonight was just the kind of night that Otto had warned him about time and again—a moonless, starry night, the sort of night that The Blood People drove Desolation Road, too.

Maybe a '59 Ford Galaxy, he thought, as he floored the accelerator and the coupe moved with reluctant speed past a particularly insistent hitchhiker whose thighs were far more appealing than her skull.

Eight cylinders, two hundred and fifty horsepower, three hundred foot pounds of torque. Speed, speed, and more speed!

And then he heard, even above the whine of the Ford's straight six, *their* engines—the engines of The Blood People, low and guttural and, in that moment, thankfully distant.

But the moment was bound to be brutally quick, he knew. And Desolation Hall was still a good five minute drive, even at the coupe's top speed. "Shit!" he whispered, and heard, from the empty passenger seat, "Don't panic, John. Just keep your cool, okay?"

He looked toward the voice, saw, as he'd expected, only the seat and the window, nodded, said "Okay!" and glanced quickly in his rearview mirror, watched headlights round a curve maybe half a mile behind him. "Okay," he said again, and the voice from the passenger seat said, "You can do this, John. You know you can!"

"Sure I do," he said, and floored the accelerator. He didn't take his eyes off the road to glance at the speedometer, but knew, from the ragged low growl of the engine, that he was nearing its top speed of eighty, in third gear—not fast enough.

The voice from the passenger seat said, "You need to slow down, John."

"Huh?" he said, eyes fixed on the narrow road, the line of dead oaks on either side, the now more-than-occasional hellish hitchhiker. "Slow down?" he shouted. "No way!"

"You really do need to slow down right now, John!" the voice from the passenger seat said, "If you don't, you'll lose this race!"

He glanced very quickly at the passenger seat, saw nothing, as he'd expected, focused hard on the road again, took a quick glance in the rearview mirror, at the headlights there—closer by half than what they had been moments earlier, so their glare filled the interior of the Ford with cold light.

"*Now*, John!" cried the voice from the passenger seat.

He quickly looked at the road, saw no more than he'd seen moments earlier.

"*Now*, for Christ's sake!" cried the voice from the passenger seat.

He nodded once, whispered, "Yes!" because, Jesus, she was *always* right, and took his foot off the accelerator; the car slowed immediately—from eighty, to seventy, to fifty-five, forty-five . . .

Another quick glance in the rearview mirror showed him only blinding white light, and he heard only the throaty, deafening roar of massive V8's. *But this time*, he thought, *she's wrong!*

He turned his gaze to the road again, touched the accelerator—fifty-fifty-five . . . , saw something rectangular and dark green moving slowly into the road ahead, not more than a hundred feet away! He hit the brake. The Ford swerved hard right; he let off on the brake—the Ford drifted back, but now his vision was obscured by road dust rising around the car. "Goddammit all!"

"*Left, left, left!*" shouted the voice from the passenger seat.

He nodded quickly, veered left, felt the right side of the Ford graze something metallic, looked quickly, saw a pair of close-set headlights speed by, the words "John Deere" in gold on a green background—"Jesus!" he breathed.

The hellish machines so close behind him weren't so lucky. The thunder of their engines became the thudding roar of gas tanks going up—*One! Two! Three!*—in a fireball.

He looked in the rearview mirror, saw the conflagration, smiled, heard, from the passenger seat, "Next time, don't second-guess me, John, even for a moment."

Otto said, "You are responsible for that, aren't you." He nodded north, at a fire-red glow at the horizon.

John grinned a little, as if pleased with himself, then shrugged. "Blood People," he said, and grinned again. "They're nothing to worry about, now."

"I see," said Otto.

John looked questioningly at him.

Otto said, "And much more than you might believe. It's my job, after all. And you do realize, don't you, that The Blood People rather enjoyed what you did to them. They didn't *like* it, and they'll want their revenge, of course, because"—he shrugged a little—"they're The Blood People, after all. But they did enjoy it! You do realize that?"

"Sure I do," he said, though it was a lie.

Otto harrumphed. "You have a lot to learn, my foolish friend."

John sighed. "Doesn't everybody."

"Indeed," said Otto.

Desolation Hall was a circular, wooden, three-story structure without windows and only one door—the entrance framed to the left and right by two softly shimmering blue lights. Tonight, from where John and Otto stood, the building was simply a huge black shape against the starry sky.

John nodded at it. "Are we going in there?"

"No," Otto said.

John cocked his head: "I don't understand," he said. "Why did you ask me to meet you here?"

A not-very customary chuckle erupted from Otto, and he said, "I simply wanted you to experience Desolation Road on a night such as this." He lifted his head to the sky, then looked at John, again.

"You *what?*" John said. "Good Lord, I could have been killed."

"But you weren't, of course," Otto said. "And that's the point. You listened to the woman." Short pause. "Not that your passing, so to speak, would have been of much import."

John sighed.

Otto said, "Young man, *death* is the very soul and purpose of this place."

John thought a moment, then said, "You mean it's the soul and purpose of Desolation Hall?"

Otto pursed his lips, as if in annoyance, pulled a piece of folded paper from his back pocket, said, "Read this. And read it more than once. Read it a dozen times, at least. And pay very close attention to *every* word. Your . . . place here, in Nyxon, and your very soul, hang in the balance," handed the paper to John and walked quickly to his car, a four-door Chevy parked near John's Ford coupe. He looked back and shouted, "One thing we don't much tolerate around here, John, is bullshit! It just ruins everyone's *fun!*" Then he got into his Chevy and roared off down Desolation Road.

John scanned the piece of paper quickly, saw little because of the dim light, shrugged, stuck the piece of paper into his back pocket, went to his Ford coupe and drove home at top speed.

"I'd like you to come over," John said into the phone. "Can you do that, or should I come and get you?"

"I don't think it would be smart to come and get me at this hour of the night," Donna J. answered.

"Yeah, yeah," he said, "I know. It doesn't matter. I'll come and get you if you want."

"It's not necessary," said Donna J. "I'll be there soon."

"Good," John said.

A moment's silence, then Donna J. said, "Am I staying the night?"

"Yes," he said. "You're staying the night."

"Good!" she said.

When he hung up, he heard from the living room, just off his kitchen, "That's the stupidest thing you've ever done."

He nodded, wondered if the woman could see the nod, said, "Yes, I know," and, minutes later, Donna J., all-but unencumbered by clothing, arrived at the front door.

He looked open-mouthed at her.

She gave him a slight, but massively erotic grin: "Are you going to invite me in?" she said.

"Yes," he said. "I certainly am."

And he did.

———————

But, hell, she didn't stay the night, mostly because of the prodding insistence and cajoling of the anonymous and invisible *other woman* in his life—who had come to him six months earlier and who had saved his ass more than once.

A pouting and clearly next-to-explosive Donna J. left his house at not quite twelve midnight, and as he watched her move deliciously—despite her anger—to the beginning of the fifty-foot stone walkway that led to his front door, and then vanish into the darkness, the *other woman* in his life tapped his shoulder, which made him turn his head quickly to catch a glimpse of her (though he had never caught a glimpse of her), and whispered into his ear, "You're not quite as stupid as you want people to believe, are you?"

He sighed. "Probably not," he said.

And she said, "Do you want to know my name?"

This surprised him because he'd never thought to ask her name: he cocked his head, as if in confusion and said, "Shit, I think I do, yes. Tell me your name."

She chuckled a bit; it was pleasant and infectious, and he smiled: "Your choice," she said.

"My choice?"

"Yes. Of course. Choose a name. Any name. And that will be the name you will call me and know me by. How could it be otherwise?"

"I don't understand," he said.

"You don't need to," she said.

He sighed. She was right. He didn't need to understand. There were lots of things he supposed he didn't really *need* to understand here in this very, very strange city, he realized—things about the city itself, mostly, and (Yes, he realized) things about himself (memories of his past life seemed to come to an abrupt end, and he didn't know why, and when he tried to envision his future, here in Nyxon, it was as if he were looking at it through cloud). "Okay," he said. "How about Sheila?"

A moment's silence, then, "I don't like it," she said. "It's too . . . elastic."

"Elastic? What does that mean? You told me . . ."

"Try another one," she said. "Sheila doesn't work for me."

He sighed again. "Okay, okay," he said, thought a moment and added, "How does Gwen sound?"

"Gwen?" Another chuckle, less pleasant, more caustic. "Do you think I'm as old as the hills? No, Gwen is not right." She sounded petulant. "Try again."

He pursed his lips. "Abigail?" he said.

She laughed; it was very high pitched, almost painful to his ears. "Maybe you see me riding a horse into the sunset. No, no, no. Abigail! Abigail! It's ludicrous, *jejune*, absurd! Try again."

And so he came up with one female name after another—Nancy, Janice, Rosemary and Linda, Michelle, Elizabeth and Melissa, for instance—and she shot down each one with a chuckle, or a laugh, or a deep and echoing sigh, until, at last, she said, "You're no good with names, are you, John?"

"Apparently not," he said, and she said, "There's a reason for that, I suppose," paused and added, "Then why don't you just call me Abercrombie and we'll both be happy."

"Abercrombie?" he said. "Are you serious?"

But he got no answer, though he said "Are you there?" time and again into the darkness, until, finally, he shrugged, sighed, and went to bed.

Otto called at six and woke him from a dream of hayrides, Christmas trees, and soft ice cream, which encompassed all the comforts of his childhood, which seemed very distant, indeed. After John's barely audible and weary, "Hello," Otto said, "Have you perused the piece of paper I gave you? If not, then do it at once and get back to me before you eat breakfast."

"Okay," John said.

"I'll be waiting," Otto said, and hung up.

"What piece of paper?" John whispered to himself, and went back to sleep at once.

He dreamt of being caught in a water-filled tunnel deep within the earth and when he woke he found, to his horror, that Stuff the cat was on his face, purring loudly, licking his forehead, suffocating him. He tried desperately to pull the cat off, but its claws were firmly implanted in the pillow: he tried yelling, "Stuff, stop it!" but could barely hear himself through the thick fur covering his mouth and nose; he tried rolling over—surely he, a one hundred and ninety pound man, was at least as strong as a house cat—but that didn't work, either, because everything below his chest seemed oddly useless, beyond his control, and, when panic appeared inevitable, he called out, "Abercrombie! I need you!"— which sounded like gibberish mumbled into a sponge, so he felt certain that Abercrombie, wherever she was, wasn't going to hear him, either, but, a moment later, he heard from near his left ear, "He *loves* you, John! Simply love him back, of course!"

"Umf?" John said.

"Stroke him," Abercrombie whispered. "Show him he's a good boy!"

"Umf!" John said again, because he didn't completely understand what Abercrombie was saying, but he brought his right hand slowly up and, gasping in vain for air, stroked the back of Stuff's head and mumbled "Good boy!" again, and again, until, almost magically, Stuff leaped from the bed and trotted off to the adjoining room. John took a deep, much-needed breath and whispered on the exhale, "What in the hell was *that* all about?" and heard, at his ear, "You expected maybe Garfield in this place?"

An hour later, he was on the phone with Otto.

"I don't understand," John said, "what's written on this piece of paper you gave me."

"Of course you don't," Otto said. "You're not meant to understand it.

At least not at first." Pause, then, "Just think this: think bullshit versus reality." Slight pause. "No, think *utter* bullshit versus *fantastic* reality."

John sighed. "So it's a riddle?"

"No, it's a conundrum." Brief pause. "I'm sure that if you check your Merriam Webster . . ."

"I don't need a dictionary, Otto. I know what the hell conundrum means."

"Good," Otto said. "Then when you've successfully dealt with this one, you'll know what you *need* to know—the difference between utter bullshit and fantastic reality. And your place in it."

"My place in it?" John said. "My place in what?"

"Good Lord," Otto said. "I'm speaking to a stone cold moron!" He paused very briefly and added, "In utter bullshit, of course. Or in fantastic reality."

"I doubt that," Otto said, chuckled quickly and added, "Which is precisely why you've been given this particular conundrum. And also because some of us aren't really sure you know what you're doing here. In Nyxon."

"Huh?" John said.

"Prove that you *do* know what you're doing here, John. If you don't, then you'll be, unfortunately, one of the lost. Forever."

John looked up "conundrum" in his Webster's Collegiate and found that it actually *was* a riddle: The dictionary definition read:

> Conundrum: noun:
> 1: a riddle whose answer is or involves a pun
> 2 a: a question or problem having only a conjectural answer
>   b: an intricate and difficult problem

Otto's "conundrum", John thought, didn't seem to involve a "pun" (which, he remembered from his high school English teacher, Mr. Fredrick, was the "most despised form of humor"), though it did involve a question, and it appeared to be quite a difficult problem:

Otto's conundrum read:

> *If chaos cannot exist without order, can order exist without chaos?*
>
> *And if chaos and order do coexist, what is the purpose of, or sense in, the existence of either?*
>
> *And if there is no purpose of or sense in either, with what are we left in Nyxon?*
>
> *Clue: You must, of course, consult the Master of Chaos Himself before you can successfully deal with* this *problem:*
>
> *An archaeologist uncovers two sarcophagi in what was once known as Mesopotamia. He takes the lids off the sarcophagi and discovers two naked bodies—male and female—perfectly preserved. "Good Lord," whispers the archaeologist, "I've discovered Adam and Eve!" How did he know?*
>
> *John, if your poor intellectual powers cannot successfully deal with that incredibly non-difficult problem by the tenth of the month, then you will find yourself walking Desolation Road alone on the first moonless, starry night thereafter. Sorry, but to release you into the world from whence you were plucked would, for reasons of security, be ill-advised.*
>
> —Otto

"Abercrombie?" John called out. "Are you there?" He got no answer, so he repeated himself once, then again, and again, but still got no answer. Shit, where was she? He thought she was supposed to be near him always—a sort of guardian angel (though no one in Nyxon had told him as much; she simply "appeared" (after a fashion) when he was in great,

existence-threatening difficulty, such as the night before, on Desolation
Road, when The Blood People were almost upon him, and earlier that
morning, when Stuff was *actually* upon him. He raised an eyebrow; that
was the key, wasn't it? She appeared to him only when there was an imminent threat to his existence, and Otto's "conundrum" wouldn't amount to
an imminent threat until the tenth of the month; he made some quick
mental calculations. Jesus, the tenth was only a week away—he had work
to do!)

He called Otto, who picked up the receiver on the first ring and said,
"Yes?"

"Otto?" John said.

"Yes?" Otto repeated firmly.

John withdrew, from his back pocket, the sheet of paper Otto had
given him: "Who is the . . ." He glanced at the sheet of paper. "Who is
the 'master of chaos'?"

He heard a quick sigh, then, "Oh will you please try to use what's left
of your poor, addled brain! You know perfectly well who the Master of
Chaos is!" and he hung up.

"Dammit!" John said, and hung up, too.

He called Donna J., asked her the same question, got a "Huh?" in
response, followed quickly by, "You know something, John—among your
other obvious . . . difficulties, you're a real shit!" followed by a dial tone.

"Good Lord," John said. There was no one else to call.

While eating a mediocre breakfast at The Eatin' Hole, he asked Sally, the
waitress, "Do you know anything about someone called the 'Master of
Chaos'?"

Sally shrugged. "I sure don't," she said, and John left the diner, got
back into his Ford Coupe, and drove to the intersection of Desolation
Road and Painswell Boulevard. The intersection was empty; the sky was

overcast and threatened rain; no problem—he could make the short drive to Desolation Hall without fear. Perhaps someone there could help him; it was, after all, where Otto had given him the "conundrum."

He turned right, floored the accelerator, and heard, almost at once, from the passenger seat, "Big mistake, John!"

He glanced at the passenger seat, saw nothing, looked through the windshield again, saw derelict houses to either side, and, further on, massive oaks reaching across the narrow road; "It's daytime," he said. "There's no danger."

"You know, of course," he heard, "that it is never *really* daytime here in Nyxon."

"Huh?" John said.

"I *said*," said the voice, and John cut in:

"I heard you the first time!" and brought the Ford to a screeching halt, put it in reverse, prepared for a quick U-turn, but looked in his rearview mirror, first, saw movement at the horizon, in the center of the road: "Shit!" he whispered tightly.

"The Blood People!" he heard from the passenger seat. He echoed the words, slammed the car into first, floored the accelerator, muttered "Shit!" again, tried to double-shift into second, heard grinding from the old gears, glanced once more in the rearview mirror, saw the suggestion of headlights, now, and a blur of red: The Blood People were moving *very* fast!

"Abercrombie?" he shouted, to be heard above the ragged roar of the Ford's engine, "I need your help here!"

"Sorry," he heard, "I'm all outa mashed potatoes!"

"Mashed potatoes!" he shouted. "*Mashed potatoes!*"

No response.

"Shit!" he breathed, and pushed the column shift into third—he was doing close to sixty now, and, to his horror, he realized the engine was at its top r.p.m.

"Should'a gotten that oil change, my friend!" he heard, though it was a man's voice, not Abercrombie's. He glanced at the passenger seat, saw a huge muddle of dark gray topped by equally muddled flesh tone, shouted, "Who in the fuck are you?" and heard, as the flesh tone widened where the head should have been, "I'm Able the mechanic and I'm here to help you outta this pickle!"

"Huh?" John said.

"Pull over *now!*" Able said.

"Huh?" John said again. "Pull over? What are you talking about? I can't do that!" He glanced very briefly at the speedometer: it read only sixty-two, and he had the pedal to the metal.

Able laughed heartily: "You think you got a choice?"

John glanced in the rearview mirror, saw the small, oval rear window and, *Jesus!*, framed within it, headlights, two massive hoods—cars side by side—Chevy emblems, and windshields as dark as midnight.

"What'd I tell ya?" Able said.

John thought dismally, *So this is how it fucking ends!*, pulled the Ford sharply onto the shoulder of the narrow road, brought it to a jarring stop, glanced to his right, saw the passenger door fly open, watched the mass of gray and flesh-tone jump from the car and move—almost instantly—to the hood, saw the hood raised, and then, from behind him, heard the two Chevys screech to a halt, heard their doors open, close, heard shouting:

"Able, you sonofabitch, whatchoo doin' with that hood there?!"

And, simultaneously, "Able, you asshole, what in the snot are you doing in that *Ford* with someone you *know* we gotta have at?!"

And, "You're gonna die, Able! Again!"

Then, in Able's voice, "Shit, he's just some fool lost on a bad road in a lousy fucking car and I'm helping him out, so don't think you're going to *do* anything to him—"

"Able, you *know* we gotta do *somethin'* to him!"

"Yeah, Able, 'cuz look what he done to *us!*"

A short chuckle, then, "It's an improvement, I'd say!"

"You're a shithead, Able! But we still gotta do this thing!"

"Uh-huh, well you'll have me and mine to answer to!"

Silence.

"I guess you heard me, right!"

Silence.

John's door opened suddenly.

Able yelled, "Get outta there, Marion!"

"You think I'm afraid of you, Able? I ain't!" John heard from just beyond the door, although, when he looked, he saw only the wide, gnarled trunk of an old oak, what appeared to be broad shadows moving swiftly on it, and he smelled the suffocating odor of fresh tar, which reminded him fleetingly of his days on a road crew, and then he felt what could only have been an incredibly strong hand grab his upper arm. "Able!" he called out, and the odor of fresh tar grew even more suffocating, and, mixed with it, he smelled onions, meat cooking, beer . . .

"Marion!" he heard. "You bastard! Get outta there or your next death will be your fucking *last!*"

"Christ, help me!" John called, and realized, in the next moment, that the shadows were gone, the strong hand, too, and the odor of tar, meat, onions and beer, as well, and Able the Mechanic said, from near his door, "That's gonna cost you, my friend!" and John knew, from Able's tone, that it was true. "Shit!" John whispered. Nyxon was a place even lunatics would run from, screaming. So why in the name of God wasn't *he* running?

At his house, later that day, he heard words being spoken to him, but he was asleep, so the words filtered through a dream of Donna J. in a very pink, very brief bikini, and, consequently, he heard only every other word—"—are—master—chaos"—and besides, Donna J., in the dream, was covered in tar, beer and onions, which her usually delicious smile said she seemed to like, and that made the dream ghastlier than centipedes cavorting on ice cream, so he woke muttering to himself, "*Who's here? Who's speaking to me?*" over and over, until, at last, he fell silent and listened. No one answered him. A rain fell straight and hard beyond the windows and he thought, for a moment, that what he'd heard had merely been the harmonics of the rain and wind, but he knew at once that he was wrong. Voices always spoke from nowhere in Nyxon; it was one of the city's themes—disembodied voices that spoke gibberish to fools who slept when they should have been running.

On Desolation Road, Able the Mechanic had told him, "They'll be after you, my friend. And I can't protect you no more. This was my one shot. There are others who could help, but they gotta be convinced. It's all a matter of potatoes." Then he'd vanished, *poof*, and John had driven at top speed (sixty-one m.p.h.) back to the relative security and comfort of his bed, where he fell almost immediately into a fitful sleep.

He got a call not long after waking: it was Sally, the waitress at The Eatin' Hole:

"Everyone's looking for you, John," she said.

"Everyone?" he said.

"Everyone in Nyxon, sure. Well, almost everyone. Winslow Homer's looking for you, and someone named Marion, and your girlfriend, too—what's her name?"

"Donna."

"Sure. Donna. She's looking for you. And Otto. What a creep!"

"I don't understand. Why don't they simply come to my house, or call me? And who in the hell is this guy named Marion?" As soon as he asked the question, he remembered where he'd heard the name before: "Jesus," he whispered.

Sally said, "Damned if I know who he is. He came in like an hour ago, big, smart-assed grin on his face, ugly as a popped boil, you know, and he

says he's looking for you, and I say, 'Who are *you?*' and he says his name's
Marion, and walks out. Slams the door real hard. Cracks the freakin'
glass. First guy named Marion I ever saw."

"Did you tell him anything?"

"Like what? I don't know where you live."

"Then how'd you get my number?"

She chuckled. "Shit, John—everyone's got your number. Everyone but
you, that is."

"Huh?" he said.

"Just wanted to warn you," she said, added, "Have a good one," and
hung up.

It was then that John noticed that he was, yes, in his bed—he recognized the soft mattress, the smell of the bedding, the lumpy pillow—but
he wasn't in his bedroom. The windows were wrong (too small and
square, not tall, rectangular and graceful).

The walls, also (dark green on white striped wallpaper, with jarring
metallic flourishes throughout).

And the ceiling (not nearly tall enough) as well as the doors (too
narrow even for his thin frame, and made of cheap pine, not oak), and the
floors—littered with carpet swatches of many colors (red, green, orange,
yellow, blue). It was a room that seemed to have sprung from a bad dream
in the making.

"Jesus! What's going on here?" he whispered.

And heard, at his ear, in a woman's voice he did not recognize, "This,
my friend, is the *beginning* of chaos," followed by a quick, hollow laugh
that made his short hairs tingle. He turned his head sharply toward the
voice, saw nothing, said, "Who's there?" decided at once that it was foolish
even to ask, and got out of bed.

The carpet swatches were cold against the soles of his bare feet. He
bent over, picked one up: it looked like carpet, felt like cold skin. "Jesus!"
he whispered, and threw it down.

He heard, at his ear, in a young man's voice, "What can you depend on, John? Certainly not your five senses, anymore. And *that* is the beginning of chaos!"

He turned his head sharply toward the voice, saw nothing, felt foolish, afraid, as lost as a penny; he said, nearly at a whisper, "Stop talking. Please. Stop talking!"

"Certainly," he heard, in a multitude of voices. "At once!" And there was silence.

He focused on one of the small, square windows in one of the ugly walls, went to it, looked out:

He saw rain. Nothing else. No bare trees or narrow road, no dirt driveway, no brown fields, no decrepit Ford coupe. Only an impenetrable wall of relentless, hard rain.

Marion the Maniac was as focused as a snake, as homicidal as a hurricane, and as dead as last year's tomatoes.

He loved being dead and homicidal, dead and focused. He remembered the life from which he'd escaped many years earlier as if it had been a bad movie. He remembered that he'd killed in that life because, he'd told himself then, he "had no choice," as if he should be sad or filled with remorse and that was *bullshit*—killing was what he *did,* just like the man who made widgets, that's what that man did, he made widgets, or the man who fished all day, that's what that man did, he fished all day, or the man who put on a big nose and painted his face and entertained God-damned kids at Goddamned parties, that's what that man did, he was a fucking clown. So he—Marion the Maniac—went around and killed people because, shit, it made him *feel good* to kill people. And that's what *he* did. He killed people.

John read aloud to himself:

"If chaos cannot exist without order, can order exist without chaos?" He sighed. He hadn't the foggiest idea what Otto was getting at. Order, chaos, order, chaos, *blah, blah, blah*. It was so far beyond him that getting to the bottom of it would be like trying to pass a watermelon. He read on:

"And if chaos and order do coexist, what is the purpose of, or sense in, the existence of either?" He shook his head. That was just so much crap designed to sound intellectual. Or maybe not. Maybe he simply wasn't smart enough to understand it. Maybe he was simply stupid. Maybe he had no right to breathe even the toxic air in Nyxon because he was so stupid. He read on:

"And if there is no purpose of or sense in either, with what are we left in Nyxon?" Again, he shook his head. Hell, if he couldn't understand the conundrum in the first place, how was he going to understand these questions? And he desperately needed to understand them, or, apparently, his existence—such as it was, here in Nyxon—would continue to fall apart: his house itself would finish becoming someone else's bad dream, and *he* would become just a tiny, and eternal, part of it. He read on:

"Clue: You must, of course, consult the Master of Chaos himself before you can successfully deal with this problem." He pursed his lips. Hell, for all he knew, *he* was the fucking "Master of Chaos." He read on:

"And, finally; an archaeologist uncovers two sarcophagi in what was once known as Mesopotamia." He stopped reading. That was nothing, just a stupid brain teaser like the kind his brother-in-law, in that other place (so very far from here), had thrown at him all the time. To hell with it! It had nothing to do with *this* place! It had nothing to do with *Nyxon*!

Back to the beginning of the conundrum, he thought. Otherwise, he wouldn't even be able to find a way out of his own bedroom (which was, obviously, not even his own bedroom any more).

And who knew what this creature named Marion was all about?

Who knew what *anything* and any*one* here was all about?

Hell, he was simply what passed for the law in Nyxon, so why was he even required to *think* about it?

"Good question," he heard near his ear, in a scratchy, high-pitched voice.

He turned his head sharply toward the voice, saw, fleetingly, the craggy, sharp-edged face of a woman well into her eighties, began to say, "Jesus, who the fuck are *you?*" but got only as far as the first word—"Jesus"— when the face vanished, then the room, too, and he found himself standing in the relentless hard rain, on soggy earth that may as well have been made of pudding.

"Dammit to hell!" he whispered.

Marion the Maniac didn't much care for Able the Mechanic, though, at one point, they'd been thrown together by circumstance—First Infantry, third platoon, on an anonymous island in the South Pacific (Island 13w, it was called), Marion a grunt private and Able a second lieutenant due to a battlefield commission. Able was large and powerful and Marion was short, thin, and difficult to pin down, though, on Island 13w, they'd both been pinned down, along with half a dozen other men in their platoon, by withering machine gun and mortar fire. *Sploosh!*—half of the half-dozen got sent packing to eternity. *Sploosh, splat!* the other half of the half-dozen went there, too, leaving Marion and Able to worry about their own mortality and the grim possibility that there was, indeed, a hell.

"Ain't no such place!" said Marion. "And if there was, it wouldn't be so bad."

"Why not?" said Able, and a dime-sized piece of a mortar shell moving at a couple million miles an hour tore off his right earlobe: "Shit, fuck, hell!" he screamed, and clamped a huge hand down hard on what remained of the ear.

Marion said, "Has to be a lotta stuff to do in hell. That's what I think."

He grinned. "I think all those Goddamned preachers got it all fuckin' wrong. Hell is for *fun*, Able! That's why every one of those Goddamned preachers is trying to keep it all for themselves!"

And Able said, hand still to his ear, "*This* is hell, Marion, and it ain't fun, and that ain't *bullshit*! This is the real deal—it's *reality* with a capital F!"

He took his hand away from his ear, saw the blood, sighed, whispered, "Shit, more blood," and glanced at Marion, who was lying back in the foxhole, arms wide, mouth open, and the top half of his head gone.

And then Able felt another small piece of mortar shell hit him, and he blinked once, then again, and again, and heard, in Marion's voice, "Because in hell you get to do whatever the fuck you want, Able! Shit, you can be a fucking maniac, and there ain't no one can stop you!"

Able stared open-mouthed at Marion a moment: Marion's mouth— all that remained of his face—was wide in a grin: Able said, "Well, shit, you got *that* wrong!"

And Marion's mouth said, "We'll fucking see about that, won't we, Able? Looks to me like we got more fucking time, now, than a two-dollar whore's got *social* diseases!"

And so, after many years—literally no time at all in the eternity they shared—Marion and Able found themselves in Nyxon, where life was worth living, but death was worth a hell of a lot more.

John Ortne was certain he'd get sucked into the soggy earth, sure he'd be lost within it, forever, dead and searching, blind, tormented and useless. A Flying Dutchman without sails or ocean.

You think of that yourself? he heard from near his left ear. It was a young man's voice and it was thick with sarcasm.

"Huh?" John said.

You know, you ain't even begun figuring out the stuff you gotta figure out! the young man said.

John turned toward the voice, saw a mound of spiky dark hair, nothing else. "Figure out what?" he said.

Figure out Otto's fucking conundrum, that's what, said the young man's voice. *Damn, you're about as dimwitted as a slug on a beer hangover.* Laughter, caustic, high-pitched, annoying.

"Shit on you!" John said.

"*Uh-huh,*" said the voice. "*Well, you ain't gonna be shittin' nowhere but in your union suit unless you put your head to the grindstone and your feet in the air!*"

"Jesus!" John whispered.

Could be, said the young man. *Could be. But you're sinkin' like an old man's hard-on and you don't even know it.*

John looked quickly at the soggy earth around his feet, saw that he was already at least six inches into it, and that his ankles would soon disappear, too. "Shit!" he breathed.

Yeah! said the young man's voice. *You got that right!*

"Abercrombie!" John screamed. "Jesus Christ—Abercrombie!"

Looks like mashed potatoes to me, said the young man's voice.

"He knows where he is," Otto said. "He just doesn't *know* he knows!"

Donna J., seated across from him at The Eatin' Hole, said, "Yeah, he's like that."

"And isn't it a pity!" Otto said, then looked at Sally the waitress, who was standing behind the counter, pouring salt. "Another cup, as good as the first!" he said, and held up his empty coffee cup.

Sally nodded quickly, said, "Gimme a sec," and Donna said, "I wanna live with him, Otto. You know—I wanna be his wife, I wanna make tuna sandwiches and stuff for him. All that shit! Maybe even have his babies." She smiled broadly, invitingly, as if she had just discovered the smile.

Otto shrugged. "Some things just aren't going to happen, and that's one of them," he said.

Donna J. stopped smiling abruptly, sighed, said, "Yeah, I guess," sighed again, looked out the window, at the first soft orange glow of sunrise, said, "Gotta go. Thanks for the food," stood, and left the restaurant nearly at a run.

Chaos! John thought desperately. *Chaos! Shit, where* am *I?* and felt himself sink another inch into the soggy earth. *Order, chaos, chaos, order!* he thought desperately. *Can one exist, can "one exist"*—he was beginning to talk to himself, now, though at a low, nearly incoherent mumble—*"without the other, can one exist—fuck! Can one exist, order and chaos, order or chaos, can one exist"*—

"*What in the name of all that ain't holy is* this *bullshit!*" he heard at his ear. He felt himself sink another inch into the soggy, dark brown earth. He turned his head toward the voice, saw fog, a pair of deep green eyes, and he said, "Shut up! I'm dying here! So just shut up!"

The eyes disappeared at once.

"Chaos," John said, and looked down at his legs, covered to just above his ankles by the soggy earth. "What is it? What is it? And who is . . . who in the *hell* is the master of . . ."

"*Fuck!*" he heard near his ear. "*You don't know shit from Shinola, my friend!*"

He turned toward the voice, saw a long, thin nose, very red, pursed lips, pale blue eyes full of humor, though all of these parts were in all the wrong places: he looked away, said, "I know what I need to know."

He heard laughter, shrill and mocking.

He said, "I'm dying here. I know that. And you're laughing."

"You can do the improbable, John, but you can't do the impossible."

"Huh?"

"Never mind. Just get yourself out of this bullshit you're sinking in and you'll be all right."

He looked toward the voice again, saw fog, and, beyond it, as if he were seeing no more than the desperate workings of his imagination, the suggestion of his house, his yard, an open door: he shook his head quickly, took a deep breath; *This was nothing. Only* chaos, *which was nothing. Order and chaos, order, which was everything, and chaos, which was nothing*—He took another deep breath. *Christ, what was that Godawful smell? Where was he—in a fucking barnyard?*

That's bullshit, dimwit! he heard near his ear. *And you're sinking in it!*

And then he heard, from further off, near what could have been his house, "*And the preachers got it all wrong. Hell is for* fun!"

Able hated feeling unable, and that's what he was, he knew—unable, weak, old beyond telling, and with no excuse at all for drawing another breath (even if he *could* draw another breath). So many long, long years he'd been chasing Marion and all the others in this Godforsaken place just so they wouldn't enjoy themselves quite as much as they wanted, so they could enjoy themselves *this* much but not *that* much!

What did it matter? he was finally able to ask himself. "What does it matter, Able? You are what you are—merely a whisper in the harsh winds of eternity." He liked that. It was profound. He'd put it on parchment and show it around to his dead relatives. They'd like it, too. They'd pat him on the back and say, "Good work, Able," and, "You're more than able, Able," and, "Able, you know as well as anyone here that these Blood People can't simply be allowed to . . . run amok."

But he didn't know that. Why shouldn't they be allowed to run amok? *Because then you'd have chaos!* he answered himself. *So what?* he answered himself. *Because chaos simply breeds chaos!* he answered himself.

He thought about that a moment, wondered where it had come from, if it was crap, or if it was part of angst, and, if it was, then if it was *angst* he was feeling, because he was *merely a whisper in the harsh winds of eternity.*

"Bullshit!" he shouted out loud, surprising himself at the beautiful depth and volume and resonance of his long-dead voice.

"Bullshit!" he shouted again: *Merely a whisper in the harsh winds of eternity, huh? Well, for God's sake (or whatever) he was a* thunderous roar *in the harsh winds of eternity, and that surely had to count for* something!

"Bullshit!" he shouted again, and looked down at his feet, which he could not see: "Bullshit!" he whispered, and looked at his knees, barely visible above the soggy, dark brown earth. "Good Lord," he whispered, "I'm sinking!"

"That, surely, you are," he heard.

"Oh yes," he heard, in a different voice, "sinking forever!"

So many people in such a tiny space! he thought.

As dimwitted as a slug having a beer hangover, he heard.

Hell is for fun! he heard.

The fog parted for just a moment and the open door to his house became, for a nanosecond, clear and approachable.

Donna J. looked at herself in her floor-length mirror and liked what she saw very much. Good, strong curves, a face that could launch at least half a dozen ships, and *moxie*, too. And who didn't like moxie?

So what was she doing *here*, pining for a man who couldn't even spend a night with her, because . . .

To hell with the *becauses*. What did they matter? So what if her skin aged a little when she was near him. So what if he made her forget her own name, and not because he was to-die-for handsome (though he was), and so what if making love to him would, she'd been warned, draw her forever, and ever, and ever ("eternally," she thought) into the strange and chaotic and grim and gloriously painful universe he inhabited. And so what if their babies would come out of her monstrous and aged and dead.

Maybe Otto didn't know what he was talking about.

Maybe "You can talk with him, Donna, and you can even kiss him and hold his hand, but you go beyond that point and you'll regret it forever. And so, possibly, will he!" was just so much . . . bullshit!

Maybe she could take a chance. Many chances. Spend the night with him. Many nights. Give herself to him, again and again and again. Become what *he* had become (how long ago? Who knew?).

"There's no one else like you in this city, Donna," Otto told her. "You're unique. You need air, sunshine, mashed potatoes, snow and lemonade and a change of seasons. And that's why we need you here."

"I don't understand," she said.

"*We* understand," he said. "And that's what's most important." He'd paused and added, "And there's this, too, of course: he must never understand, completely, who he is, and *what* he is."

"Why?" she asked.

"It's simple, I think," Otto said. "Because if he did understand who and what he is, he would simply not be what we here in Nyxon *need* him to be. Because, after all, how in the heck can someone who isn't one of us live among us? And watch over you, as well?"

"But he *is* one of you, Otto?"

"Of course he is. And as long as he doesn't know it, everything's fine."

I'll never see her again! he told himself. *I'll never touch her again. I'll never need to touch her again.* It was so sad. So very sad. Here he was, sinking in bullshit (almost literally), and he'd be gone forever, he'd never see her again, never get into his ancient Ford coupe and drive Desperation Road again, never try, in vain, to make sense of his conversations with Otto, again, never be sent on a fool's errand in a spooky damned house, never hear the voices of . . . whoever, whispering, cajoling, shouting at his ear, telling him all about his shortcomings, saving his life (whatever it was), drawing him into their universe, however briefly. Christ, it was almost . . . *fun!* And all because of Otto's stupid fucking conundrum, all because he, John, didn't have the sense to figure it out: chaos, order, chaos, order. It was all so far above him, he might as well try and pass a watermelon.

Bullshit! he heard at his ear. *Bullshit!* He recognized the voice, he realized. He'd heard it a million times, though never, he thought, *outside* his own head.

Good God, it was *his* voice!

Bullshit! the voice said again. *And you're sinking in it.*

"I don't understand," he said aloud.

Bullshit! said Able's voice.

Double Bullshit! said Marion's voice.

Bullshit! came a chorus of voices.

Read the damned conundrum again, and read it as if you actually had a brain!

Because you do!

He shook his head, felt the soggy, dark, and foul-smelling earth reach his kneecaps, felt his back pockets, left, first—nothing—then the right, still nothing. "Good Lord," he said. "Where the hell is it?"

Shirt! he heard.

He checked his shirt pockets, left, then right. There it was, in the pocket; he plucked it out, began reading the conundrum aloud, sighed, began to weep, whimpered, "I don't *get* it! I don't *get* it!"

It's no fun, is it? he heard.

There's hardly any fantastic fun there! he heard.

Read further! he heard.

So he did, silently, then, after a moment, aloud:

"*And if there is no purpose of or sense in either, with what are we left in Nyxon?*

"*Clue: You must, of course, consult the Master of Chaos himself before you can successfully deal with* this *problem:*

"*An archaeologist uncovers two sarcophagi in what was once known as Mesopotamia. He takes the lids off the sarcophagi and discovers two naked bodies—male and female—perfectly preserved. "Good Lord," whispers the archaeologist, "I've discovered Adam and Eve!" How did he know?*

"*John, if your poor intellectual powers ca not successfully deal with that incredibly non-difficult problem by the tenth of the month,*"

"Get it?" a voice at his ear asked.

"No," he answered dismally.

Then the bullshit will swallow you up! he heard. "*And us, too, of course. How could it be otherwise?*"

He looked at his legs; the soggy, dark brown, foul-smelling earth had reached the middle of his thighs. "Oh my God," he whispered.

Pretty soon, he heard, *it will reach your navel.* Then he heard laughter, sharp and self-pitying. *And ours, too, of course.*

"Navel?" he said.

Navels! he heard.

After a month, Donna J. decided he was never coming back, so she focused her, albeit not very sincere, attentions on a young man named Clyde, whom Otto had hired a few weeks earlier as, Otto explained, "Constable in charge of the Fantastic." Clyde was good-looking enough, despite the fact that one eye was alarmingly larger than the other, and he was bald, too, but he had an air of confidence about him that John Ortne never possessed (and which she usually required of the men in her life).

Their second early morning at the Eatin' Hole, Clyde pulled a sheet of paper from his sports jacket pocket and showed it to her: "Got this from Otto," he said. "He told me it was a sort of test, but it seems like a lot of horse puckie to me."

She took the piece of paper, glanced over it, handed it back. "It's Otto's little joke," she said. "Everything with Otto is a joke. He's a very funny man—you'll see. And he really hates it when he's taken seriously."

Clyde looked at the sheet of paper, said, "Who do you think this "Master of Chaos is?" and Donna J. said, "He's actually an old friend of mine, Clyde. Someone you may meet, sooner or later."

STORY CREDITS

Rainy Day People" was first published in *PostScripts Magazine*, Issue 10, 2007.

"Circularity" was first published in *Cemetery Dance Magazine*, Issue 37, 2002.

"New York Poet," was first published in *Writer Online*, 2010.

"Mr. Death" was first published in *The Devil's Wine*, an anthology edited by Tom Piccirilli, and published by Cemetery Dance Publishing, in 2004.

"The Music of the Night" was first published in *The Devil's Wine*, an anthology edited by Tom Piccirilli, and published by Cemetery Dance Publishing, in 2004.

"The Man Walking," was first published in *Bone Soup*, published by Cemetery Dance, 2010.

"His Mother's Eyes," was first published in *Twilight Zone Magazine*, 1988.

"After Time," was first published in *Bone Soup*, published by Cemetery Dance, 2010.

"Cradle" was first published in *Writer Online*, 2010.

"At Rikki's" was first published in *Writer Online*, 2010.

"2035 Redux" was first published in *The Devil's Wine*, an anthology edited by Tom Piccirilli, and published by Cemetery Dance Publishing, in 2004.

"The House Under the Street" was first published in *The Rochester Democrat and Chronicle*, Oct. 26, 1986. Variant title: A World Without Toys, first appeared in *Shadows* 10, 1986, edited by Charles L. Grant, republished in *The Year's Best Fantasy and Horror*, edited by Ellen Datlow & Terri Windling, 1988.

"The Lightwater Hawkins Story" was first published in *Brutarian Magazine*, Issue 47, 2006.

"The Sign at Vera's Restaurant" was first published in *The Devil's Wine*, an anthology edited by Tom Piccirilli, and published by Cemetery Dance Publishing, in 2004.

"One of Those Poems Aging Writers Write," was first published in *Bone Soup*, published by Cemetery Dance, 2010.

"Sunsets in 1962" was first published in *The Devil's Wine*, an anthology edited by Tom Piccirilli, and published by Cemetery Dance Publishing, in 2004.

"A Visitor Encounters the Small Screen," was first published in *Bone Soup*, published by Cemetery Dance, 2010.

"Only Two Legs and No Silk" was first published in *The Devil's Wine*, an anthology edited by Tom Piccirilli, and published by Cemetery Dance Publishing, in 2004.

"Gratitude," was first published in *Bone Soup*, published by Cemetery Dance, 2010.

"More Middle Age Craziness" was first published in *Exit Online*, 2004.

"The Godly Greeting of Dogs," was first published in *Bone Soup*, published by Cemetery Dance, 2010.

"Process," was first published in *Bone Soup*, published by Cemetery Dance, 2010.

"The Marybell Women" was first published in *Cemetery Dance Magazine*, Issue 47, 2003.

"The People on the Island" was first published in *Brutarian Magazine*, Issue 42, 2005.

"All at the End of Mid-Evening," was first published in *Bone Soup*, published by Cemetery Dance, 2010.

"Clocking the Moment," was first published in *Bone Soup*, published by Cemetery Dance, 2010.

"Weldon Kees" was first published in *The Devil's Wine*, an anthology edited by Tom Piccirilli, and published by Cemetery Dance Publishing, in 2004.

"Tower Man" was first published in *Flesh and Blood* magazine, 2004.

"Tomorrow, 25 Years from Now," was first published in *Bone Soup*, published by Cemetery Dance, 2010.

"The Screamers at the Window" was first published in *Shivers IV*, an anthology edited by Richard Chizmar and published by Cemetery Dance Publications in 2006.

"Breakdown" was first published in *The Devil's Wine*, an anthology edited by Tom Piccirilli, and published by Cemetery Dance Publishing, in 2004.

"Tomato as Metaphor" was first published by *PostScripts Magazine*, Issue 7, 2006.

"Sally Pinup" was first published as a chapbook by Squid Salad Press, 2010.

"Otto's Conundrum," is original to this collection.